PENGUIN BOOKS

T0363521

Red Sand Sunrise

Fiona McArthur has worked as a rural midwife for many years. She is a clinical midwifery educator, mentors midwifery students, and is involved with obstetric emergency education for midwives and doctors from all over Australia.

Fiona's love of writing has seen her sell over two million books in twelve languages. She's been a midwifery expert for *Mother&Baby* magazine and is the author of the nonfiction works *The Don't Panic Guide to Birth* and *Breech Baby: A Guide for Parents*.

She lives on an often swampy farm in northern New South Wales with her husband, some livestock, and a blue heeler named Reg. She's constantly taking photographs of sunrise and sunset and loves that researching her books allows her to travel to remote places.

fionamcarthurauthor.com

ALSO BY FIONA MCARTHUR

The Homestead Girls

FIONA McARTHUR

Red Sand Sunrise

PENGUIN BOOKS

PENGUIN BOOKS

UK | USA | Canada | Ireland | Australia
India | New Zealand | South Africa | China

Penguin Books is part of the Penguin Random House group of companies
whose addresses can be found at global.penguinrandomhouse.com.

Penguin
Random House
Australia

First published by Penguin Group (Australia), 2014
This edition published by Penguin Group (Australia), 2015

13 5 7 9 10 8 6 4 2

Cover design by Alex Ross © Penguin Group (Australia)
Text design by Samantha Jayaweera © Penguin Group (Australia)
Cover photographs: Woman by Peter Zelei/Getty Images, tent by Charles Yacout/Getty Images,
Sky by Grant Faint/Getty Images, birds by Robert Adrian Hillman/Shutterstock.com
Typeset in Sabon 11/17 by Samantha Jayaweera © Penguin Group (Australia)
Colour separation by Splitting Image Colour Studio, Clayton, Victoria
Printed and bound in Australia by Griffin Press, an accredited ISO AS/NZS 14001
Environmental Management Systems printer.

National Library of Australia Cataloguing-in-Publication data:
McArthur, Fiona, author.
Red sand sunrise / Fiona McArthur.
ISBN 9780143572909 (paperback)

A823.4

penguin.com.au

To my husband, Ian, my family, and my writing family too.

PROLOGUE

Eve

Sunrise promised a new day, and Eve Wilson hoped it would ease the weight of impossible grief in her shoulders as she followed her feet to the Brisbane Botanic Gardens. This was her sanctuary. Among the trees and the wildlife and surrounded by the flowing waters of the Brisbane River. Here she could let some of the anguish wash away with the tide, and find peace when things went bad.

At moments like this she wished she had her family to lean on. As if aware of her need, the iridescent green coolness soothed her as she backed up against the knobbly bark of the nearest trunk and allowed her tears to well and sting and drip in time with the nearby fountain.

Just yesterday, in the ward, vibrant and excited, Roslyn had spoken to Eve of her plans. Family dreams mulled over while Eve checked Roslyn's observations, gave her medications, and encouraged her away from boredom. They spoke about how the blood clot in her groin had made her leave her job earlier than planned. How Jason worried they wouldn't be able to buy the expensive pram they wanted. Little anxieties, tiny concerns, none of which registered in the scheme of tragedy now that Roslyn was irrevocably gone.

Words from the midwifery textbook rang in Eve's head: 'If the mother's heartbeat cannot be restarted within four minutes of cardiac arrest dramatic action must occur to save the woman.'

Well, an emergency caesarean section on the ward had been dramatic, complete with curtains between patients and blood on the floor, but it hadn't saved the mother. Incredibly it *had* saved the baby, yet as Eve had walked away from the scene she knew the image of the heartbroken father would be imprinted on her mind forever.

Why? Why did tragedies have to happen? What good could possibly come of this ghastly event? She just wanted to go home and sleep for a week, but tomorrow she would have to forget today's shift in high dependency and front up to the birthing centre, go back to being holistic.

Trust in the body. Trust in the women. Trust in herself.

The irony was that work was the place she most trusted herself. To her late mother and high-achieving sister she'd always been 'Poor Eve', the one who couldn't get her life in order. No matter that she had her friends, her flat, her love of music and nature – heaven forbid she call that happy. She just wasn't successful enough, high-flying enough, in their eyes. And now she was almost thirty.

She patted the gnarled tree at her back with open hands like she would tap the bottom of an unsettled baby. Obviously none of that mattered when you compared it to this, she thought as she lightly knocked the back of her head once against the hard trunk.

Could she have done anything differently? If there was a next time, would she be able to help save the mother? How?

If only there was something she could learn from this.

Callie

More than 800 kilometres away, sitting in her smart office in Sydney's Double Bay, Dr Callie Piper glanced from her computer screen to her patient.

'The test came back positive. Congratulations! You're pregnant.' Callie smiled at the ecstatic woman and subdued the tiny ache inside her own chest. This was great news for the couple after their traumatic miscarriage last year.

The young husband patted his wife's hand as if he didn't know what to do first. 'Thank you so much.'

All Callie had done was read out a result. 'You two are the clever ones. I'm very happy for you.'

He leaned towards Callie. A new, serious responsibility rested on his youthful shoulders. 'We've talked about what we'd do if the test was positive. We'd like to come to you for our antenatal care instead of an obstetrician.'

Crikey, no. What if something went wrong? Like it had for her. 'I'm so sorry. I leave babies to the specialists who deal with them all the time. But I'll give you a referral to an obstetrician. Or there is the hospital if you want to go through the midwifery clinic. They have visiting specialists every week if anything crops up.'

The new mother-to-be chewed her lip, and Callie stifled the guilt.

She used to do antenatal clinics, years ago.

'Can't we just come back here?'

Callie printed out the referral and smiled apologetically as she handed it over. 'You can still come for anything that's not pregnancy related. Make sure you all come visit me as soon as you're settled at home after the birth. I can't wait to meet your baby.' And she did look forward to that. She couldn't meet enough healthy, bouncing babies.

The father understood. Saw her concern, probably. 'We will.'

Callie stood, and felt propelled around the desk to give her young patient a brief hug, though it wasn't her usual practice. 'I'm so pleased for you.'

As the couple walked out, hands clasped, whispering to each other, Callie waved with a smile on her face – until she saw her husband, a dark shadow of impatience, moving aside to let them past as they made their way to reception.

'Did you want me, Kurt?'

'Why else would I be here?' Kurt said, striding towards her office.

Callie felt her stomach drop. She hated it when Kurt had that look on his face. The whole ambience of the room changed with the downward turn of his mouth, like someone had just blown a cold wind right through her body. It hadn't used to be like this, had it?

'Of course. Come in.'

Five minutes later, in some deep part of her brain she wondered what would have happened if she hadn't invited him in. The sounds of the busy street outside faded as Kurt's words stabbed Callie like tiny knives.

'She's *what*?' Callie turned to her husband of almost fifteen years and stared at his patrician profile. He tapped the sole of his Italian leather shoe on the marble tiles. *Tap, tap, tap.* Then repeated his bombshell.

'Pregnant. You know Stella. From next door. I'm sorry, Callie, but I want a divorce.'

Kurt seemed exasperated at her lack of understanding, but then, lately Kurt was often exasperated, at the very least. *Because he didn't enjoy the guilt of adultery*, some detached part of her soul whispered.

He was quite aptly named, really. Kurt. Frequently curt. And it rhymed with hurt.

Callie felt bile rise in her throat and she glanced helplessly at the door through which her last patient had passed not five minutes earlier. Callie was the patient now. Her symptoms – and apparently the diagnosis – were irrevocable because it seemed her marriage had just miscarried.

Suddenly she became that plain, bespectacled girl from outback Queensland again. The one with the publican father who'd had the affair. The nerd who'd left the remote township of Red Sand behind to study medicine, and never felt like she belonged at university even though she'd graduated with honours.

Callie looked back at her husband. Kurt had been the one to suggest firmly that they settle in an exclusive part of Sydney, when she would have so much preferred a country setting. Maybe she should have fought for somewhere halfway. Somewhere away from other women?

'Stella? Pregnant?' She shook her head. This wasn't happening. This had not been factored into her settled life, her ticking of boxes that should have added up to an untroubled marriage. She thought she'd done everything possible so this *wouldn't* happen to her, as it had to her mother.

Her eyes were drawn with horrible fascination to the shared wall between her office and the coffee shop next door. Stella could be a few metres away, brewing a latte. Pregnant with the child Callie had always wanted.

Was it because Callie had had a Down syndrome daughter who had died at birth? Kurt never spoke of it and had made it clear he didn't wish Callie to either. She blinked and looked away from the wall, wondering bitterly if Stella felt in any way bad that Dr Callie Piper's world had just imploded.

There was a knock, then the door from the waiting room opened and her practice manager's head appeared. Callie focused on her like a lifeline. 'Yes, June?'

'I'm so sorry, but your mother's on the phone. She says it's an emergency.'

'Can't she ring back?' Kurt's dismissive arrogance made Callie frown.

He really was a prick. She blinked again. She never normally used bad language. Even mentally. As she lifted the receiver Callie nodded at her apologetic secretary to hang up so the call could come through.

Before she could say, 'Are you all right, Mum?' her mother's distraught words dealt an even worse blow.

'Oh, Callie, I'm so sorry to be calling like this.'

Callie thought she heard a supressed sob and her belly coiled in sudden dread.

'It's your dad. He's had a heart attack, my darling. And I'm afraid . . . your father's dead.'

Callie closed her eyes and felt the howl rising in her throat like a wave. *No.* It couldn't be true. Who could have known there was greater agony to suffer? But her mother needed her. She fought through a blanket of pain and focused on the receiver in her hand.

'Hold on, Mum. I'm coming.'

Sienna

In an operating theatre at the Greater Melbourne Research Hospital, 800 kilometres further south again, Sienna Wilson tied the end of the continuous suture and lifted the knot so her assistant could trim the extra material. She checked the closed wound before she stepped back and waved for the scrub nurse to wipe down the suture line and apply the dressing across the abdomen.

Stretching her shoulders, Sienna drew off her double-layered sterile gloves and smiled at the radiant mother and her newborn. *Breech birth lower-segment caesarean section successfully navigated.* She doubted she'd ever have a child, but if she did it would definitely be the caesarean way. Calm, ordered, swift and sure. Not sweating and panting while her body took control. Like those births her sister, Eve, laboured through with her patients. Poor Eve. Sienna couldn't imagine how exhausting that must be.

Now where had that come from?

That phone call last night – that's where. Sienna remembered where she was and nodded at the proud father. 'Congratulations. Everything went very well.'

She'd made sure it had.

The father shook her hand and she thanked the staff, surveyed her patients one last time, and then pushed open the theatre door while those left behind sorted the recovery.

Sienna glanced at the clock. 9.15 a.m. This time the next day the funeral would start. She wondered if poor Eve would arrive in time. She rarely did. Sienna hoped that one day her sister would wake up and get her life in order. It wasn't that hard to do if you were single-minded.

No way would she travel to a place like Red Sand just for a funeral, even if Eve was going. Eve had told her that Red Sand was so outback that despite being in Queensland it was an almost equal distance from Melbourne and Sydney

But the distance didn't matter because Sienna wouldn't be celebrating the life of a man who had walked away from his daughters without a backwards glance.

She had a memory flash – 'Happy birthday' in his scrawled handwriting – but she evicted the thought. Their family was well rid of the country bumpkin. Her mother had said that time and again, and Sienna believed her.

She just hoped the other woman's family were kind to poor Eve, who was such a softie. And a little bit eccentric. Sienna shuddered to imagine what she'd wear to the funeral, or if she'd even think about it before she jumped in the car. Her sister's rose-coloured view of the world frustrated the life out of Sienna. Well, maybe this trip would fix that.

She refused to feel guilty. She had her own life, her own plan, and she was almost there.

She *deserved* to be the youngest director of obstetrics in Australia, and the position was so close she could taste it. Only Wallace Waters stood in her way. She'd begun to wonder if the delay was because she was sleeping with his son. She didn't want to marry Mark, for goodness sake, and Mark was just as happy to keep it casual. But she had the feeling Wallace was waiting for grandchildren and a pregnancy would put paid to Sienna's promotion in a flash. Well, not this little black duck.

Sienna strode through the automatic doors to the doctors' car park and sought the flash of her red sports car in the sunlight. She was happy on her own. Happy with her career. If being with Mark was holding up her promotion then he'd have to go.

ONE

Red Sand township sat pretty well slap-bang in the middle of Australia. It was outback with a capital O. Hot enough to heat your coffee in the summer and dry enough to make you wish you'd brought your own water to make it with. A little wild on a Friday night, a little quiet through the week, Red Sand was a small, dependable, hard-working hub in the Channel Country of western Queensland.

I should have stayed here, Callie thought. She would have had more time with her dad and less with Kurt.

She swallowed the jagged lump in her throat and watched the coffin being adjusted until it was resting on the planks they would soon remove.

Callie stared at the hovering wooden box as she waited with her mother for the rest of the congregation to arrive, for the minister to start. Dad had never liked religion – or not since he'd committed one of the cardinal sins, anyway.

People were still drifting in from the car park and across from the dirt airstrip as she watched the sun flicker through the top of the nearest gum tree. A pink and white cockatoo landed with a crackle of foliage and a brown-green gumleaf floated towards the assembly. Callie's throat closed over and she imagined herself somewhere else – maybe on a high ridge?

She remembered a relaxation mantra she'd heard once that talked about worries turning into leaves, leaves that rested on her shoulders. A breeze would come up behind her and blow those leaves and all her cares into the wind to be neutralised. She imagined that floating leaf falling on her shoulder and then blowing away over the endless brown plains.

It didn't help.

Sylvia Wilson shuddered beside her and Callie lifted her arm and hugged her mother close. Her mother seemed thinner than she remembered, and Callie tightened her embrace.

She had no idea how either of them would survive this. Of course they would, but at this moment the darkness was overwhelming and it wasn't surprising she could barely think of Kurt or how she could possibly salvage her marriage. Or even whether she wanted to.

Deja vu. Her mother had survived when her husband thought the pasture greener away from the ochre hills and flat expanses of Red Sand. But four years later he'd come back.

Mum had even encouraged Dad to send birthday and Christmas gifts to the two daughters he'd left behind when he returned, so Callie knew about the half-sisters she'd never met.

Remarried to her childhood sweetheart, Sylvia had refused to let anyone ridicule his weakness. In return, Callie's dad had spent the rest of his life making it up to her mother, to her, and to the town that had grudgingly forgiven him for following a passing political journalist to Brisbane.

Growing up, Callie had absorbed all this like the red sand soaking up longed-for rain. She'd shied away from her own light-hearted childhood sweetheart, who had wanted to marry young like her parents had. She'd believed a jealous friend who told her that young love would never last, and run to the city. Chosen the steady and cool-headed man from medical school who planned their life together with perfect logic and precision.

Kurt had been so different to her dad and to the farmer's son, Bennet, that she'd believed herself . . . safer? Now look where that had ended.

The cockatoo let out a shrill cry and soared off in search of mates. Callie savoured the familiarity of the sound and mentally returned to the sun-baked surrounds of the graveside.

When she'd arrived in Red Sand two days before, her mother reminded her of their obligation to those never-seen sisters, and Callie had phoned them both. One was even coming for the funeral. Eve Wilson. So strange that her half-sister had her father's surname name and Callie didn't. She glanced around again. Eve couldn't be here yet; Callie recognised everyone else.

The minutes ticked by. If Eve didn't get here soon she'd miss it.

Eve felt as though she'd never get there. She'd been told she was mad to drive 1500 kilometres for the funeral of a man she couldn't remember. Eve didn't think she was mad, but she'd let herself down by not coming while her father was alive.

She'd blown it. She had always wanted to see the town her dad came from, meet the man who'd left when she was still in nappies, who she would only have recognised from the two photographs her mother kept for the girls. She hadn't expected him to die before she got there.

Eve couldn't remember him, the man who'd fallen for their mother, stayed long enough for two daughters to be born and then left, but she'd always wondered at the sadness in her father's eyes in the photos. It was the sadness of a choice gone wrong, her mother had said, and those eyes suggested life hadn't been smooth for any of them, at least not until he'd chosen to return to the world he'd abandoned for their mother. Mum had certainly seemed happy being single in the final years of her life.

Today Eve would finally meet the half-sister she'd never seen – though it would have been easier if Sienna had come too.

Another car and caravan passed the other way. The straight road was ridiculously narrow so she was getting good at slowing and moving half off the strip and onto the red dust at the side whenever a car – or, heaven forbid, a gigantic road train – passed, then swinging her all-wheel drive back onto the strip again.

Finally the ribbon of tar curved a little and a shimmer of white, sand or salt or maybe even water, winked in the morning light between two distant red sandhills. Eve glanced at her GPS hopefully.

Not a lot of talking from Irish Sean, the GPS voice. He'd let her down on the conversational side; no forks in the road. But that mirage had to be a lake surrounded by the red sand the town was named after.

Eve chewed her lip. She still had ten minutes until the funeral started, and there wasn't long left to wonder what her half-sister, Callie, was like. She'd sounded upset but sensible on the phone, and in her mind Eve could still see Callie's signature, the perfectly formed, girlish handwriting, added under her father's on their birthday cards. So hopefully there wouldn't be too much awkwardness between Eve and her father's other family.

Was Callie like her mother or their dad? Imagine if she was even a little like Eve herself?

Eve snorted. Her mother had always said, 'Eve is different.' She guessed she believed her. And not just because she had no desire to be a doctor like her sister, and wasn't obsessed with climbing to the top of her profession like their mother. Outside the birthing environment Sienna reckoned Eve's favourite clothes designer was 'Spur of the Moment', and her life goal, 'Whatever Comes'.

But Eve just loved her job – seeing the wonder in a mother's eyes when she'd achieved the incredible birth of her baby. She remained convinced women could do anything if someone believed in them.

In her work she was the low-profile presence in purple scrubs at the back of the room, silent until needed, there to support women in harnessing their inner strength, and to keep them safe. Her job was to stay confident that the mother had the power of birth in her own hands – and Eve *was* confident of that.

And maybe, just maybe, this half-sister of hers would see the value in what Eve did too. But she was sending her love anyway, even if they weren't kindred souls. She just kind of hoped they were.

A signpost offered a welcome, though no buildings appeared, then a small ruby-red sandhill, a slight rise, a few scrubby trees and . . . Eve sighed in relief. Was this the town?

Except for Quilpie, the town she'd passed through hours before, Red Sand township looked more substantial than any place she'd seen since Charleville eight hours ago. From what she could observe as she drove past, there was one short main street of shopfronts, a few boarded-up establishments, and one pub – a long, low verandah-clad building in the middle of the main street. 'The Imperial Hotel', its sign read, and Eve wished she'd seen it when it was her dad's.

She spied the drunkenly askew sign to the cemetery, turned in through the peeling white gates and roared up a dusty track.

One helicopter and three light planes were lined up in a paddock opposite the cemetery, and the crowd of dark-garbed people under scrubby trees gave the instruction she needed as she pulled in behind the hearse and glanced at her watch.

She undid her seatbelt and sighed. *Ten minutes late. Again.*

There was a ripple of movement behind the trees at the edge of the gravestones, and the gathered mourners parted to allow a tall purple-fringed woman in a crumpled orange dress to hurry through.

Callie stepped forwards and lifted her hand until Eve saw her, changed direction and arrived in a little stumble of dust.

Eve awkwardly held out her hand. She was certainly not what Callie had expected. Callie glanced at her mother, who was blinking at the streaks of violet in Eve's hair, then took the proffered fingers and shook hands while her gaze lingered on her new sister's face.

As if driven by an unseen force, Callie's other hand closed in as well. Somehow she knew her father would be smiling. She wasn't sure what she felt, but it wasn't coldness, and she noticed her mother squeeze her shoulder.

'Hello, Eve.' Sylvia Wilson held out her own hand, and to Callie's surprise and probably everyone else's, Eve stepped forward and hugged her.

'I'm so sorry for your loss.'

Sylvia smiled sadly. 'And yours, my dear.'

Eve blinked away tears. 'I'm afraid I didn't really know him.'

Sylvia stroked the coloured fringe from Eve's eyes. 'Then your loss is greater than mine, dear.'

The presbyterian minister coughed and the assembled mourners dragged their eyes away from the fascinating drama unfolding in front of them.

*

Twenty minutes later it was done. The boards were removed and Duncan Wilson was lowered into the ground.

Callie felt her mother's fingers slip out from under hers as she bent to throw the first sod.

The red-earth wad landed with a horrid *thunk* on the lid of the coffin and scattered into marbles. Callie bit down hard on her lip as she bent down for her own contribution to 'dust to dust'. She'd never thought about the words before and she didn't like thinking about them now. Her hand stilled and she swallowed. Couldn't do it. Eve didn't throw a wad either.

Then it was time to go, and the three women stood in awkward unity to say thank you to the mourners.

Sergeant McCabe, new in town since Callie had left, was a tall tough-looking man in the blue shirt and dark trousers of the constabulary. He inclined his head and shook Sylvia's hand.

'My condolences. I'll miss him.' He patted Sylvia's shoulder and nodded to Callie and Eve. 'Your father was a larrikin – but the best kind.'

'Your father was a good man. A character.' Mrs Saul from the post office patted Callie's arm as she moved past. She nodded at Eve. 'He'd fix my roof any time the tin came loose and would never take anything for it.'

'And he trained all five of my boys at pony camp.' Mrs Saul's daughter, Fran, sighed as she too patted Callie's arm.

'Don't know who'll organise our leg of the Desert Races this year.' An old stockman shook his grizzled head as he ambled away, bow-legged, eager to put his disreputable hat back on his head where it belonged and secure his favourite bar stool at the pub.

Callie stood beside her mother and intriguing new sister as people filed past, each with an anecdote about how her father had organised or comforted or rallied around their needs or misfortunes and, with a swell of bitterness in her throat, wished her husband could hear the accolades for a man he hadn't understood.

TWO

Duncan Wilson's wake was held at the Imperial Hotel. Eve followed Callie's car to the pub as she mulled over her first impressions of the two women in Duncan's life.

Funny how she'd assumed Callie would be tall and slim like her and Sienna, but Callie was like her mother. Sylvia was small and dark-haired, almost pixie-ish, with the kindest eyes Eve had ever seen, and Callie had her mother's build and eyes in an elegant package.

There had been none of the stand-offishness she'd expected to receive as the representative of Duncan's other family. Maybe it was a good thing Sienna hadn't come; if anyone could instantly get up people's noses it was Sienna.

Eve turned into the pub's crowded red-dirt car park and pulled up in front of a post-and-rail fence that looked like it'd had one too many drinks itself. She could almost hear Sienna's condescending comment: 'Very *rustic*.'

Well, Eve loved it. The building sat back a little from the red dusty edges of the tarred road, its most distinguishing feature the silver tin roof that hung over the encircling verandahs. A flag-pole stood to the side, and Eve felt her eyes sting as she took in the Australian flag hanging limply at half-mast, forlorn in the hot, still air. She wondered how many times the father she couldn't remember had run his fingers through the rope at the side of the flagpole.

A couple of wooden steps led to the main doorway, which lay on the diagonal. It looked like someone had snipped off a corner of the pub just as they would a packet of frozen peas.

The heat from the sun soaked into her hair as if someone had pointed a blow dryer at her head, and when she touched her crown she was astounded at the burn beneath her fingers. This place was insane.

She looked down at the little clouds of red dust puffing up around her sandals as she hurried across to where she'd only just realised Callie was waiting.

Callie's face appeared serene, but the unobtrusive twisting of her fingers proclaimed her tension. Eve's heart squeezed.

'Sorry. I vagued out. Don't worry about me. I'll be fine. You see all the people you need to and we'll catch up later.'

Callie nodded and touched her hand. 'Thank you. But come to find me or Mum if you feel lost.' Her gaze rested briefly on Eve's face as if she'd been going to say something else, but then she took a deep breath and turned to face the crowd within.

Eve watched her go and spoke to her receding back. 'Likewise.'

Poor thing. Callie had looked so fragile that Eve wanted to gather her up and tell her she understood. She had the sudden thought that being strong through a death was pretty similar to being strong during a difficult birth, except there was no prize of a baby at the end. There was a lot of hard-to-control emotion and pain, and even though you didn't think you could get through it, you just *had* to.

Eve looked again at the entry to the pub. The hotel catered for overnight visitors in the ten air-conditioned rooms out the back, all of which apparently opened onto the wide verandahs. She'd booked one for herself online before she'd left Brisbane, and after the all-night drive, bed was starting to look enticing.

Get bag later, she decided, drawing in a big breath and stepping into the dim and crowded room where the strong odour of beer swirled.

A large blurry photo of Duncan Wilson had been hung crookedly above the long red cedar bar and Eve found her eyes drawn to it every time there was a lapse in the stream of people who introduced themselves to her.

Her dad had been a handsome man.

Sienna resembled him, especially around the eyes. Both Sienna and their dad had those thick, long lashes and eyes as blue as the sea he'd lived so far from. The only things the three of them shared were the long nose and the blond hair. Eve had her mother's short, sparse lashes and hazel eyes, but at least she had her father's height. More than she needed, really.

The Duncan above the bar looked a heck of a lot happier than the man she had a picture of, but then, Eve had liked Callie's mother instantly, so maybe that was it. She'd loved her own mother, though she gave up on seeking her approval, even when she'd nursed her in her last days, and Eve wasn't sure she'd actually liked her. A funny way to be, when you thought about it.

Someone pressed an icy glass of lemon squash into her hand, and she turned to see a smooth young player grinning at her.

'You can tell a good pub by the genuinely welcoming atmosphere,' he said. There was even an outback drawl. Eve suppressed a smile. He waited patiently for an answer as if used to women being flustered by his attention. 'Don't you think?'

*

Callie was trying to keep an eye on her new sister as well as deal with the scores of people who had travelled long distances to pay their respects to her dad. Her mum had the right idea, sitting down in the ladies' lounge and letting people find her. Callie edged along the walls of the taproom towards the glass-paned door that led into the back rooms. Then she felt an imperious tap on her shoulder.

Tall and thin, something like an avenging flagpole, Blanche McKay could strike fear into the heart of the toughest stockman, let alone a softie like Callie's. Blanche had always made her nervous, but at least Callie was old enough now not to show it.

Today the immaculately groomed matriarch of McKay Holdings was in respectful social mode; tomorrow she might be riding at a gallop along a boundary fence with a gun jammed in her saddle. Either way she was a force to be reckoned with.

Blanche's family owned Diamond Lake Station, the largest cattle station in the Diamantina, sitting 160 kilometres to the north of Red Sand, plus an enormous slice of Western Australia's Kimberley country that included a part share in a diamond mine.

Blanche looked down her magnificent nose at Callie, who was surprised to see real sympathy in her eyes. 'You know we offer our condolences on your loss.'

Callie wasn't sure if it was the whole McKay family or the 'royal we' who offered the kindness. The unexpected glitter of unshed tears in the older woman's eyes made her choke up again. She moistened her dry mouth and imagined those leaves blowing off her shoulders again. Eventually she could get the words out.

'Thank you all for coming.'

Blanche went on. 'He was a very good man, despite his lapse.'

Callie glanced uneasily over her shoulder and saw that Blanche's youngest son, Henry, had distracted Eve.

The older lady blinked and her eyes sharpened on Callie. 'There's something I need to talk to you about. For the future.'

Callie didn't want to think about the future. Today was bad enough.

'Did you know we suffered our own loss, last year? My darling Victoria died, not long after her baby was stillborn.'

Callie gathered her scattered thoughts. 'Yes. Of course. It was terrible. I'm so sorry for your loss. How are you all now? Mum said you were unwell with the grief.' She couldn't remember what her mum had said about Blanche managing her loss lately. 'I haven't spoken to Mum for a few weeks.' Or her dad. And she never would again. Callie swallowed as her own sorrow welled.

But Blanche was on a mission. Not unusual. All the McKays were larger than life, Callie thought distractedly, and she couldn't imagine any of them doing something as mortal as dying without Blanche's express permission.

'You knew my step-niece Jennifer had married?'

Callie nodded. Her mother had told her, but she'd read about the outback wedding of the year in the weekly magazines too.

'Jenni and her husband lost their baby last month, three months before it was due. Complications from prematurity. Our first baby in the family since Victoria's death.'

Callie's heart squeezed with remorse at her flippant thoughts in the face of further tragedy. She reached out to touch Blanche's hand. 'I'm so sorry.' Callie knew only too well how the loss of a baby felt.

Blanche's eyes glittered again. 'She's been so kind to me since my Victoria went, that girl.' She straightened her spine. 'So I have decided to do something about medical coverage out here. For people like your father, and Victoria and Jenni, and all the young women.'

She paused to add emphasis. 'The company has pledged to fund a proper medical centre here in Red Sand, for all medical emergencies. And I'd like to see good care offered close to home for pregnancies, if not for actual births.'

Callie blinked. The town just wasn't big enough to warrant that, was it? The 200 people who lived here, or even the 600 in the shire, didn't need a doctor that often. She couldn't see a clinic happening, no matter how much money Blanche pledged. And obstetricians didn't stay in the outback to give antenatal care to just a few women. But this was Blanche and you didn't say that.

'That's an admirable idea.'

Blanche nodded. Of course it was. She'd thought of it. 'I need your help to find me staff.'

Callie didn't know what to say. In fact, with the devastating loss of her father she didn't want to think about babies who had died as well.

Thankfully Lex, Blanche's eldest son and the current managing director of McKay Holdings, appeared beside Callie and bent to speak in his mother's ear. It was reassuring that someone could look down at Blanche, and Callie tried not to listen in.

'You do realise you're monopolising Callie at her father's funeral, Mother. A discussion for later, perhaps?' The words were quietly spoken, but there was no 'perhaps' in his tone.

Lex towered, broad of shoulder, the sun-creased lines at the corners of his wide-set eyes deepening as he glanced sympathetically at Callie, but she still felt herself shrink. Lex was scary. Capable of riding the meanest stallion, or shearing as fast as any ringer, he could toss a nearly full-grown heifer with a heave of his arm. He wasn't arrogant, just too overpowering for Callie's world. She had to admit Lex was also the quiet achiever who juggled the station, the involvement with the mines, and the financial empire handed on by his father, but she'd never felt comfortable in his presence.

His mother raised her brows at the interruption; there was a brief shoot-out between two pairs of pistol-grey eyes, and then Blanche smiled ruefully and nodded.

'Forgive me, Callie. We'll catch up before you go back to Sydney.'

Lex steered Callie away through the throng. 'I'm sorry about that. Mother can be very single-minded.'

Callie had heard more than once that he could be too. Not her kind of man. She winced at the thought. But then, Kurt apparently wasn't her type of man either. Neither was Bennet from her youth.

Bennet wasn't here, but she wasn't going to dwell on a disappointment she really had no right to feel. It was bad enough that she had to lie to those who asked and say her husband hadn't been able to make it.

She just wanted this day to be over. Callie cast one last glance around for Eve before the Lex Express directed her through the doorway and towards the ladies' lounge.

THREE

Back in the bar, Eve took the offered glass and, forgetting where she was, lifted the iciness to her cheek, leaned against it, and sighed at the bliss. The fact that she hadn't slept the night before had begun to take its toll. She allowed her stinging eyelids to close for a long moment. *Ah. Sleeeeep.*

Then her eyes snapped open. 'Sorry. Nearly dropped off there. And thank you.' She inclined her head towards the drink. Wicked grey eyes watched and waited for her attention to return to him. How young was this guy? She felt like she was a hundred years older than him.

'I'm that exciting then. You just go to sleep in my presence.'

'Yep. No offence.' Eve glanced at the drink. 'Non-alcoholic?'

'Afraid so.'

'Excellent. I'm not much of a morning drinker.' Eve returned his engaging smile, but players had never really done it for her – let alone ones only a few years out of high school.

'Henry McKay.' He held out his hand and Eve put her free one in his and tried not to laugh as he squeezed her fingers suggestively. 'Of course, everyone knows who you are. We just didn't know you'd be tall, blonde and gorgeous.'

Oh, brother. Well, he got the first two right. 'Should you really be flirting with me at my father's funeral?'

Henry smiled. 'You know what they say. Everyone flirts at funerals.'

'Is that so?' she said coolly.

He wasn't put out at all. 'I'm just teasing. And I am truly sorry about your loss. Your dad was a great bloke. He was a bit of a hero of mine.'

Uh-oh. This Henry guy was anything but heroic. Amusing, definitely, and as smooth as Eve was not. She had never thought of her dad as a player, just blinded by her mum in a weak moment. Maybe that wasn't true. 'For all the right reasons, I hope?'

An unexpected seriousness crossed Henry's face. 'Absolutely.' He gave a determined nod of the head. 'Loved by all.'

'Okay, then.' Surprised at how relieved she felt, Eve relaxed. Amazing how you could build up someone you didn't know in your imagination, and now that her dad was gone she didn't really want to tarnish that image. 'Tell me about other ways to pick a good pub.'

Henry brought his head closer as if to impart a state secret. 'Icy cold beer.'

'And that's all?'

'Well, complimentary locals are an added bonus.'

'Wow. Do you have shares in the pub or are you trying to sell it to me?'

'Neither. We sold it to your dad before I was born. It's worth a mint now; it has the only liquor licence for 500 kilometres.'

When she didn't look impressed, he battled on. 'So what do you do, Enticing Eve?'

'I'm a midwife, Hotshot Henry. What do you do?'

'As little work and as much fun as possible. So Duncan had two daughters in the medical profession?'

'Three. My sister's an obstetrician.'

'Really?' He spluttered back a laugh and, with difficulty, pulled himself together.

Something had mightily amused Henry, but Eve was distracted by the sight of her new sister being maneuvered out the doorway by a stern-faced giant. She forgot to ask why he laughed because she was confronted with a different curiosity.

'And who's the hulk who just left the room with Callie? He local?'

Henry turned his head as the couple disappeared, and grimaced. Eve waited expectantly. Obviously he was not Henry's favourite person.

'Catch of the shire,' he said dryly with a tiny shrug. 'My big brother, Lex. Managing director of McKay Holdings.'

'Whatever that is,' Eve murmured, and Henry's smile flashed again. A naughty boy's grin.

'I like you.'

Eve had to smile back. 'I like you too, but I think I'll go find Callie now. Nice talking to you, Henry.'

He winked, and lightly touched his finger to her nose. 'You'll be seeing me.'

'Oh, brother,' Eve muttered under her breath. She pinned a subdued smile on her face and went looking for Callie and Sylvia among the throng. It was impressive that so many people from around these parts could appear in the same place. And that they thought a toast to her dad was the perfect reason to drink at eleven in the morning.

She saw Callie first. Then Sylvia. Both sat with backs straight on a low couch, their faces shining pale and exhausted even in the dim light of the back room. The black-suited minister rose from beside them and created a space for the next person who wanted to offer commiserations.

Eve felt the urge to gather them both up and hide them for ten minutes so they could catch their breath. Remembering her mother's wake, she knew there would be enough time after the funeral for emptiness so instead she went across to them and waited for their quiet conversation to finish.

'Hello, you two. It's a crush out there.'

'Sit by me.' Sylvia patted the lounge just vacated by the minister. Unconsciously Eve glanced over her shoulder to make sure there wasn't a more interesting party behind her.

Sylvia smiled with genuine warmth. 'Yes, you! Of course you, Eve.'

She patted the seat again and Eve eased herself self-consciously onto the low couch and tried to tuck in her long legs so as not to trip up the passing traffic. Both Sylvia and Callie smiled down at Eve's feet and she realised they were looking at the purple glitter on her toenails. Maybe she should have worn closed-toe shoes to a funeral?

'You have our father's height,' Callie said into the awkward pause.

'Nearly all of it, apparently,' Eve agreed, and decided Callie was a sweetie to even mention that they were related, in the circumstances. She grinned at Callie. 'And you have your mother's lovely eyes.' She looked around. 'What a turnout. Duncan was obviously popular.'

'He was a very good man.' Sylvia closed her eyes for a moment. Callie squeezed her mother's hand.

Oh, dear. Conversation was a bit of a minefield, but so was sitting there silently, and that had never been Eve's strong point. 'I'd say he was lucky to have you both. I love the pub. It's full of character.'

'Duncan was very proud of it.'

There was another painful silence. Eve tried again. 'Do you live here at the hotel, Sylvia? I know you live in Sydney, Callie.'

'Close. I live in the house behind the hotel. It looks over the flats towards the river.' Sylvia sat forward. 'Which reminds me – you must stay with us, not in the hotel, Eve. We have plenty of room at home.' She looked worried for a second. 'Though not if you'd prefer the hotel, dear.'

Eve held up her hand. 'I think you'll want to relax when this is over. Not put up with a guest. And I've booked my room. I'll be fine.' She glanced at Callie. 'Though I'd love to spend some time with you and Callie tomorrow, if I could. But I don't want to be a nuisance.'

Callie shook her head decisively. 'Nuisances don't drive twelve hours to go to a funeral. It was a huge effort and we appreciate it. When do you go back?'

'I'd like to stay an extra day or two. I have a few days off. I thought I'd spoil myself and take it slower on the way home.' She grinned. 'My respect for long-distance truck drivers just went up a few notches.'

'My respect for *you* has gone up.' Callie gestured vaguely at the door. 'I flew to Longreach and then drove down in a hire car. I've never driven from Brisbane, let alone Sydney. My husband refused . . .' Her voice faded and she closed her eyes.

Now that Eve thought about it, it was strange that Callie's husband wasn't by her side.

Callie changed the subject abruptly. 'I saw you talking to Henry McKay.'

'Henry.' Eve thought about that one. 'Yep. Guy with the lemon squash and hunky brother.'

Sylvia turned her head Eve's way. 'You don't think Henry is hunky?'

'My impression of Henry is that he's a fun bit of fluff. Younger-than-me fluff. Good for a laugh. I imagine the brother might be too much the other way.'

'Perceptive Eve.' Callie smiled.

A shadow fell across the doorway. 'And who's the handsome, horsey-looking lady in Dior making a beeline for you?'

'That would be Blanche McKay,' Callie said without glancing in her direction. Mother of Henry and Lex.'

'Wow. Imagine her as an M-I-L.'

'Don't even think about it.' Callie shuddered and Sylvia shushed them both as Blanche strode towards them with determination on her long face.

She seemed to be heading for Eve, but at the last minute she swerved to face Sylvia. 'My condolences, Sylvia. We will all miss Duncan very much.'

The genuine regret on Blanche's face had Sylvia's eyes filling again. 'Thank you, Blanche,' she said, her voice quiet but composed. She gestured to Eve. 'Have you met Callie's half-sister, Eve?'

'How do you do?' Blanche nodded but didn't offer her hand, and Eve remembered reading somewhere how people in the outback were often more comfortable nodding to strangers than shaking hands. They weren't constantly brushing up against humanity like people in the city; maybe it was something to do with that.

Blanche went on. 'Henry tells me you're a midwife?'

She felt Callie stiffen beside her and resisted the temptation to look to see why. 'Yes. In Brisbane. I go between a free-standing birth centre and casual relief in high-dependency.'

Blanche turned to find a chair, and Henry, arriving from the bar with another squash for Eve, winked as he passed the glass to her, then pulled an over-stuffed chair across for his mother.

Blanche settled herself, and her patrician nose wrinkled. 'Birth centre. I've heard of those. Babies born underwater and all sorts of nonsense.'

'I imagine it's very different from where you had your children,' Eve agreed.

Blanche's eyes sharpened. 'Had to defend that before, have you?'

Eve had to smile. 'A few times.'

'Henry said you were different.'

Eve glanced at Henry, who grinned at the contest. But the conversation went no further, as the last of the McKays arrived.

Blanche's lips tightened as she was thwarted once again. 'Have you met my other son, Lex?'

The guy towered over her. Eve thought about standing up but it would be embarrassingly awkward from so low down.

'Hello, Lex.' She inclined her head in a passable Blanche impersonation but couldn't keep the amusement from her eyes as the hunk nodded back coolly. He was obviously distracted by something but he did stern very nicely.

His voice was as dry as one of those creek beds she'd passed this morning as he looked pointedly at his mother.

'I'm afraid I'll have to break up the party.' He didn't sound sorry, Eve thought flippantly, and she couldn't help being a little disappointed she didn't have a chance to enjoy the eye candy. 'There's a front coming across and we need to fly home before the turbulence hits.'

Blanche opened and closed her mouth and then lifted her chin. 'As you say.' She stood, and Callie and Sylvia also rose gracefully.

Henry stepped forwards and discreetly put out a hand to help Eve, who was deep in a struggle to disentangle her legs and not spill her drink.

She glanced at him from under her fringe and whispered, 'Thank you.'

Blanche and Sylvia embraced briefly. She saw Lex squeeze Callie's hand in his, and then collectively the McKays nodded at Eve as they turned away.

Voices called goodbye and the crowd thinned magically, as if all were allowed to leave now that the McKays were going. People began to drift out to cars or hitch rides out to the aircraft parked opposite the graveyard. Those staying on would no doubt continue their enthusiastic send-off into the night.

Five minutes later, Eve leaned against the rustic internal wall and watched Sylvia and Callie work the taproom, pleading Sylvia's need for rest.

As she waited for her turn to say goodbye, she caught the eye of an old bushie, his sun-wrinkled face its own life-lived channel country, shaded by an akubra. One wiry elbow was propped up on the bar as he clutched his glass of dark beer.

She vaguely remembered his corrugated face from the funeral. Or she remembered the hat, held then in gnarled hands. Eve mentally bet herself he'd ride a horse as well as he rode the three-legged stool he was saddled on now. She crossed the room to put her empty squash glass on the bar.

'You one of his other daughters, missy?'

'Eve Wilson. How do you do?' Neither offered to shake.

'Lost me mate.' He raised his glass to the portrait over the bar. 'But his beer tastes good.' He looked her up and down. 'You drive?'

'Only from Brisbane.'

'Fair way.'

'Nice drive.' She found herself abbreviating her sentences in unconscious mimicry, and the thought made her smile.

His eyes brightened, even if the expression on his weathered face didn't change. There was a long silence, then, 'You have the look of Dunk.'

'Thank you.'

He lifted his glass and looked at her through it. Nodded. Then looked back down at his glass. Eve guessed she'd exhausted his need for conversation and, truth be told, she was crashing a little herself after the drive. She had a lot to think about, surrounded by the remnants of her father's life.

FOUR

The next morning Callie woke to the raucous sound of cockatoos, a whole pink and white orchestra of them, and she could picture them, beak to beak, squabbling and shuffling sideways up and down the overhead telephone wires. She wondered how her new sister had slept and mentally shushed the noisy birds. She'd always loved the Major Mitchells and there was a familiarity about their sound that cemented her decision: she wasn't going back to Sydney. Ever. She'd just have to make the transition happen.

The biggest concern was Mum. She was bone-thin, and was it Callie's imagination or was her mother a little bit jaundiced? She'd follow that up today and check if she'd seen anyone about it. Maybe it was due to the horror of losing Dad. His sudden heart attack had shocked Callie, shocked everyone. She could only imagine the depth of grief her mum was feeling.

She had no job but was surprisingly unperturbed by the idea of selling her lucrative medical practice in Sydney. Maybe a conversation with Blanche McKay about her fantasy outback medical clinic could provide an option for the future? But definitely with less emphasis on Blanche's idea of incorporating antenatal care.

It might not be feasible – realistically, how much work was there here for a GP? Although until they tried they wouldn't know, and at least Blanche might employ her while they found out. She'd ring her soon to clarify a few things before she wasted too much thought on it.

Callie threw back the quilted cover she'd grown up with on her bed, and padded across the timber floor in bare feet to the window to gaze out over the red-dirt paddocks that led down to the creek. A clump of trees hid the pump house. Not much water in the waterholes as usual, but on the rare occasions of flood she'd seen the banks of water rise almost as high as the house.

She glanced back towards the street and the roof of the hotel. Maybe she could just work in the pub. The vision of an undemanding occupation beckoned like utopia after the overload of the last few days – and, if truth be told, the last few years.

Either way, she wasn't going back to see Kurt. There was an incredible simplicity to that thought, and she wondered how long she'd been suppressing the knowledge of the inequality in her marriage.

There would be no suppressing his infidelity once Stella's pregnancy started to show, and Callie had no desire to be the subject of sympathetic looks. There had been times when she'd been suspicious about other women. Had she been blind for years? Since the loss of the tiny daughter she'd never seen?

Her throat closed as old grief for her lost baby swelled. No, she wasn't going back. Her father had always been reserved around Kurt and would have stood by her decision.

'Divorce,' she said out loud, and winced. She, who was never going to have a marital break-up. *Ah, well.* The best-laid plans of mice and men – or wives of adulterous men – often went astray.

She'd ring June at the surgery today. June was more than a secretary. She'd never said anything against Kurt, but hadn't been one of his fans, no matter how nice he'd tried to be to her. Maybe Callie would offer June a temporary job out here, because the woman could organise anything, and she might come for an extended holiday if she didn't stay on with the new doctor.

Financially Callie would be fine.

Such a thriving city practice shouldn't be too hard to sell but she would miss her clients, the families she'd shared moments good and bad with over the last eight years, and would probably never see again. Like the young newly pregnant couple – was that only a few days ago? It felt like a lifetime.

The cockatoos screeched again and Callie trod the familiar hallway to the kitchen to greet the day.

It seemed there was no chance of making her mum tea and toast in bed because Sylvia already had the teapot on the table.

'Morning, my mum.'

'Morning, my daughter.' Their eyes met, filled and they both sniffed. Dad had always added the 'my', and they would never hear it from him again.

Sylvia lifted her chin and Callie saw again the strength in her mother that had drawn her father back to them. Tough, resilient, uncomplaining about the things she couldn't change, born to survive floods and droughts and extreme heartbreak, she epitomised the outback pioneer soul. Her whole world was providing a warm and welcoming home for her family and friends, and she'd always found joy and fulfilment in that simple goal.

Callie had never been so proud of her – or, now that she really took in the gauntness of her mother's frame, so terrified of losing her. Callie crossed the room and hugged the one small solid rock in her world, felt the bones beneath her fingers, then put Sylvia at arm's length so she could examine her more clearly.

'So, apart from the last week, how have you been, Mum?'

Sylvia shrugged. 'The truth is, a little more tired than usual.'

Callie studied the lined face in front of her. 'You still look beautiful.' Her mother's dark eyes were a little red underneath, but then so were Callie's, from crying and trying not to cry. 'I'm worried about you.'

Sylvia smiled. 'Of course you are.' She looked away and half turned her shoulder. 'But there's nothing you can do.'

Callie's heart plummeted. 'What's that supposed to mean?'

Sylvia straightened and turned back to look into her daughter's eyes. 'Are you sure you want to talk about this now?'

Did she? 'I love you more than anyone else in the world.' And wasn't that true. 'If you can talk about it now, then yes – please, tell me.'

A weary lift of thin shoulders and then, 'Dr Graves says I have stage-four breast cancer. Obviously an aggressive one. I don't want an operation. Or chemotherapy.'

Callie felt the floor tilt, and she put out her hand to steady herself on the edge of the big kitchen table, a table that had seen so many changes and joys and heartbreaks – and which now bore witness to this bombshell. It had been leaned on, slapped, laughed around, and cried on. It held in its wooden boards the history of her family.

Her fingers dug into the scrubbed wood. Stage four? She moistened her lips and straightened. How could she not have known this?

'Did Dad know?'

'No. It would have killed him.'

Her mother's lip trembled at her poor attempt at humour, and Callie moved to enfold her again.

'Oh, Mum. Terrible joke.'

'I know.' Sylvia stepped back and with determination poured Callie a cup of tea. 'But he'd been talking about a manager for the pub, so I guess he could see I wasn't well. It was your dad who said I had to go to the doctor.'

It all began to make more sense. 'So that's why Kelvin could come at such short notice to work at the bar after Dad . . .' *Died.*

Sylvia nodded. 'I've offered him the lease until we sort it out but he can't sign it yet. And there's something else we need to sort out. Apparently there's a hitch with the will. Mr Stiles is away for a week, and I said I'd wait for him rather than talk to someone else about it.'

'The will is nothing. Everything is yours.' Callie took the cup and cradled her mother's hand. 'How long have you known you were sick?'

'A fortnight. Since the doctor's last visit. I have to see him tomorrow.' She brushed the tears away from her face. 'It's easier with your dad gone. I'm content to follow, but I hate to think of leaving you. Especially now.'

'Then don't.'

But they both knew that it was too late for anything but an empty promise. And a few fiercely treasured months to come.

'Dr Graves suggested we treat the pain with radiation as it comes. He said I could fly to Brisbane for a quick day or two and then come home, but unless it gets too bad, I'm happy to just soak in the sun.' She patted Callie's hand. 'Especially now you're here. It's not like I don't know a doctor.'

'I'll be here. I'm not going anywhere.' It seemed big, bad, horrible things did indeed come in threes.

As if she'd read her mind, her mother patted her arm. 'So where is Kurt?'

There was no easy way to say it. 'He's run off with a girl from the coffee shop and they're having a baby.'

Sylvia blinked, but that was all the surprise she showed. She shook her head and patted her daughter's arm. 'I always did hate coffee,' she said dryly. 'I don't think he's been kind to you for a long time, has he, Callie?'

Callie reached in for another hug, pressing her cheek into her mother's and feeling the warm softness of her skin against her own. Callie wanted to tighten her grip. Hold her so she couldn't go.

Bugger Kurt. This was what mattered.

Stage-four breast cancer. The poorest prognosis. She dealt with this at least a couple of times a year in her practice, but that didn't make it any easier. Maybe it was a whole lot harder because she knew the way it would go. Her brain screamed for treatment; what if a new drug was found? Radical surgery? But moving Mum to a centre where she knew no one just wasn't going to happen. And in her heart she knew it was too late. Stage four. Palliative. Make her comfortable. Create memories that would make them both smile. Treasure every second because there wouldn't be that many left. Indeed she would. Her throat stung. She would be here and be thankful for it.

'Okay. We'll do it your way.' She kissed the top of her mother's head. 'And savour every moment.'

Sylvia shook her head. 'You can't stay. What about your practice?'

'Kurt wanted to live in Sydney. I didn't.' It was easy when you knew what was really important. Shame she hadn't grasped the concept earlier. 'I want to live here. With you.'

'Sell your surgery, you mean? What about a job?'

'Blanche McKay might have one for me.'

They both sat down with their tea and, except for the painful emptiness of the chair at the head of the table, it was like old times.

Callie squeezed her mother's hand. 'I have enough money for a long time even if I don't work. So don't rush away.'

FIVE

As she'd been instructed to the night before, Eve walked across to the house for breakfast.

She was surprised that the dew was heavy on the packed ground beneath her shoes and the morning was so chilly. She glanced up and smiled at the vast pale-blue sky with its promise of heat to come.

Pink and white cockatoos dotted a spotted gum tree like Christmas decorations, and two dogs headed importantly down the red-stained gravel that ran alongside the road and into the distance.

When Callie opened the door she looked crushed, almost hunted. Eve frowned and opened her mouth to ask what was wrong, but Callie shook her head.

Later, then. And then she smelled it. The unmistakable aroma of bacon and eggs pulled her in and her mouth watered so badly it almost made her slur her 'Good morning' to Sylvia as she was waved towards the table. She couldn't help glancing back at Callie but her sister was looking at Sylvia.

Callie put a large plate in front of her, and Eve did a double take at the size of the meal. Luckily she was one of those people who burned off fat just by talking.

Callie must have seen her eyes widen. 'I know. It's a lot. But I made too much. Guess I have to get used to Dad not being here.'

Eve's heart squeezed for her. It had taken Eve six months before she stopped tearing up whenever she spoke about her mother after she'd died, and she had no doubt that Callie would have been closer to her dad than Eve had been to her mum. She really needed to drop the guilt she felt about that.

'Don't apologise. Breakfast is my favourite meal of the day. And bacon and eggs is my fave breakfast.'

'Tea or coffee?'

There was a huge teapot in the middle of the table. A white ceramic spout poked out from under the funny knitted tea-cosy, as if the pot had on a snuggly dressing gown. Eve had never seen one in real life before. No sign of coffee.

She grinned. 'Tea in the mornings, thank you. I can help myself.'

'How did you sleep?' Sylvia passed the milk.

'Like a top, thanks. It's so quiet.'

'Except for the cockatoos?'

'Even with the cockatoos.'

Callie sat down at the table and opened her mouth and closed it a couple of times before she blurted out, 'Can I ask you something? Don't feel pressured, but if you could just think about it . . .'

'Sure.' Eve glanced at Sylvia for a clue but there was nothing she could draw on so she sipped her tea and waited.

Callie spread her fingers and looked down at them before she met Eve's eyes. 'I guess I need to start with this: my husband and I are divorcing and I'm moving here to live with Mum.'

So that explained why Callie's husband wasn't here to support her. It also explained the abrupt end to their conversation when the husband topic came up. Poor Callie.

'I'm sorry to hear that.'

Callie looked up and Eve saw a remarkable expression of peace on her face. 'Things work out in strange ways.'

Eve's favourite sentiment. She could have hugged her. She felt the beginnings of a tiny thread of hope: maybe she and this new sister did share some basic philosophies that she and Sienna didn't, a kindred spiritedness she'd felt from the first moment and hoped she hadn't been imagining. But Callie had already moved on, so maybe there was a bit of Sienna in Callie as well. Eve's mental attempt to play families made her smile inside.

Callie said, 'Blanche McKay wants to set up and fund a permanent medical centre here. She's motivated by three family tragedies. One of the conditions is that we have an antenatal-care component and I'm not happy to take on that responsibility.'

Callie straightened, as if now that it was out, it was one hurdle she didn't need to worry about. 'So are you interested in hearing this?'

'Sure.'

She drew breath. 'I wondered if you knew of any midwives capable and interested in that side of it,' she paused and then said in a rush, 'or even if you'd consider it yourself? There might be a lot of on-call first aid, though.'

Eve live and work in Red Sand? Now that was out of left field. Eve saw Callie glance at her mother, who nodded encouragingly. So Sylvia knew Callie had been going to ask.

Callie went on hurriedly, as if still not sure whether she thought it a good idea or not. 'Blanche's niece lost a baby last month, and her daughter suicided a year ago after she also lost her first baby. Both were premature. Blanche thinks that if we'd had more antenatal care, as well as what was provided by the flying obstetrician, it might have prevented both tragedies. Or at least it will encourage others to seek help earlier in future. She's come to the idea that those babies and mothers might have had different outcomes.'

Callie shrugged, and Eve got the impression Callie wasn't anywhere near convinced. 'She's willing to put a lot of money into staffing and supplying the medical centre. I'm keen to be a general GP. Maybe if there had been one of those then my dad would still be here.'

Callie gripped her teacup but didn't lift it to her mouth. 'I'm not sure she's right about the need or the benefits antenatally, but I think I'd like to see how viable it would be if we included all the stations around the area and offered multi-purpose services.'

'Wow, ambitious project,' Eve said. 'So on the women's side of things, just antenatal care?' She couldn't help imagining tiny, bush-born babies. 'No future for planned births? Not even low-risk?'

'No.' Callie's response was accompanied by a sharp shake of the head. She obviously felt strongly about that, and Eve wondered if there was a history there. 'We don't have the coverage of support. I can't be anyone's backup for births.'

Eve didn't agree. Callie could back up if she had to. She was a GP, wasn't she? They were only talking about unexpected babies and keeping them well until help arrived. Newborns didn't need a lot.

'So you don't think the women will decide that because there's a doctor here they won't have to go away to give birth as early as they usually would?'

Callie rolled her eyes. 'I sincerely hope not. At the moment, every pregnant woman around here leaves at thirty-six weeks and waits for labour in Longreach or Charleville. The higher-risk women go to Brisbane or Toowoomba. All accommodation's paid for by the state if you leave on time, but you pay for your own if you're late getting away.'

Eve smiled at the autocracy in government health. One way of ensuring compliance. 'Nasty.'

'It seems to work. If women have relatives they can stay with they sometimes leave it a little later. But nobody would be birthing here!'

Eve shrugged. Where she worked in Brisbane, some patients' lives were so chaotic they hadn't had antenatal care or organised a place to birth; they'd just walked in when they went into labour, or carried in a newborn after an unexpected birth. It happened. It still seemed strange that Callie was so terrified of unplanned birth. She wondered if Sylvia had gone away for her confinement.

'Okay. But you're a doctor. Did you get any experience with obstetrics in your training?'

A reluctant nod from Callie. 'I did my Obstetric Diploma before I married, to round out my GP training, and a bit of anaesthetics, and I've been doing a lot of well-women care.' She shook her head. 'But I'm no obstetrician and the two babies I actually delivered myself were years ago, as a resident.'

She fixed her gaze on Eve's face. 'I'm not planning to deliver babies.' Then she shrugged. 'I just wondered if you knew of any-one who'd even consider coming out here while I get settled? For at least six months? I think we'd need to have a few pregnancies to see whether there was a real need. But while we set it up we could look for a replacement if the midwife who came needed to go back earlier.'

Eve wasn't thinking of looking for someone else. She was think-ing *Eve Wilson: Outback Adventurer*. A change. A challenge. A break from the sadness at work that she couldn't seem to shake.

She shrugged. 'I am thinking about it. But to be honest I was thinking of me rather than someone else.' Eve looked at Sylvia and then back at Callie. 'It would be a chance to get to know you both, spend a bit of time learning about a father I never knew, and I'd like to do that. If it's okay with Sylvia?'

'We'd love to get to know you more, darling.' Reassuringly,

Sylvia looked more pleased than dismayed. It was a pretty wild thing to contemplate and Eve wondered what Sienna would say about it. But then, she hadn't seen her sister since their mum's funeral twelve months ago, so it wasn't like she'd notice if Eve left Brisbane.

What the heck was she considering? Eve glanced out the window at the red barren landscape stretching away to the horizon, then back at this woman she felt a rapport with already. She liked very much what she saw.

Callie was smiling. 'You might be sorry you said that.'

'Nah.' Eve grinned at her half-sister. 'But I guess you'd have a lot of work to do before you need me sitting around, waiting to talk babies, so I have a little time to decide definitely.'

If she was really thinking about this there'd be a month or two of organising of her own life to be done first. Arrange leave from work. Sublet her flat. The concept began to take shape. 'Must admit, though, I like the idea very much.'

There was flattering enthusiasm on Callie's face. Eve hadn't realised she was so needy for someone to really want her company.

'Okay,' Callie said, 'let's leave it there. At least I have a lovely option to discuss with Blanche, if she doesn't go cold on the idea – which, I might add, is unlikely.' Callie gestured with her hand at the window. 'When you've finished your breakfast, we might take a drive around, show the place off before it gets too hot, although it's March and cooling down a little. At least then you won't be able to say I didn't warn you how it was going to be if you decide to come.'

She glanced at the clock and then at her mother. 'Would you like to come, Mum?'

Sylvia seemed to wilt at the thought. 'No. You girls go. I'll stay. Have a rest.' She smiled at Eve. 'But I want to hear what you think when you come back.'

After they'd washed the dishes and cleaned the kitchen, Sylvia sat on the verandah with her feet up, and Callie and Eve started with a walk down the main street. It was hot. Not unbearably so, but there was a dry breeze different to in Brisbane, like a pizza oven door was open.

Callie named the buildings Eve had seen when she first arrived, some of them empty, and they meandered along the footpath from one end to the other. More than half of the shopfronts were closed, and Eve began to wonder if there were enough people in the vicinity to need a medical centre, let alone enough pregnant women to need a midwife.

They came to a hairdresser's and Eve grinned at the photo of riding boots and a pair of shears. 'Scissors Outback.' She peered in the window of the shop. 'So you have a hairdresser?'

'And apparently she has a new girl who does nails.'

'Woo hoo. Wish I didn't bite them.' She glanced down at her hands. 'But Sienna would be pleased.'

'I'm sorry she couldn't make it for the funeral.'

'Mmm.' They hadn't really talked about Sienna. *Might have been for the best that she couldn't make it*, Eve thought. Sienna probably would have just spent the time complaining about the lack of amenities. About how dumb Eve had been to come and how it was disloyal to Mum to like Duncan's other family. 'I'll let her know how it went and that you and Sylvia were really mean to me.'

Callie glanced hurriedly across at Eve, saw the grin and laughed with relief.

'Seriously. You guys have made me so welcome. I didn't expect it.'

'No hardship.'

They passed a newsagent's and a small bakery with the enticing aroma of fresh bread rolls drifting from the door. A lean-jeaned cowboy waved a pie in Callie's direction.

Eve admired his loose-limbed stroll and easy, understated fitness, so different to the gym-built guys in the city, and felt her cheeks warm when he winked at her. Then he climbed, mouth ecstatically full of pie, into a disreputable truck with an equally disreputable dog in the back and drove away.

She could feel it, something raw and welcoming about the little town, and could imagine a short time getting to know it. The feeling had been helped no doubt by the genuine solidarity of the townsfolk and friends of Duncan's as they'd rallied around Callie and Sylvia after their recent loss.

Decision made. 'It looks a little quiet to actually need me, but if you do, I'd really like to try it, Callie. I can't see myself here permanently, but helping set up your centre could be good experience.'

'That's hopeful.' Callie laughed. 'Thank goodness we had a hairdresser to entice you.'

Eve touched her home-coloured fringe. 'Made all the difference.'

Two boys rode past on pushbikes with schoolbags on their backs. They pedalled furiously along the street and disappeared down a dirt track that seemed to have nothing up ahead.

Eve looked for their destination. 'Where's the school?'

'That track goes in the back way. It's half a kilometre out of town. Funny story.'

'This place is full of funny stories.'

'Well. Typical outback, but the truck that was towing the schoolhouse in got bogged and they couldn't get it out with the building on the back. So they put the school there instead of in town.'

'They never moved it?'

'They would have but the truck driver had a blue with the builder. Loaded up his truck and went back to Brisbane.'

'You're kidding me.'

Callie shook her head. 'So the school's out on a back road and the kids are told to take the shortcut instead of riding on the main road. Keeps them out of the way of the road trains and tourist traffic.'

'You guys crack me up.'

'If you'd seen the old school you'd understand – we were so happy to have the new classrooms we just decided to say thank you.'

'Let's hope this new medical centre of yours doesn't get bogged before we get it where we want it.'

By the time Eve was ready to leave Red Sand she knew she'd miss Callie.

Callie put it out there first. 'I'll miss you, Eve.'

Eve wanted to cry. She swallowed and plastered a fake grin on her face. 'I was just thinking the same. Crazy, huh?'

'Very.' Luckily Callie wasn't looking at her; she was looking at her mum. 'I've never had a sister before. I might not be good at it but I'd like to try.'

Eve watched Callie struggle with her words. She knew the feeling when you wanted to make something clear and you couldn't. Story of her life.

Callie went on. 'My only best friend as a kid was a guy, but Mum and I have always been close, and I think you and I could be close too.' She looked at Eve, who had herself back under control.

'When I married I was so busy with work I didn't have the opportunity to make friends . . .' Callie's voice trailed away.

It didn't sound like her husband had encouraged Callie to have a life. 'You're here now. You'll love spending the time with your mum.'

Callie had whispered Sylvia's prognosis in a quiet moment the night before. They looked at each other and an understanding passed between them. Eve just wanted to hug her.

Callie sighed sadly. 'Yes. Precious time. I've got a lot to get my head around.'

Eve swallowed down a lump in her throat. 'Your mum is amazing. And so are you. I'll look forward to coming back. Don't wait too long to call me.' Eve marvelled at this persistent feeling that she'd found someone who understood the things she couldn't put into words, despite the ten-year age difference between them. 'I know you have good networks here but ring me if you need me. Leave a message at work if I don't answer my mobile and I'll ring you back.'

They both glanced at Sylvia, who was resting on her swing chair on the verandah with goodbyes already said. Neither mentioned that she had dropped off to sleep.

SIX

Sienna walked away from another successful caesarean operation in Melbourne and as she clicked across the corridor in her high heels she felt her phone vibrate in her pocket. *Damn.* She'd wanted to complete the ward round before the gynae list started in her rooms. What new crisis did her registrar have for her?

She glanced at the caller ID and saw it was Eve. She sighed.

'So how was the funeral, little sister? Did you get there in time?'

'The funeral was short but eloquent.'

Eve sounded a long way away. Sienna glanced at her watch.

'And yes, I was late but only ten minutes and it hadn't started yet.'

Of course she'd been late. 'And his other family?'

'Callie and Sylvia are amazing.' Sienna could hear the excitement in Eve's voice and it left a bad taste in her mouth. These were the people their father had chosen over them. How could Eve get pleasure out of that meeting? But then, Eve seemed to find excitement in the strangest ways. There was a rumbling roar from her phone and she missed what Eve was saying.

'Are you on speakerphone? Where are you?'

'Just leaving Red Sand so the phone will lose service soon. Just wanted to let you know it all went off well and I'm on my way home.'

'The funeral was two days ago.'

'It's a long drive, Sienna.'

'I told you that. I can't believe you went in the first place. Look, I have to go, message me when you get back and I'll call you. Okay?'

'That's fine. See you.'

'Bye.'

Sienna's phone vibrated again and this time it was her registrar. Eve was forgotten as she took the call.

Callie watched the Subaru until it was a dust ball in the distance. She'd miss Eve. Which was odd; two days ago she could have passed her in the street without recognising her.

This morning, after their talk, Callie felt less small, despite the fact that her younger half-sister towered over her. She turned back to the house and as she climbed the verandah steps she could see her mother, grey fringe across her eyes, veined-hand loose in her lap, asleep in the chair.

It all became damply blurry after that as she rested her head against the verandah post and let the grief swamp her.

Her dad. Gone.

And soon, her mum.

The burden of responsibility weighed Callie down like an iron hand pushing her into the ground and she wanted to beat her chest and ask, *Why me? Why Mum?*

But then she straightened, remembering how her mother had done the same thing after she'd shared her prognosis. Callie too could stand straight and strong. Women out here did that all the time. Women everywhere, Eve would say, and she was right. Funny how they both had similar outlooks.

But the idea of sitting still and waiting for the worst to happen would destroy her and she didn't want to take over her mother's life. Just to be here quietly in the background, soaking up all the time she could. She'd ring Blanche McKay and discuss the potential of a permanent medical centre. That could be something to distract her from the future she didn't want to think about.

Blanche arrived the next day, at the first sniff of interest from Callie. Apparently Henry was around somewhere, flirting with the local girls as he waited to fly his mother back to the station.

Callie and Blanche walked the dusty main street, much like she and Eve had done the day before, to consider which of the deserted buildings left over from the last opal rush they could possibly revamp into a medical centre.

Blanche had deemed the present one-room clinic, which operated once a month, too small to work with. She was keen on using the old saddlery, complete with a sun-bleached horse tie-rail out front. Callie thought the building too big.

The structure had half a dozen small rooms, plus enough space for a double parking bay inside and a carport outside. 'You'll have to have a reliable four-wheel drive, for emergencies, and in case you want to visit new mothers after their births when they come back home. I'll see the government about an ambulance.'

Just like that? See the government about an ambulance? Callie bit back the smile. 'I wouldn't be involved in going out to see the mums. A registered nurse or midwife would have to do that.'

'Hmm.' Blanche let that go as she strode across the dusty wooden floor. 'We'll knock out some walls, but the ones at the back can stay. I like the option of extra rooms. An emergency medical centre, as well you know, could need them.'

Lordy, Callie thought. What was she encouraging here? Blanche probably had visions of a full hospital and a dentist as well. 'We can leave them shut if we don't need them.'

'I already have someone in mind for the renovations.' Blanche's eyes were bright with determination. 'Bennet Kearney.'

Bennet. Typical of Blanche not to care that Bennet had been the man she'd left to marry Kurt. 'I thought he was a vet in Melbourne now?'

'Of course you know Bennet's wife died last year and they have a young son.' Blanche cast her an impatient look. 'Did your mother tell you they both moved back last month and they're living with his sister at their parents' station?'

Sylvia hadn't mentioned it. If he was back, why hadn't he come to the funeral? She pushed that hurt away to look at later but it cast a pall over the conversation.

Blanche was on a mission. 'Anyway, our good fortune is that apparently he's taken up carpentry in his spare time. He's good.'

Callie could believe he'd be good at carpentry. He had great hands.

Unwillingly her mind drifted to a time she'd lain in Bennet's arms on a bed of curling wood shavings in his father's workshop. She'd had a fetish for the bouquet of wood and varnish ever since.

She blinked. *Whoa, there.* Crazy thoughts. She needed to think about the magnitude of Blanche's dream, not about Bennet Kearney. Despite Blanche's confidence, she doubted he'd be that keen to work with her.

In the real world she wasn't so sure she was ready to be the doctor of all trades Blanche seemed to be envisaging. Still, she reassured herself, she wouldn't be alone: Eve might be here, and the RFDS would be on the other end of the phone if she had a major emergency. At least she had enormous faith in the flying doctors' ability to talk someone through a crisis.

Striding beside her, arms waving enthusiastically, Blanche was saying, 'I've spoken to several similar centres in Western Australia and they recommend a mini theatre be included.'

Callie trod very gently. 'I'm not doing operations, Blanche.'

'Of course not.' A long-fingered hand brushed that aside innocently. 'I was thinking, just for minor emergencies. Stitching an arm. That sort of thing.'

'Emergency suturing is fine, but I need different insurance for operations. I thought this was to be similar to when the flying doctor does an outreach clinic? Basic.'

'McKay Holdings will pay for your insurance. That was Lex's main concern and I've sorted it out with a close friend on the board of an insurance conglomerate. You'll be working for us.'

Callie wasn't too sure how she felt about that. 'Well, maybe. Maybe not. This whole idea is still on paper.'

Blanche straightened and met Callie's eyes. 'Not for me, it isn't. There's a real need, Callie.' She gazed with determination around the musty space. A zealot for the new world. 'I was thinking of a mini hospital.'

Callie went even more gently. 'I know you were. But staffing is a big issue. And my mum is seriously unwell, Blanche. This is a part-time job for me, not a vocation.'

That stopped Blanche for a moment. 'Yes. She looks unwell.' She wasn't blind, just one-eyed about her own project. Which suited Callie because she didn't want to talk about her mum's future.

Blanche even squeezed Callie's shoulder and there was real empathy. But only for a moment.

'Yes, well, if your sister came back as a midwife she could run the antenatal side and the emergencies with you as backup. I did some investigating last night when you said she might be interested – strictly confidentially, of course. Apparently she's extremely qualified and she's a nurse practitioner with her own Medicare provider number. Couldn't believe our luck.'

How the heck had she found that out? Callie hoped Eve had been sincere when she said she'd think about it and didn't mind Blanche checking up on her, because clearly Blanche was oblivious to being too forward.

'And we'll find an administrator for the paperwork. A really good PA.' Blanche was getting to her point. 'So you wouldn't have to worry about that side at all. Eve could liaise with the flying obstetrician and gynaecologist and you could be the one in charge of the general practitioner side and work whatever hours you liked.' Blanche paused for breath.

Callie just stood there, visions of Blanche's sky-high expectations passing in front of her eyes. The enormity of it began to curl in her stomach.

Blanche's patience could be stored in a matchbox. 'So? What do you think?'

'Will we have enough patients to justify this kind of service? I mean, the shire is huge, I know, but the population's only around the 600 mark. What are we going to do the rest of the time when there are no patients?'

'You have your mum and a practice would soon build. Plus there are the tourists. Grey nomads and the not so grey. Driving past all the time. You know that. Women's health issues for all ages would keep you busy, let alone the men who never make the time to see someone.' Blanche rubbed her hands together. 'Eve could do outreach clinics for the new mothers and babies.'

Her gaze swept the dusty rooms and Callie truly believed Blanche could see the finished centre in her mind.

'The young women could have most of their antenatal care here and wouldn't need to go away much at all until their thirty-sixth week. We'd have a secretary, and a couple of the local girls could be nursing assistants. I'd send them away for some training.'

And Bennet would build it all.

Callie gave herself a mental shake. This wasn't about her and Bennet, this was about creating a mini hospital.

'You have shareholders, Blanche. You're talking a lot of money.'

An elegant shrug. 'The mine's been very good this year. Making it faster than we can spend it. And those board members are all relations. They can invest what's left when I'm dead.'

Callie couldn't see Lex ignoring all the financial implications. She was starting to feel browbeaten with the strain of keeping up. So much going on. Her dad. Her mum.

'As long as you know I don't do babies and birth. It's been years since my training and I don't remember anything.'

'I don't believe that. You always were as smart as a whip. Brush up on the books, girl, if you feel ill-equipped. Apply for any course you like and I'll pay for it.'

Stop. Please. Where was Eve when she needed her?

'I'm not leaving to go anywhere for a while, Blanche.'

Something must have got through because Blanche stopped.

'Your mother? Of course. Which reminds me. What about your husband? Is he coming out here too?'

Typical of Blanche to only just remember she was married. Callie resisted the impulse to laugh. It really wasn't that funny.

'Actually we're in the process of divorcing.'

'Man's a fool. So you are staying. Good.' And that was the end of that conversation, and of Blanche's interest in the topic.

But Callie had been doing some thinking too. 'Midwifery-run clinics are the way of the future. I'm not ruling that out. Maybe Eve could liaise with the flying obstetrician. We could see how we go adapting a model from there. It all depends if Eve really is keen – maybe I could be the doctor on call only if a woman needed to be transferred out.'

She closed her eyes at the thought. Maybe an emergency obstetric course was called for.

SEVEN

Bennet arrived the next morning. With his tools.

Bennet Kearney stood at medium height but topped Callie by a hand's width, a lean-muscled man with the crinkled eyes of a thinker. Today, whatever he was thinking didn't amuse him.

When Callie opened the door she flew back twenty years and her mood soared with the pleasure that expanded in her chest. She'd forgotten how warm seeing Bennet had always made her feel.

'Bennet! Come in. Mum's in the kitchen. I can't believe Blanche has dragged you here so quickly.' Then she shook her head. 'Of course I can. Blanche could move mountains.'

She laughed. Felt silly and self-conscious as she saw his eyes widen as he took her in – recognised the sudden flare that had her responding in an instant. She imagined she could smell the intoxicating aroma of wood shavings that she'd first encountered all those years ago in that cosily private workshop.

Then the flare was gone and his face became expressionless. No crinkled eyes. No matching smile. Callie's euphoria shrank.

'You okay?'

'Fine. Thanks. You?' He turned the battered akubra in his hands, tucked it under his arm, and waited for her to precede him.

'Good, thanks.' There was an awkward pause and Callie spun towards the kitchen.

'Mum, Bennet's here.' She knew he was following despite his silence and that strange tension about him that had stopped her first impulse of demanding an embrace. Disappointment curdled in her stomach.

'Bennet!' Sylvia wasn't holding back. She rose and hugged him, and Bennet gathered her in close to his chest, bent his head and kissed the top of her hair.

'Sylvia, I'm so sorry I didn't make it to the funeral. Had a foal trying to enter the world sideways and I couldn't get away. How are you? You look well.' But Callie heard the hesitation. His brows rose and his eyes met Callie's with concern.

Sylvia stepped back and looked at him. 'Still numb at the shock that he's gone.' She straightened and eased the lines from around her mouth with a determined smile. 'But happy to have Callie here.' She glanced at her daughter. 'It is good to see you, Bennet. And I'm so sorry to hear about your wife.'

'Thank you, Sylvia. It's been ten months now.'

'How is your little boy?'

'We're getting there. My sister's good with Adam.'

'Callie says you might be looking at doing some building? Your father was an amazing carpenter. I always remember the pride he took in that workshop of his.'

Callie's eyes flew to Bennet's as the heat ran up her cheeks. There was a brief flash of mocking humour on his face before he looked back at her mother, but Callie was too embarrassed to be amused.

Had her memories of Bennet been lying between her and Kurt all these years and she hadn't realised? Was it her fault too that her marriage had withered and died? She thought she'd blocked out their childhood romance but seeing Bennet at the door made it all come rushing back in technicolour detail.

Thankfully Bennet had carried on the conversation with her mother because Callie's cheeks felt hot.

'I don't know if I'll ever be a master builder, but I do enjoy the feel of wood shavings under my fingers.'

Callie stared fixedly at her feet but she felt his glance. A little dig at the past? She guessed he had the right.

'Do you have the time?' Sylvia glided around, assembling teapot and cups, her face alight.

'Lucky it's been slow on the veterinary front since I came back.'

Sylvia waved him to a chair at the table and poured him a cup of tea, organising refreshments with new purpose. Callie hung back outside the circle of easy conversation, fighting the memories that crowded in despite herself. She diverted her mind forcibly. Joined the conversation.

'But you're getting enough veterinary work?'

Their glances collided and he looked away at a point over her left shoulder.

'I've started to help the bloke up at Longreach with the stations nearer to me than to him, but I need to drum up some business of my own. Might have to get a couple of litters of puppies and drop them off at the school down here. Get the kids to take them home. Find some work that way.'

Sylvia laughed and it was so good for Callie to hear the sound it was almost worth the confusion in her own mind. In fact, Sylvia seemed more animated than Callie had seen her since her arrival. She decided to ask Bennet over as much as she could while her mother was well enough. If there was awkwardness between him and Callie then they'd both just have to get over it.

She watched Sylvia clasp her hands. 'And now Blanche has you working on Callie's medical centre.'

Callie shook her head. 'It will always be Blanche's medical centre, Mum.'

No smile from Bennet. 'Blanche said she was setting it up as a trust. In memory of Victoria. Giving it to the town. I'm supposed to email Blanche some ideas tomorrow.' He glanced at Callie. 'So can we have a walk around after this? I'll need to start on the drawings.'

Half an hour later Bennet's vibes stayed coldly official as he walked beside her. It was like being escorted to the local cop shop by Sergeant McCabe for a misdemeanour. She didn't like it one bit. She was a professional woman, not a chastised child.

'How old is Adam now, Bennet?'

'Six. He's a good kid.' He stopped and turned to face her, but she still couldn't read his expression. 'Why isn't your husband here to support you?'

Rumour usually flew like the wind around here and she'd told Blanche about Kurt yesterday. Not that Blanche would bother talking about Callie's private life.

'We're not together. He's decided to start a family with someone else. I'll file for divorce as soon as I can.' Twice in two days she'd said that. She needed to look into it but she had a sinking feeling she couldn't do paperwork without a year living apart at least.

'What about your practice?'

She shrugged. 'I'm selling it. Moving back here to be with Mum.'

His face softened. 'Your mother's lost a lot of weight since I saw her last. Is she okay?'

Callie swallowed the sudden lump in her throat. 'No. She has advanced breast cancer, metastases through her body. She's declined treatment.'

He froze, then shook his head with a muttered curse. 'I'm sorry to hear that.' He sighed and started walking again. 'She'll be glad to have you here.'

The subtext said that he wasn't, and Callie couldn't help but feel a little stab of regret. But she had enough on her plate – boy, did she ever – without guilt about Bennet and lost opportunities.

They turned into the old saddlery and the conversation became business focused. Gradually they relaxed and unconsciously fell into their old banter.

'You're using your brains again, Callie,' he teased, when she couldn't keep the tape measure straight. 'Some people just know how to use their hands.'

She blushed and they both pretended that his words didn't bring back memories.

They talked about what Callie wanted versus what Bennet could achieve, and as had happened in the past, there wasn't much difference.

She slanted a glance at his profile. 'So you can build a floor, pull walls out and put them in. Even fit bathrooms?'

Bennet rubbed the underside of his chin with his thumb. He'd always done that when he was thinking.

'I can plan it and build most of it. I'll get in some young blokes from around here to help out with the manual stuff for a few days. Or the girls if the boys are out at muster camp to speed things up.' He waved the electronic tablet he'd been sketching on.

'We'll get tradesmen in from Brisbane for the specialist stuff like electrics and plumbing. Quicker that way, and Blanche wants it done yesterday.'

Callie had to laugh. 'I can believe that. She's roped me in and I'm trying to do the same to Eve.'

Bennet gave her a quick look from under those dark brows. 'Eve? I hear a half-sister came to the funeral.'

She thought about Eve and even she could hear the smile in her own voice. 'Yes, Eve. The other one couldn't make it.' The smile fell away as the reason she was here flooded back.

Bennet cast her a look and for a brief moment she saw the understanding. He lifted his hand to touch her shoulder but stopped before he got there.

She straightened her neck. It was okay, she could live without Bennet's sympathy, but she did regret the distance between them.

Think about something good. 'Eve's a midwife, and if all goes well she might be working here while we set up and get established.'

He looked away for a moment. 'Must be strange. I hear you two seem pretty friendly considering the angst her family has caused yours.'

'Her mother. Not her family. It was all a long time ago. So, strangely it's not like that. And Mum has always been amazing about it.'

She accidentally brushed against him, just a light shimmer of her fingers on the back of his hand as they measured a wall. She couldn't deny the frisson. Bennet jumped back as if she'd burned him and snapped shut the cover of his tablet.

'I think I have enough to sort out preliminary drawings. Say goodbye to Sylvia for me. I want to get home to Adam.'

Callie watched him spin around and stride away, and tried not to think about the young man she'd poured her heart out to all those years ago. What had she expected? She'd been the one who walked away.

EIGHT

Sunday morning a week later, Eve looked out over the Brisbane River as she listened on the phone. She'd known Sienna wouldn't like the idea of Eve relocating to their father's town.

'You're going back to live there?'

Eve sighed. 'Not for a while, but Callie's setting up a medical centre and she needs a midwife. I've said I'll go for at least six months.'

'You're going to the outback?' She could hear the disbelief in Sienna's voice. 'What about your birth centre work? Your lovely flat and friends?'

'It's western Queensland. Not the moon. And it's not for a couple of months yet.'

A CityCat ferry shot across the middle of the Brisbane River and, looking out of her kitchen window, Eve knew she'd miss the water. But she didn't need Sienna to tell her that.

Sienna was still disbelieving. 'You'd leave your tai chi class?' There was a pause, then, 'I know you.' Sienna's voice flattened. 'Did something happen at work?'

Eve closed her eyes. 'That was two weeks ago.' It felt like years. 'But anyway, I am over high-risk for a while.' She tried not to get lost in thoughts of a baby who would never know her mother. She'd never known her father and she wished she had. She wanted to know her new sister. 'Callie's in for a tough time. Her mother's dying and I want to help.'

There was silence from Sienna until, 'And you would be a help, with your experience.' Eve heard her sister sigh. 'In all of it. Dying mothers included. I didn't help you much with ours.'

Eve waved that away. Palliative care wasn't Sienna's strong point. 'Red Sand is an amazing place. I found it more interesting out there than I expected.' *Well, a little more interesting, anyway.* She readjusted the phone and her tone. 'I'll be fine. It's time for a change. And I have a lot to offer.'

'And your sanity to lose.'

But Eve could hear the beginning of resignation in her sister's voice, and she allowed herself to relax a little. Sienna could be terrifying when she bent her intellect to dissuading you.

Get it all out. 'I'm waiting for the building to be completed but I'll go earlier if I'm needed.

She heard the intake of breath. 'Don't they have a registered nurse?'

'They do now.'

'You're rushing into this.'

'No, I'm not.'

'All I can say is, make a contingency plan. A date you need to return to work, for example, so your soft heart doesn't strand you there.'

Eve thought about the idea and decided it was a little calculating, considering she hadn't given Callie a time limit. But maybe she could mention it.

'I'll think about it.' Eve's eyes followed a sleek regatta shell scull up the river. No doubt the girls at the rowing club would think she was mad too. And Ross, their coach, who she dated casually. But they'd really only been friends, no matter how much he'd wanted to change the status quo.

'My boss will approve leave without pay for six months, and one of the girls at work might sublet my flat.'

Sienna's sigh drifted through the phone from Melbourne. Eve could tell she was tiring of the conversation. She'd always had a short attention span for other people's problems, especially if the solutions she suggested weren't fallen on with approval.

'You'll go mad in the outback. Get your friend to rent your flat and be back before Christmas. I might even fly to Brisbane and have lunch with you. Talk next week. Bye.'

In fact they talked again the next night.

'Callie asked me to phone you. Apparently we both need to be in Red Sand for the reading of the will on Wednesday.'

A small huff of disbelief from Sienna. 'There is no way I'm flying out to western Queensland for an inheritance I don't want. If our biological father has left me anything, though it would more than likely be some debts, then you can have it.'

Eve hated the way Sienna called Duncan 'their biological father'. Eve had never seen it like that: there had been written correspondence and all those cards. She was trying really hard not to become annoyed. It was difficult when Sienna was being stubborn.

'Apparently we both have to be there to answer some condition or Sylvia can't settle the estate.'

'Not my problem.'

'Sienna.' Eve was exasperated. 'Sylvia's dying. She doesn't need you being difficult on top of her grief and neither does Callie. Just fly here. Please. We'll fly to Longreach and drive down together. We can do it in a day if we leave early enough on Wednesday morning.'

'I can't cancel a weekday.' Eve could hear the surprise in her sister's voice and she almost smiled through her frustration. Sienna wasn't used to Eve being forceful. It spurred her on.

'If you were sick you'd have to. Melbourne will still run without you.'

Sienna was not happy. She'd had a huge Tuesday as she tried to see two days' worth of patients in one afternoon, and she'd been up after midnight with a birth that ended in emergency caesarean. Eve had been late to meet her in Brisbane and they'd almost missed their connection to Longreach.

The only car they could hire was a bone rattler, because the one they had requested had apparently suffered from a computer meltdown.

As would she very shortly if they didn't get to this damn town.

'Another half an hour.'

She glanced at Eve in surprise. 'Did I say that out loud?'

Eve flashed her teeth in a smile. 'No. But I could read the vibes.'

Sienna closed her eyes on the barren red landscape with the standing termite mounds peering at her from behind scrubby trees. Counted to ten. How on earth could Eve be so bloody cheerful all the time?

'So what are you so happy about?'

'I can't believe you are actually here. I seriously didn't think you'd come.'

'Don't I wish I'd known that earlier,' she said dryly and cast an exasperated glance at her sister. 'She's dying, Sienna. You have to come,' she mimicked.

'Sylvia *is* dying and you *did* have to come. I'm glad you did. That's all. And aren't you even a little interested in what our father wanted us to have or know from the grave?'

'God, no!' She watched Eve's face fall and she felt like the baddie again. How did Eve do that? 'Wake me when we get there.'

Sienna glanced at her watch and ran her tongue around her teeth. The tea she'd been given on arrival had been strong enough to stand a spoon up in and she normally drank weak Earl Grey. *Yuck.* She was so tired.

The appointment was for twelve, to give them time to head back to Longreach before the last flight out – thank God for small mercies – and they'd made it with fifteen minutes to spare.

Though, made it to where? That was the question. How on earth did a city girl like Eve think she'd be happy here? The place was practically a ghost town.

Sienna had to admit, though, in other circumstances she might have got on with the half-sister, Callie, a sensible GP who appeared to be no fool, and their father's widow, a kind-eyed, sparrow-like woman dignified in her contained grief.

They were all seated around an ancient table that could have been made out of a tree a hundred years ago in a room at the back of Duncan Wilson's pub.

The solicitor, whose name she'd already forgotten, reminded her of those pitted anthills they'd passed; he had much the same shaped torso, a weathered face and officious stance.

'Thank you all for coming.'

Some came further than others, Sienna thought sardonically, but she appreciated him opening proceedings at the stroke of twelve.

'This is the last will and testament of Duncan Simon Wilson . . .'

Sienna tuned out, almost physically unable to listen due to a combination of engulfing tiredness and rebellion. Glanced around the room. She seriously wasn't interested. Except for the drone of the anthill man this whole place was too quiet. She could just hear some kids playing in the distance. And now a truck reversing fairly close. Probably supplies for the pub.

Her father's pub. Which made her think, even if she didn't want to, about the man she barely remembered. Even from the grave he managed to disrupt her life.

'Is that acceptable to you, Dr Wilson?'

'I'm sorry.' *Damn.* Microsleep. 'I left Melbourne very early this morning.'

'Of course.' Anthill man repeated himself. 'Duncan left the hotel in equal parts to his three daughters but the income remains the property of his wife, Sylvia, until her death. Your two sisters have agreed to offer the lease to a third party but we need unanimous permission before we can proceed to the next stage.'

That was all? 'I could have given that over the phone.'

'You had to come here to personally hear the conditions or the will would need to be confirmed in court.'

'Surely you could have waived that.'

'It was Duncan's wish that the four of you meet. This was his way of encouraging that.'

'Encouraging? Good word.' And she'd bet he was laughing right now. 'Fine, done. I agree. Can we go?'

There was a strained silence and she could feel Eve squirm beside her. Sienna sighed and reminded herself these people were grieving; they'd done nothing against her and didn't deserve rudeness.

'Look, I'm sorry. I was up after midnight with a complicated case and at the airport at 4.30 a.m. I'm really not at my best today. I apologise for my bad mood.'

The tension in the room lightened and the solicitor nodded, appeased.

'I had hoped you'd at least have lunch with us before you headed back?'

The way Sylvia asked made it impossible to refuse and Sienna made a supreme effort to lift her game after promising herself she'd kill Eve later.

'Of course. Our plane doesn't leave until 7.30. Thank you.'

Lunch – fresh rolls with avocado – was surprisingly pleasant in the little beer garden out the back of the pub. The garden even had patches of green grass where it had been watered, lots of hardy roses, and a shady tree with tables and chairs. Sienna watched Eve as she fussed over Sylvia.

'Your sister's lovely.' Callie's voice broke through Sienna's foggy thoughts.

'Yes.' Sienna stifled a yawn. 'Eve's been given the warm and fuzzy bone I don't miss.'

Callie smiled. 'Perhaps that's useful as an obstetrician – to be able to make clinical decisions at the right time. I'm sure you're very good at what you do.' Callie hesitated. 'Last night? Were the mother and baby well in the end?'

Sienna glanced at the woman beside her and saw the genuine concern. She remembered suddenly that this woman was her half-sister. Despite all the kicking and screaming she'd mentally indulged in, half of the same blood ran in their veins. It was a bizarre thought.

'Yes. Both fine. A true knot in the cord caused the baby's heart to slow. A good call was made at the end, before it pulled tighter during birth. Could have been nasty.'

Callie shook her head. 'Terrifying.'

'For the mother, of course. Do you have children, Callie?'

'No. Too old now.'

Sienna had to laugh. 'Half of my clients are over forty. Though, much to my sister's dismay, statistically they do have more caesareans.'

The door from the pub opened and a tall, well-dressed older woman strode across the grass towards them.

Sienna saw Callie close her eyes and straighten her shoulders as if preparing for battle. Sienna glanced at her watch and gathered her bag. They'd have to go in the next few minutes.

Callie stood up. 'Blanche. How nice to see you. You've met Eve.' Eve lifted her hand but didn't leave Sylvia's side.

'And this is Sienna, Eve's sister. They're catching the 7.30 from Longreach.'

'Ah ha.' Blanche looked very pleased with herself, though after glancing at her own watch, not so pleased with the limited time. 'You're the obstetrician?'

'I am.' Who was this odd woman? Sienna returned the once-over and stood up herself. They were almost equal in height.

'I'm Blanche McKay. I'm funding the new antenatal clinic.'

'Really. How nice.' As the words left her mouth she caught the look on Callie's face as she rolled her eyes. Eve stopped fussing and came to stand beside her.

'You could help me.'

'But unfortunately not today.' Sienna reached into her purse and removed a business card. 'You could ring my secretary to arrange a time and we can chat on the phone.' Sienna glanced at Eve. 'You ready? I really can't miss that plane.'

NINE

Five days after the reading of the will, Bennet came again. Callie opened the door, and this time she was the one who didn't return the smile. She'd given herself a stern talking-to after their last meeting.

'Mum's in the kitchen. She'll be pleased to see you.' She didn't say, *I'm not so sure whether I am*, but it was probably on her face.

He didn't move. Just waited until she looked to see what the delay was. 'How are you today, Callie?'

Callie met his blue eyes blandly and fought the urge to lose herself in them. She looked away with a vague smile. 'Oh, you know. Good.'

'I'm sorry I was a pain the other day. You didn't need my baggage. It was cruel of me.'

'Like kicking a dog when it's down?' Callie put her hand over her mouth. Where had that come from?

He winced before giving a wry smile. 'I see you're feeling stronger.'

'Sorry. How are you, Bennet?' What a silly conversation for two people who had grown up together.

'Tired today.' He shrugged and rotated his strong neck as if the stiffness there bothered him. Callie tried not to look. 'Adam was up with nightmares last night.'

A small child who had lost his mother. All distance forgotten, Callie leaned impulsively towards him and plucked at his sleeve.

'Come in, you poor thing. And poor little Adam. Does it happen often?'

'Less since we moved to Delta's.' Bennet led the way as she shooed him in.

'Go right through into the lounge. Mum's got her feet up.'

Sylvia lifted her cheek for Bennet to kiss and he bestowed on her a smile that Callie wouldn't have minded for herself. But, tough. *Get over it.*

The afternoon passed pleasantly, a little nostalgically, as memories spun around them like the willy-willies outside while they pored over his plans. Sometimes she could guess what he was going to say before he said it, and sometimes he would smile at her when she used her favourite exclamation of 'Whoa'. As if he remembered all the times she'd said it, years before.

Schematically, they shifted a few walls and windows in the new medical centre, but the undercurrent they both knew was there – the brush of her shoulder against his, their fingers touching as they pointed out the same idea on the screen of his tablet – was way warmer than a married woman and recent widower should be.

'Callie?'

They turned together, and Sylvia smiled with delight at something Callie couldn't see.

'I'm tired. I might close my eyes for half an hour.'

'No problem. We'll go for a walk.' She'd be glad to stretch, create some space before the preliminary plans were emailed to Blanche.

'If it's not too much bother, could you check the pump down at the creek? Sometimes it doesn't work properly after a long dry spell.'

'No problem at all,' Bennet said.

*

As they walked down to the creek Callie could feel the years peeling back like layers of skin – or clothes. Now where had that thought come from? She ducked her head to hide her face.

It was almost as if she were sixteen again and discovering the incredible fact that hunky Bennet Kearney was unmistakably attracted to *her*, dorky Callie Wilson. Bennet had always made her feel special. Today there was a vibe between them that had started with warmth and friendship and drifted towards a tingling awareness of the other that she hadn't experienced for years.

She bent to slide carefully through the fence, and of course Bennet held the wires apart with his hand and foot. As she eased between the two barbed strands, she wondered how many hundreds of times he'd done that for her over the years. It seemed she was out of practice because a rusty barb caught her shirt and she froze.

'Wait.'

She felt the release as Bennet freed it and then her hand was in his as he helped her straighten up. His strong fingers were so warm as they curled around hers and it was crazy, the surge of protection she felt from just that clasp of his hand. She tried not to think about how this could have been an everyday occurrence if she'd come back here after uni and married Bennet, instead of Kurt. What a useless, stupid thought.

His fingers loosened, dropped away as they should, and a few steps later Callie and Bennet skidded down into the hollow that held the little pump house and, incidentally, shielded them from the rest of the world.

On the eroded bank she stumbled over a river gum root and his hand shot out to steady her, but the motion continued and before she knew it he'd swung her around and she was hard against his chest.

Instinctively her eyes shut for a second and then opened as she breathed in deeply. He smelled so good. It felt like she belonged there, snuggled up against his chest, protected from the pain and distress of the outside world. She stared up into the dear face and the words came out in a whisper, more to herself than to him.

'Maybe I should have trusted you all those years ago.'

'We'll never know.' His voice had regained that bitter little twist that was new to her. It reminded her that this wasn't a fairytale, it was real life.

'The way I feel at this moment . . . now's not a good time to trust me.'

She felt the jump of insight in her belly. Unfamiliar, and yet wonderfully enticing. In a world where bad things were piling on top of each other, all she knew was that Bennet felt wonderful.

'You feel good.' She buried her nose in his chest. His bulk was so different to Kurt's fine-boned athleticism. Bennet's chest was much more reliable. Bennet was solid. Dependable. Gorgeous. Her soul cried out that Bennet thought her a desirable woman, instead of the thoroughly disposable one her husband had.

She buried deeper. 'You smell good too.' Like fresh soap, thankfully unadorned by some flash aftershave. She could feel his warm breath on her hair. Hear his intake of breath.

'Stop it, Callie.' He tried to steer her away from him and she could feel the reluctance in his hands. Fighting with himself, and with her.

She lifted her head out from his chest and stared up into his face. The strong bones of his jaw stood out in sharp relief. 'Why? Nobody can see us. We're both unattached. We care about each other and we both need comfort.'

'I think we'd better —' he looked down at her and the intensity faded from his eyes '— check the pump.' He moved her away from him.

Take that, forward woman, she admonished herself silently and hoped he couldn't see the red in her cheeks. How could sensible, professional Dr Callie Piper feel as ridiculously unsure of herself as she did at this moment?

She wanted to grab his hand back and make him look at her – look and then do more. Just how much more was she imagining? Instead she meekly followed him down to the pump house and helped him lift off the cover so they could check it.

There was no accidental hand brushing on either side, and when they went back up to the house he was careful not to get too close.

'Bennet's here, Callie.' Sylvia's soft voice carried through the bathroom door and Callie glanced in the mirror. She'd found herself doing that a lot whenever Bennet's name was mentioned over the past three days.

She hadn't done it when Kurt phoned the day before to say he'd had the removalist pack her belongings. Funny how the only thing she'd felt then had been relief that she didn't have to go back and do it herself. Every day that load felt lighter and she wondered if the surge of attraction she felt for Bennet was the cause.

'Okay. I'll be out in a minute, Mum.' Her hands tightened on the edges of the sink. There really was something particularly seductive about a man who could build stuff with his hands. She grinned at the woman in the mirror. Would she like to romp around in the wood shavings with Bennet? Her cheeks heated and she turned away. What a goose she was.

Her thoughts flew to the incident by the creek. He had said she couldn't trust him. She'd rolled those words over in her mind so many times since then and decided it meant he was attracted to her but didn't want to be. Weren't such complications the last thing she needed with so much else going on? And she didn't want Bennet to feel disloyal to his dead wife because of her. Or maybe she did?

Then there was the fact she was still married, even though in her head she had, far too easily, closed that door. Maybe instead of blaming Kurt she should be thanking him for jerking her out of wasting her life. Had he been getting half a wife for years?

She glanced in the mirror again and chewed her lip. Hiding in the bathroom wasn't solving anything. She pulled a face and then resumed the facade of the sensible Dr Callie Piper.

Bennet was standing near the table. Sylvia hovered beside him, holding a cup and saucer; apparently Bennet had refused tea.

'Here you are.' Her mother glanced at Callie with a smile when she entered the room, then put the cup down on the table and subsided into a chair as if suddenly tired.

'Morning, Bennet.' Callie reassured herself her mum was okay before she turned to Bennet. His shirt was done up to the second-top button. She hadn't noticed that before and a wickedly delicious thought twirled in her brain: was he buttoning up against his attraction to her? Or was he just chilly?

'Morning, Callie.'

'Is it cold out?'

His fingers came up to self-consciously loosen his neck button.

'Not that I noticed.' His cheeks tinged pink and Callie didn't know whether to be deliriously happy or embarrassed because her mother was present.

'Something wrong?'

'No. Just came to say goodbye. Probably won't be back for a week. The planning's done and we need to wait for the orders of materials to come in. I've things to do in Longreach.'

'Oh. Of course.' Her chance was lost. She looked at her mother and then back at Bennet again. He almost vibrated with intensity. 'Well, you've certainly done an amazing job here.'

'Thanks. Your input was good.' He shifted his solid stance. 'I've enjoyed discussing it with you.' Lifted his chin. 'Wondered if I could speak to you for a minute outside?'

Sylvia stood up. 'If you go for a walk would you check the pump again, please? It worked last night but stopped this morning so my garden is gasping.' She waved them away. 'I'm going to have a lie-down.'

It was Callie's turn to blush. *Not subtle, Mother.* Just what was her mother thinking? Hopefully not the same thing she was: Bennet down by the river. The two of them. Just the frogs and soft red sand.

'I'll do it after Bennet goes, Mum.'

'No.' Bennet's voice startled them all. 'I don't like the idea of you down there on your own. Could be snakes. We can do it now.' He turned and waited for her to precede him out the door.

'So I can't handle snakes?'

'You don't handle snakes, Callie.'

'Ha ha. As if I didn't know that, Mr Smarty Pants.' She looked at him sideways as they went down the steps. 'What did you want to talk about, Bennet?'

'It can wait.' They went across the yard to the back fence. He stepped over it.

'For what?'

But he didn't answer, just held the fence for her. She was getting nervous. It wasn't a bad feeling. But she definitely had butterflies. At forty years old. *Crikey.*

'We should really put a gate in here,' she said.

He reached out and took her hand to help her stand as she came through the wire unencumbered. He kept her fingers in his and tucked her hand into the crook of his arm.

'Why? Who needs a gate? I like it this way.'

She looked down at his big hands, work-worn and capable. She resisted the urge to look back at the house to make sure they were out of view. She knew they were. 'What did you want to talk about?' she asked again.

'Everything. Nothing.' He shrugged. Laughed at himself. At her with less humour. 'It wasn't talking I wanted to do.'

I'm hearing you, she whispered silently. 'So, what did you want to do?'

'Kiss. You.' He was a straightforward man. 'Feel your face under my fingers.' His grip tightened a little and she leaned into him. 'And you look so beautiful, Callie. More beautiful every time I see you.'

She thought of her husband, who had made a baby with another woman and was leaving her.

'I don't feel beautiful.'

His hand trailed over her cheek, soft as a drifting feather from one of the black kites circling overhead, a caress and an expression of wonder.

'I assure you. You do feel beautiful.'

Damn, she wished that Bennet wasn't so honourable because she thought she just might love the man at this moment. Nothing would happen. And she'd go home frustrated and angry with herself for not making it happen.

Except something did happen. Bennet let go of her arms and cupped her chin in one strong hand, tilting her face up to his.

'You should never have left me.' And then, with an unmistakable thread of distant pain, he kissed her, and thankfully he didn't stop.

*

Callie lay in bed that night and tried to understand what had happened. She'd never been so foolish or irresponsible, or as impulsive as she and Bennet had been today.

She was mad!

They both were!

Making love down at the creek like a pair of teenagers. They were lucky they hadn't been bitten by ants, let alone been caught by someone. She giggled then sobered. She could just imagine that: Dr Callie Piper spotted naked under the gum trees. Now there was some gossip that could fly around.

Then she sighed. Bennet had regretted it as soon as it was over. He'd tried to hide it but she could see his sudden introspection, the weight of guilt. It'd been less than a year and he'd betrayed his dead wife. She didn't like that he felt that way, but she could certainly understand it, and sympathise. It was different when your wife had died, different to when your husband had just decided he didn't love or fancy you any more.

He'd dressed quickly afterwards. She'd been too stunned – or was that dreamy? – to do anything but watch. Truth be told, she'd been turned on all over again just watching him button his shirt over his impressive chest. She had to bite her lip to stop her mouth from leading her into more trouble; she could see that Bennet had issues.

Oh, why couldn't anything be simple? But that wasn't her life. Of course not.

He'd reached a strong hand down to help her up and she'd found herself standing with no effort. She'd been hoping for another kiss but he picked up and brushed off her clothes and handed them to her one at a time, as if she wouldn't put them on if he didn't keep passing them over.

He didn't meet her eyes. 'I'll just check that pump for your mum while you finish . . .' He gestured with his hand and her heart squeezed at the look of anguish she glimpsed in his eyes.

She sighed. 'I'm sorry, Bennet.'

'I'm sorry too.' He looked at her, narrowed his eyes against the cloudless blue sky. 'Not because you aren't beautiful – but because you don't deserve my baggage.'

'That bad, huh?' She spoke softly to his retreating back but she knew it hadn't been bad. Far from it. And she guessed that had made him feel even worse.

Well, dammit, she wasn't going to regret the absolute magic of lying in Bennet's arms, especially if it was never going to happen again.

TEN

It felt bizarrely like coming home as Eve drove around the back of the pub eleven weeks after she'd first visited. She pulled up in the yard of Sylvia's old Queenslander, which was silhouetted against the sky. The wide verandahs looked blessedly shady under bullnose iron, while strands of blooming crimson bougainvillea entwined around the wooden pylons in a flamboyant display she hadn't expected.

She saw Callie wave from the verandah, then fly down the steps to greet her. 'Welcome back!'

'Hi there, sister.' Eve climbed out of the car slowly and stretched her shoulders before she hugged her. It was so good to see Callie. She looked again. There was something different about her that Eve couldn't pick.

It had been almost three months since Callie arranged the funeral of the father she loved, so the gentle passage of time would have helped with the overwhelming grief but there was something else – an excitement that Callie glowed with. Maybe she really had been throwing herself into this project?

They hugged again and then stepped apart a little self-consciously. 'How's Sylvia?'

Callie followed Eve around to the rear of the laden Subaru and took two of the smaller bags from her.

'Determinedly bright. Likes your idea of excluding animal products from her diet. She says it's been easy because she wasn't eating much anyway, so now when she eats she just uses a vegan option. And it's the only thing I've read that gives good scientific backup for remission.'

Eve heard the voice of the sceptical doctor and grinned. 'As long as she's feeling better, that's great.' She looked Callie up and down. 'And how about you? You look like you've been on a health kick too.'

Callie rolled her eyes. 'I've been busy. Blanche is relentless.' She climbed the steps in front of Eve but glanced back. 'It's so good to see you.'

Eve grinned to herself. 'I'm pleased.'

She paused at the first landing, put her suitcase down for a moment and turned to stare out over the brown paddock below and towards the scrubby creek. The red sandhills glowed in the distance.

Callie came back and stood next to her. They turned to look the other way. The black ribbon of road cut across the red earth like an exclamation mark with blurry edges as it disappeared into the distance out of town.

'It's as beautiful as I remember.' *And as isolated*, Eve thought, but she didn't say it. She'd said it enough as she'd lain in bed the night before in the cabin in a Charleville caravan park. And again this morning as she'd driven on. Back of beyond, all right.

In the distance a man on a horse with half a dozen dogs was rounding up some cattle in a haze of dust. What the heck had made her think she would fit in out here?

'You okay?' Callie looked worried for a moment and that was the last thing Eve wanted.

'Fine. Just soaking it in.' She couldn't even ride a horse. 'So it's been fun watching the clinic take shape?'

Callie nodded enthusiastically. 'It surprised me how excited I am about it.'

Eve smiled. 'And how's Bennet the Builder going?' Callie had mentioned on the phone that Bennet had been her boyfriend years before.

Callie looked away, and they picked up the bags and started up the steps again. 'That man has serious skills, and not just as a vet. I can't believe what he's achieved and I can't wait to show you.'

Yeah, but you avoided the question. Eve didn't say that either. 'You do look relaxed, Callie.'

'I can't believe how good it feels to be back in Red Sand. And being with Mum.'

Maybe it was just that. Stars in the eyes because of no horrible husband.

'Away from Kurt?'

'Surprisingly that too. The practice sold and all my stuff has arrived. So it's all fading into the past already.' She grimaced. 'The break from work is good. I hadn't realised I'd worked without any time off for years.'

She pushed open the back door, and Sylvia rose carefully from her seat at the kitchen table as they walked inside.

'Don't get up.' Eve hugged her gently. 'You look a little rosier in the cheeks.' *But thinner. Much thinner.*

'Hello, darling. How lovely to see you. How *are* you?'

The warmth of Sylvia's greeting brought tears to Eve's eyes. This woman made you feel you were just the person she'd hoped would drop in and that you were welcome to stay as long as you liked – which was lucky, because Eve had brought a car full of gear.

'Great, thanks. And it's lovely to see you too.' Her own mum hadn't exhibited even a quarter of the kind-heartedness and genuine pleasure Sylvia took in other people's company. Callie must be terrified of losing her. Eve was beginning to see why her father might have felt lost with her mother and even two little girls, why he'd come back to this woman and Callie. After all, she'd just left Brisbane to do the same. What she didn't get was why he'd left Sylvia for her mother in the first place.

'We've given you the big room out the back, the one overlooking the river. But have a cup of tea first before you unpack.'

Tea! Eve knew she was back now. She was normally a chai drinker, and in the months she'd been away she surprised a few of her friends by having the occasional old-fashioned cup of tea, preparing herself for the onslaught of the Tea-Drinking Republic of Red Sand.

'Callie says there have been big developments at the old saddlery.'

Sylvia's eyes twinkled as if at a secret joke. 'Bennet's been practically living there, and every time I go down there's something new. Half the town has walked around the big container that was dropped off yesterday from the medical suppliers.'

Callie laughed and Eve stared at her. Her new sister had a great laugh. Funny, that was the first time she'd really heard it.

Even Sylvia was smiling fondly at Callie, who stopped and crinkled up her face at her mother. 'What?'

Sylvia shook her head and glanced across at Eve, who grinned back, but Callie was off and running.

'We've got two and a bit weeks until the grand opening. Unpacking the container is our first big assignment now the inside painting has been finished. Then there's sorting sterile supplies and medications, and unboxing the equipment and working out how to use it all.'

Eve knew all about that. 'I unpacked our new birth unit in Brisbane. Took us days.'

'Experience I will draw on. My old practice manager is flying out to Longreach tomorrow and Bennet's bringing her down. She's giving me a month of her skills to get us through all the paperwork and new forms we need to keep Lex's legal team happy.'

Eve thought about the long streak of gorgeous misery, Lex McKay. She'd had a few daydreams about him at the Botanic Gardens, lying under her favourite tree after work. Now she wondered out loud, 'Does Lex do happy?'

Sylvia giggled, another sound new to Eve's ears. She leaned back in her seat, feeling the expansion of an unfamiliar sense of belonging. It seemed the father she couldn't remember had given her a precious gift from the grave: a new family she was growing to love very easily. She could feel the tightening in her chest and tried to understand why it affected her so much.

She was just being a sook. Eve chose not to look at Sylvia because it would bring even more tears to her eyes.

'So your Sydney manager is coming out for a month?' she asked Callie. 'How'd you manage that?'

'She's a friend. I'm hoping she'll love it and stay. She's going to train one of the women here with the medical software we'll use. I'm hopeless at explaining software to people.'

Thank goodness Callie was hopeless at something. 'Me too.'

Three days later Eve was packing the last shelf when she heard a vehicle pull up outside. She'd learned to recognise the chugging noise of diesel engines, but she'd been expecting a farm vehicle. The sudden flash of rotating beacons coming in through the window had her dropping her box of loose syringes and heading for the front door.

'It's Lex,' she called to Callie, and that funny little excitement she'd had all day as they waited for Lex to bring the new ambulance expanded in her stomach.

It was natural to feel a little trepidation for her additional role as emergency response worker, and when had she signed up for that? *Thanks, Blanche*. So this flutter of nerves was nothing to do with the ambulance's driver, she told herself.

The four-wheel drive Troop Carrier, compliments of the Queensland government and bloody Blanche, was apparently Eve's responsibility. She knew the concept amused Callie but it darn well scared the pants off Eve.

'Afternoon, Lex.' Eve passed his window as she used the key to open the double doors to the car space.

'Eve.' A nod, laconic as usual, then he was reversing smoothly into the ambulance bay. The engine wound down as he climbed out. She'd forgotten how tall and powerful he was, and being jammed together in the cramped space made her aware of that feeling in her belly again.

Callie opened the second set of doors that led into the emergency room, and Eve backed up the ramp towards her sister and out of the confines of the bay.

'How was the drive down from Longreach?' Eve asked.

'Good. It's a beast, but you'll manage it fine with a bit of practice.'

Was that a tinge of scepticism in his voice?

'Gotta love a beast.' *I'm not scared*. She chanted the line from the bear hunt song to herself. 'So the paramedic instructor's arriving with the RFDS on Friday and will stay overnight.'

Lex lifted his hand and rubbed his neck, flexing the muscles in his shoulders as if he'd been a little tense driving the vehicle. Eve tried not to watch.

'Yep. She'll explain all the mod cons of the intensive-care side of it.

But the mechanics are great.' For Lex that was enthusiasm.

'Boys' toys.'

He raised his brows at that. 'Girls' toys, apparently. If I'd said "boys' toys" I'd be called a chauvinist.'

She felt so small beside him when he loomed over her. She had to admit she did enjoy the fact she felt more 'womanly' around Lex. Why was that?

Eve's glance was drawn back to the red and white vehicle. It looked so big and technical; she didn't even want to picture herself pulling up beside an accident scene and jumping out. And if it had made Lex tense there was a possibility it wasn't as easy to maneuver as her little all-wheel drive.

'I'm a big girl. I'll be fine.'

'I noticed that.' That came with a smile and a brief glance that made her aware another button of her shirt had come undone. Then he turned all serious again. 'I'm sure you'll manage.' But he didn't sound any more convinced than she felt, and in a strange way that stiffened her spine.

She needed to learn how the equipment worked, and Blanche had arranged for Eve to go away after that to a two-day Advanced Emergency Life Support workshop, and then to a heavy-terrain driving course. Apparently after that she'd be fine. *Bloody hell.*

To be fair, apart from close-to-town accidents, the vehicle's main purpose was to transfer patients in reasonable comfort to the airstrip a kilometre down the road. That and to traverse creeks if needed, to get to homesteads for outreach visits.

'I think we should ask around and maybe find a volunteer driver. That way you could stay in the back with the patients.'

'I'll sort it out.'

Lex just raised his brows.

'Or June will.' Callie, always the sensible one, reappeared and saved Eve from the brain freeze, and an argument she and Lex seemed to be tumbling into for some reason. 'Come in, June's made a pot of tea and put out some of Mrs Saul's boiled fruitcake.'

But the whole time Lex was there Eve felt strangely combative, on edge, and the amused glances Lex cast her just made her feel more awkward.

ELEVEN

The first Friday of June was the opening day of the Red Sand Medical Centre. Eve could imagine a disastrous financial expenditure year was drawing to a close for Lex McKay. Blanche could be one expensive mother. The thought made her smile.

They'd chosen a Friday because it meant more people would be able to come to the opening – those who came to town could stay overnight if they wanted – and any hiccups could be fixed by Monday for the fresh new week.

Dawn broke still and cool. Eve had noticed the drop in temperature in the mornings, though it was still warm in the middle of the day. She'd been writing in her diary for the past few weeks, keen to record the people she met, the gecko in her room, the snake beside the water tank. She was already aware she could grow to love it out here, and when she looked up she'd lost an hour. *Oops*. Running late again. She dived out of bed.

She still couldn't believe how much Callie had achieved in a few months, especially as it had taken Eve and her boss, Chippie, twelve months to replace something as simple as a bath in their hospital in Brisbane.

Apparently Bennet had worked at a steady pace, but Eve reckoned he must have worked night and day, judging by the photos

Callie had taken of the stages of work.

The building was slap-bang in the middle of town, and had been painted heritage colours. Somehow Eve had imagined they would have painted it white with a big red cross, but it was muted, tasteful and much bigger than she'd thought it would be.

Blanche had flown in a plumber and an electrician from Brisbane, and June, Callie's practice manager, looked like she could organise a small country. She was already talking about staying and opening up a local business, and she wanted to start an exercise class too. Eve wondered if they could make a group with the Country Women's Association. Sienna would crack up laughing at the thought.

Callie and Eve had spent several days unpacking the enormous container filled with medical equipment and supplies that the semi-trailer had dropped off out the front. Handily, every time they'd needed a new shelf or cupboard, Bennet the Builder had zipped in and created it.

Eve could have fallen for Bennet, except that he was shorter than her, and Callie obviously fancied him. She was pretty sure Bennet fancied Callie too, if those searing glances between them she kept catching said anything. Sadly, even Eve could see that Bennet hadn't only built a few walls for their mini hospital, he'd built a few between him and Callie as well.

But it was a big day, and she wasn't worrying about stuff she couldn't fix. And half a dozen CWA ladies had been baking furiously for the supporters who were flying and driving in.

'Eve, the McKays are here,' Callie called through her door, and Eve swiped on some purple lipstick, matching her new purple shirt. It was time. All their work would be on display, and she was proud of the centre, incredibly proud of her sister, and proud to be part of the concept.

The most exciting part was that after the opening she was going to hold their first antenatal clinic; they had six pregnant women booked in already. This was what she was here for.

Two minutes later Eve entered the kitchen but there didn't seem to be room for her. She'd forgotten that three McKays in one place took up an awful lot of emotional space, as well as physically diminishing the room. Talk about a larger-than-life family.

Lex, tall and handsome in his collared blue shirt, jeans and immaculate elastic-sided boots, looked like something out of an R. M. Williams catalogue. He nodded at her with a slight smile, which was an improvement on the way they'd parted on ambulance day. She'd seen him a couple of times in town this past week on errands for Blanche, and sometimes she thought he liked her and other times she felt it was all on her side. She nodded back and tried to keep the confused thoughts off her face but the guy made her more aware of little things.

Blanche vibrated with excitement and shook Eve's hand cordially, so she'd obviously moved up to actual contact with Blanche. And of course Henry crossed to her side and lifted her fingers to his lips with impeccable grace.

'Ah. The divine Miss Wilson.'

Oh, Lordy. 'Nice to see you again, Henry.'

'I absolutely agree.' The twinkle in his eyes was so obvious she laughed out loud.

'You crack me up.'

Lex muttered something that sounded like, 'At least someone's amused by Henry,' and Blanche turned to Callie.

'I'd like to walk through the building one more time before the ceremony, if you would like to accompany us?'

As usual it was an order not a request, but Eve strongly suspected Blanche might be physically missing a diplomatic bone and her similarity to Chippie actually endeared the McKay matriarch to her. So she crossed to her side.

'You've been amazing, Blanche. Everything is perfect and I can't believe how quickly you can make things happen. You should be in government.'

'Government is far too slow-moving for me, dear.' She glanced back at Callie and Lex, who were still in discussion, and frowned.

'Follow me. I have a feeling you are a woman after my own heart. Can't abide this standing around. Perhaps it will encourage them to stop considering things and get them done.'

Eve shook her head. 'Disagree there, Blanche. Callie's worked like a Trojan.' God, she was mimicking Blanche now. It was a bad habit. But she would not have Callie picked on. Funny how she could be brave for other people but not herself.

Blanche paused, taken aback. She blinked like a dazed kangaroo, then stared at Eve. 'As you say. I'm not used to people correcting me, though.'

Then it was Blanche's turn to laugh. It was a short, sharp trumpet of a noise but enough for both of her sons to stop and turn with disbelief, making Eve wonder how often their mother laughed.

Once they reached the busy end of the street there were a few early arrivals milling outside the centre and Blanche nodded regally as she passed them to enter the building with her entourage in formation behind her.

Sylvia had declined to go on tour. She would come for the opening ceremony, and Callie had promised to collect her mother before the official business began.

Inside, the gloom and dust had been replaced with air-conditioned, airy light, and the walls, eggshell blue at Eve's suggestion, calmed and soothed.

A glorious print of a blue-skied sunrise over the red sandhills outside town made first impressions welcoming and warm, and the wooden floors shone brightly beneath two ochre-swirled rugs that led to the reception desk and through to the two consulting rooms.

Each room held a large wooden desk with a laptop computer, a group of three chairs, an examination couch, scales and basic observation tools. There was a soothing print of the ocean in Eve's office, and of the outback in Callie's.

The largest of the three side rooms was the emergency room, with sliding doors and a ramp on the side where the ambulance could back up and be unloaded straight into the room. This was Blanche's baby, built piece for piece to mirror the one in WA she'd fallen in love with.

Blanche glanced around proprietarily. 'I still think we need a portable X-ray machine.'

'No, we don't.' Lex glanced at the newly painted ceiling – and probably beyond to heaven – before closing his eyes. Then he fixed his mother with a steely frown. 'We've talked about this. It requires lead-lined walls and experienced personnel.'

The two Wilson women grinned at each other.

His occasional glances at his mother were priceless, Eve decided as she tried not to laugh. It was worth it all to see the way Lex winced.

Blanche was like a kid in a lolly shop. 'The portable ultrasound and baby monitor arrived.'

Eve's good humour evaporated. She had to admit the ultrasound would be a godsend in emergencies, but that foetal monitor had been a colossal waste of money, as well as a demon she could have done without. If they had a woman requiring such close monitoring then that woman and unborn baby needed to be elsewhere. She'd just have to make sure healthy women didn't start using it or they'd be finding problems that didn't exist.

'Don't like that one?' Henry had slipped in next to her, a little too close for comfort.

Eve stepped back to increase the distance between them – straight onto Lex's left riding boot. The uneven ground tilted her and she put her hand out to steady herself, but unfortunately the trolley she chose to grab had wheels.

The trolley took off. She saw Blanche swivel to check what the noise was, but Eve was on her way down. Lex caught her, held her briefly against the rock wall of his chest until she had her feet firmly again on the floor, and then let go with unflattering promptness.

'Thank you.' She glanced at his face, which seemed to have tightened for some reason. Eve wasn't quite sure what she'd done to offend Lex McKay but it must have had some weight. Blanche's big room didn't feel so large with all these McKays in it.

They finished the walk through the three small backrooms and Eve hoped nobody could see her burning cheeks as she hung back. Henry sent her an apologetic look and she nodded that away. It wasn't Henry who'd embarrassed her.

The rear of the building housed the staff rest room and shower over a huge claw-foot bath Bennet had rescued from an old shed and restored. Another room held the sterile store, all the stock from the previous health centre that they hadn't liked to throw away until they'd gone through it, and other odds and ends they didn't know where to put.

The last was a plain bedroom with an electric hospital bed that Blanche had insisted on, just in case someone needed to lie down in a quiet place. Or stay overnight. Or, Eve decided, hide.

The opening hour approached and by the time the visiting dignitaries, the flying obstetrician gynaecologist, or FOG as he was known, and the flying doctor crew, plus assorted media had all arrived, Blanche was impatient to get it over with.

A crowd of at least fifty had gathered and among them were women, unmistakably pregnant, waiting to be seen.

June, Callie's practice manager and Fran, their new secretary, a widow with grown children who ran the local B&B, handed out information packs to the crowd.

Blanche made her speech, short and blunt, saying the centre was for pre- and post-birth care and that everyone would get at least four home visits after they brought their baby home. It was a huge innovation for such a large area, she said, and concluded by encouraging everyone to make Dr Callie and Midwife Eve welcome.

Eve glanced at Lex when his mother said that, and the amused look suggested he was thawing out a bit. He took a step towards her, but stopped as Henry called out.

'Eve. Wait. Want to meet at the pub later?' She saw a few hopeful faces turn his way as he passed, but no, he was intent on her. She just hoped he realised she wasn't playing hard to get, just blithely and thankfully uninterested. Bummer about Lex too.

'Sorry, Henry. Callie and I are holding a clinic for the women who've travelled for the opening, and we'll be here for a while. But I see lots of pretty girls keen to have a drink with you.'

His face fell. 'I want one with you.'

She resisted the urge to give false encouragement. 'I'm sure you'll manage. Bye, Henry.'

She caught her sister's eye. Callie nodded and inclined her head towards June as a young woman disappeared into the clinic.

TWELVE

Their first antenatal patient, Gracie O'Brien, eased into Eve's office, accompanied by her mother. Gracie was nineteen, with a shining ponytail the exact colour, Eve decided, of the sandhills outside town. Her mum's cropped and faded locks must once have been just as beautiful.

At first glance, Eve thought mother and daughter looked bone-thin but then decided she was just used to plumper city girls; these two were of greyhound stock.

'Hi, Gracie. I'm Eve, the midwife. Congratulations. Only fourteen weeks to go? And you're our very first patient.'

'Hi.' Gracie ducked her head shyly as she sat down. 'This is my mum, Carol.'

'Pleased to meet you, Carol.'

Carol waved a hand. 'Nice to be here. A blessing to have to drive only an hour and a half. Took us four hours to get to Longreach before.'

'The distances are amazing out here.'

Carol shrugged. 'Driving is nothing if the service is there at the end. And it is. People drive further than we did. But this is good.'

Eve liked her already. She bit back a smile and glanced down at the notes she held.

'Well, the Longreach clinic has sent a copy of the information you gave them when you booked in there so we don't have to go over all the boring stuff again with you. Today we just need to check you and baby.'

'Oh? Good. I was dreading having to do all that again.' Gracie held her arm out as Eve unrolled the blood-pressure cuff.

'So how are you? How's your bump? Is she or he moving well and poking you?'

Gracie nodded. 'I think so. I feel him move when I go to bed mostly. Is that okay?'

Eve let the air out slowly from the blood-pressure cuff as she listened for the beat of Gracie's pulse. Heard it come in. Heard it go out. Gracie's levels were normal. She took the stethoscope out of her ears.

'That's fine. Happy babies usually move a lot; it's just when mums-to-be get busy they sometimes don't notice.' She unwrapped the cuff and put it away. 'If you haven't felt your baby jiggle for a while then try to stop, and just sit and relax until you do.'

Gracie frowned. 'I never stop.'

'If you get worried, ring and talk to me. Or email and I'll get back to you. Most babies move a little at least every hour but mostly it's about how *your* baby moves. So if your baby's patterns change, give me a ring.'

She glanced up to check that Gracie had understood, and the girl nodded.

Carol leaned forwards. 'They slow down as they get closer to birth, though, don't they?'

Eve wrote the blood pressure on Gracie's card and again on the file on the computer. 'We used to think babies did move less but research has shown that's not always true. It really isn't normal for a baby close to birth to change its movement habits.'

Gracie's hand touched her belly like she'd felt a little kick beneath her baggy shirt, as if the baby had been listening. They all laughed, then Eve went on.

'Of course the movements can't be as free when there's less room towards the end of pregnancy, but if they slow down it could mean your baby isn't as happy as we thought. So that would be a cue to let me know.'

Eve looked at Gracie's mum, who nodded. 'How many children do you have, Carol?'

'Six. Gracie's the eldest. All normal births so I'm telling her there's nothing to worry about. But our Gracie isn't really a worrier anyway.'

Eve grinned at the girl. 'You do look pretty relaxed. I'm impressed. So will the father of your baby be involved with the birth, Gracie?'

'Been involved enough,' Carol muttered and Gracie cast her mother an exasperated look.

'He's not coming to the birth, if that's what you mean. He's at university.' She finished the sentence proudly, and it was her mother's turn to sigh. 'I was there too, in my first year of midwifery, when this happened.' She patted her rounded belly. 'But that's life. It will sort.'

'Midwifery. Awesome. Maybe you'll want to help out here one day.' Eve wanted to cheer out loud. *Go, Gracie!* She decided they'd worked it out pretty well between mother and daughter, and though Gracie seemed shy, already Eve could see the core of strength inside the young woman. She was beginning to recognise the outback spirit in all the women out here.

'So is your mum going to be with you when you give birth?'

'Maybe. Or if Mum can't get there the midwives will look after me and I won't stay in long.'

'Is that what you did, Carol?'

Carol nodded. 'I'll try to be with her but sometimes things crop up on the station and you can't get away. It's not like you've got neighbours who can pop in from next door. After the first time, my husband had to leave once I went into labour, and then stayed back on the station. Minded the animals and the children till he picked me and the babe up.'

Eve chewed her lip and tried not to grin at the order of the minding: animals then children. 'So you had no problems?'

'Except for being fertile?' The tone was dry but there was a twinkle in Carol's eye. Eve loved the understated humour out here, and it reminded her of Sylvia. She could stop worrying. Gracie was a lucky young woman.

Eve patted the couch and helped Gracie to lie down and pull up her shirt to expose her brown, rounded tummy.

Eve rubbed her hands together to warm them and smiled at Gracie before she bent to examine the mound. She explained the way the baby moved around, measured the height of Gracie's bump with a tape measure, then listened with the new Doppler until the galloping sound of a baby's heartbeat filled the little office.

All three women smiled. 'Your baby's head is down at the moment but they shift and wriggle. Later on it should stay head-down.' Eve helped Gracie to sit up. 'You going to the toilet more now?'

'I'll say. If it wasn't so hot I'd stop drinking. Hardly get anything done, what with running off to the loo all the time.'

'I'll take some blood from you just to check you're not anaemic.'

'So you can do that here too?'

Eve assembled her equipment. 'Yep. The sample flies out with the mail plane.'

Carol watched a little squeamishly but with morbid fascination as Eve took the blood. 'So she'll get those results next time?'

'I'll ring you if you need to take iron tablets, Gracie. You have those in your home medicine chest, don't you, Carol?' Eve knew that a trip to the chemist was out of the question so all the outlying stations had well-stocked bathroom cabinets.

'Always.'

They finished up and Gracie went in to see Callie for the first-visit introduction while Eve finished typing. Then she closed that file and opened the next.

After the last patient Eve glanced at the clock and couldn't believe it was close to five o'clock. She shut down her computer then eased back in the chair and stretched. What a huge day! But a satisfying one. The women out here amazed her, and the distance they'd travelled to attend the clinic – well, that just blew her away.

The young pregnant mum with her baby sitting in the breech position, juggling two wild toddlers under three, had been remarkable. Of course she hadn't liked that she had to go to Brisbane earlier than usual because of her baby's position, but Eve would feel the same if she had to leave a young family behind.

Eve stood up and stretched again, realising she hadn't missed Brisbane once since she'd arrived in Red Sand nearly three weeks ago. She wouldn't mind finding out if June had been able to drum up enough interest in that exercise class. She missed relaxing her body alongside like-minded people. Of course she wouldn't be here long term, but there was no reason not to start it.

Eve heard a goodbye called out, and then the front door shut after Callie's last patient. She wandered into her sister's room and leaned on the doorway as Callie switched off her own computer.

'How'd you go?'

Callie sighed. 'I felt like a fraud.' She, too, stretched and stood up. 'You did all the work. I just agreed with what you'd told them and answered a few questions. Though I did have a chat to Molly about keeping an eye on her baby's movements.'

'Irish Molly?' Eve grinned. 'She's a doll. She's been a backpacker for the last two years?'

'Yep. Used to have a thing for Henry McKay. She was working for Mum and Dad behind the bar.' Callie paused for a minute and Eve saw the wash of remembered grief across her face.

Eve reached across and squeezed her sister's arm. They both sighed for the sadness in the past and that sadness to come. Callie straightened her shoulders and drummed up a wobbly smile.

'Yes, well, anyway, she met and fell in love with Simon – his property is about an hour north-west, and they're such a lovely couple.'

'It was good, wasn't it? The clinic. Providing the service. Setting it up so they felt they could all call us at any time.'

'And we got to use our new ultrasound. Blanche will be pleased.'

Callie smiled and then sobered. 'Colleen's not keen on going to Brisbane.' She grimaced. 'Our first breech.'

'Is there anyone in Longreach who'd try to turn her baby head-first before she goes into labour?

Callie shook her head. 'It's the same as anywhere. Breech is rare enough; you lose practice. She'll have to be a caesarean.'

Eve frowned. 'That'll be hard with those two little ones.'

'It's Longreach or Brisbane.'

Eve waggled her brows. 'Or arriving here at the last minute with a breech on view.'

'No.' Callie's eyes widened. 'Crikey. Pray she doesn't do that.

Have you delivered a breech birth?'

'Three. But I didn't have to do anything.'

Callie's eyes were still round. 'Was it nerve-racking?'

'Amazing. Incredible.' Eve stared through the wall into the past. 'But you're right. I had good backup but it got the adrenalin going.'

Callie shuddered. 'I would die. The stress would kill me.'

Eve laughed. 'Not true. Everything would be fine. Just don't touch the baby unless you have to. And those mums seem to instinctively get into the right position for the birth. The natural mechanisms are still there for breech as they are for head-first babies.'

Callie shook her head. 'You're gorgeous but no, thanks. Let's hope Colleen's baby decides to do a somersault and come head-first. I'll let the FOG know and talk to her husband. Hopefully he can persuade her to go early to Brisbane. That's all we can do.'

'You underestimate yourself. Look how you managed the ultrasound.' Eve had her concerns about Colleen and what was going on at home. Colleen's unease for her husband and the way they were suffering in the drought mostly. Apparently the feed was very low. She suspected Colleen was going to go at the last minute and just hope her baby turned.

'It probably won't happen,' Eve reassured Callie. 'But if it does – then just have faith.'

Callie winced. 'Don't say that.'

There was a knock at the door and Blanche peeped her head in. 'Just dropped in to say goodbye.'

'We used the ultrasound.' Eve waved towards the hallway. 'One of the women has a breech baby and we could confirm that and discuss her care for the birth.'

'I'll tell Lex,' she said with unholy satisfaction. 'He said it was an unnecessary expense.'

Imagine that, Eve thought. There had been a few instances over the last week when she had begun to wonder if Lex could be anti the whole medical facility idea. What could he have against the clinic when the service they were providing only had benefits for the women who visited it?

THIRTEEN

By the end of the following week, both women were pleasantly exhausted and Callie could feel the peace seeping into her. Peace and healing – and a lot of that had to do with Eve.

Her new sister seemed to be able to take everything in her stride. Including the days she'd spent in Charleville's Intensive Care Unit, refreshing her knowledge of advanced life-support care for her role as ambulance officer while Callie had run the clinic. Luckily everything had been the same as the week before, and Callie was becoming less stressed when dealing with well pregnant women.

She could almost face an obstetric refresher course, but she didn't quite have the headspace yet.

As she and Eve leaned on the verandah rail of the house Callie pulled her cardigan tighter around her shoulders, the sound of boisterous laughter drifting back from the pub on a Friday night.

Sylvia had gone to bed, frail but in good spirits with the company, and Callie could feel the rightness of being here with her mum. She should have done this years ago.

'I think the clinic will be a great success.'

Eve groaned. 'I think I'm over talking about the clinic.'

'Since when have we talked about the clinic?' Callie sipped her drink and hid a smile.

'Ha. Between daylight and bedtime every day for the last forever.'

'So what do you want to talk about?'

Eve paused and then said it. 'Actually I'd like to talk about you.'

Callie shrugged in the darkness. 'I'm pretty boring.'

'Well, I haven't had a chance to find out. We never seem to have time to talk about anything else and I still know so little about you. I'd say you're anything but boring, but I'll shut up if you like.'

Callie caught a glimpse of Eve's apologetic grimace in the gloom. She felt a twinge of guilt.

'That's fair enough. I dragged you away from your friends in Brisbane, so you can't harass anyone else but me.'

'You didn't drag me out here. I chose to come. It's no hardship.'

'Okay. You chose to come.' But she still felt guilty. 'What do you want to know?' Callie waited patiently for her sister to start, in no hurry as the sounds of magpies and butcherbirds – birds that would be thinking about sleep in the city but still sang late in the cool outback evening – floated to her as the moon rose.

She could even hear the crickets down by the creek. She shied away from thinking about the creek, especially with Eve here, but her belly warmed anyway.

'You've had a really tough couple of months and I haven't wanted to pry. But you said once that you'd lost a baby, and if you think you could talk about it I really want to know what happened. And how someone as gorgeous and caring and just plain motherly as you hasn't got any other kids?'

Callie wished she hadn't encouraged Eve to ask, that she could call her words back. She looked into her almost empty glass and wished she had wine to loosen her tongue. As the silence lengthened she knew this was going to be hard.

'Bethany. A little girl.' Callie tried to keep her voice even but still it came out just above a whisper. 'I never saw her.' *If only . . .* She closed her eyes for a moment. *Move on.* Away from the thought that always pierced her.

Her voice flattened like the unending plain out there in the darkness. 'I had severe pre-eclampsia at the end of my pregnancy and she died while I was in a coma. That's why I don't deliver babies any more.'

'I'm so sorry.'

Callie heard the shock in Eve's voice. She didn't look at Eve. Couldn't. Her eyes stung anyway. That's why she didn't talk about it.

'Have you any photographs of her? Bethany?' A question Callie hated, but the tone said, *Don't answer if you don't want to.*

The pain that never really went away glowed again like sleeping embers fanned in a sudden hot breeze.

'They didn't take pictures because Kurt didn't want them to. When I woke up she'd already been cremated. All I had was a jar of ashes.'

'Shit!' Eve crossed to her and slid her arm around Callie's shoulders. 'I'm so sorry.' She shook her head. 'Shit. Shit. Shit.'

'Eve!' Callie dragged herself out of the past and glanced at her sister in mock surprise. 'That's a lot of poo happening there.'

'I need a lot . . . a truckload. I'd like to put your husband in it, head-first.'

Callie almost laughed. Kurt. *Lord.* She wasn't going there.

'He didn't know what to do. Thought he was doing the right thing. Sparing me the trauma of a funeral.' Callie sighed. 'She had Down syndrome, you know. They told me she had a heart defect incompatible with life.'

She stopped. Held the silence and finally had to fill it. 'But you're right. I think I would have coped better if I could have just held her for a while. Not just imagined what she looked like. Spoken to her, even if she couldn't hear me.'

Eve's face, so easy to read, was for once blank with shock. 'I think so too.'

But Callie wasn't hearing now. She was feeling. 'I've never been able to bring myself to make a place for the ashes.' Maybe she could make that plot now she was home, where she belonged. That idea grew.

'How about I help you make one for Kurt?'

Callie blinked. Smiled damply at her new champion. 'Stop it.'

But she could see Eve was genuinely upset. And not a little angry. Her new sister's eyes were narrowed like she wanted to confront someone. Even her fingers were tense and clenched. Callie felt a measure of comfort that someone really did care that it had happened to her.

She could hear the struggle in Eve's voice. 'What were the staff doing, not taking photos? Have you checked with the hospital? Any midwife would take pictures if the mother was unconscious. Keep a lock of the baby's hair. Put a packet in the medical records. It's what we do in case parents change their mind ten years later.'

'It's seven.' She'd never asked the hospital. Kurt had said no, they hadn't taken any. Seven long years.

'Maybe they still have something somewhere.'

Callie swallowed the sudden fear in her throat. A catch of excitement she couldn't bear to allow to grow.

'Eve, don't! Please don't say that.' Her skin felt tight across her face like a mask as she turned to face her sister. 'What if I start to think they have but when I ask them, they don't?' She shuddered. 'No. I'm not going to ask. It would be like losing her all over again.'

'I'm sorry.' Eve ran her hand through her hair. Put her glass down and gripped the rail with both hands. 'I'm sorry. I'm making it worse. I don't know what to say.'

Boy, did Callie know all about that. How you couldn't retrieve the irretrievable. How sometimes silence was all you could manage.

At least the conversation was over.

'So what did you do?'

She almost laughed. Conversation not over. Apparently Eve didn't subscribe to that theory. She so should have known that about her new sister.

'I went back to work as soon as I could and put my head down. I wanted to try for another baby but Kurt said no. That it was too dangerous health-wise, and he didn't want to lose me. But I think he was scared we'd have another disabled child. So I went on the pill, until we stopped having sex.'

She laughed but it was a bitter, sad little sound. Even she could hear that. 'Now I'm forty and he's having a baby with someone else.'

The tiny silence that followed vibrated with all the words unsaid.

Then Eve shattered the silence in typical Eve fashion. 'Well, you have to feel sorry for that poor bitch.'

Callie lifted her head in shock. And, finally, with a reluctant smile, she shook her head. 'Eve. Your language.'

'You wait. If I ever meet your husband you'll hear language. Now pour yourself a real drink and we'll toast to our sympathy for that other woman. Then let me tell you about me.'

Callie did what she was told and, incredibly, she did feel a little better. It was good to have it out in the open, she guessed. But a change of subject would be even better.

'Now that I'd like to hear.'

'Ha. Boring stuff.'

'Anything but boring, I'm sure.'

'Well, as you know, Dad left our house when I was about two. So basically I never met him. But after meeting you guys, I don't get why he left here in the first place. Your mother is much nicer than mine was.'

Callie had to laugh. 'Hush. My mother said your mum was very beautiful and that he'd never stretched his wings. My parents were married at nineteen, you know, and I was born six months later.'

'Explains a few things, I guess. How people can have a thought in their head about the grass being greener . . . Though by all accounts my mum preferred living without a man around the house. A bit like Sienna. She's very like my mother was.'

Callie had to smile with Eve. Both were obviously thinking about Sienna's brief visit for the reading of the will.

'Do you know how they met?'

Callie had asked her mum once. 'Apparently your mother stayed at the pub to write an article. When she wrote to say she was pregnant, Dad was torn. Finally he decided on a new life. Mum said to go.'

'Sylvia is one amazing woman.'

'It was a long four years later before he came back. He never left town again.'

'But your poor mum.'

'She never said much about it. I remember I was around eight and suddenly this laughing hero of a guy was gone. And Mum was stoic, still is, but I remember her crying that night. That was the only time I ever knew she cried.'

Callie straightened her shoulders. 'She might have been fatalistic, but I think I just got angrier and angrier with my dad. When he came back I didn't talk to him for a month. But over time he wore me down. Looking back now, he was incredibly patient with me, and he never stopped making it up to Mum.'

Callie gazed out into the darkness. 'I think she was happier than she'd been before he went away.'

Eve's voice was hesitant. 'But why would you bother to sign a birthday card to a half-sister who took him away from you?'

She looked at Eve. 'Mum said I had to. Reminded me that you and your sister had lost what I'd lost. I actually understood that. As things settled and I began to believe he wasn't going away again it began to feel so important to sign the cards.'

Eve nodded. 'I liked getting them. They meant I really did have a dad out there somewhere. And another sister. I created very involved fantasies of why I didn't see you. I wanted to come visit but Mum just said no. I don't remember him at all so I guess I didn't miss him. But I liked that my surname was different to my mum's. Sienna hated it.'

Callie wondered if Eve was as unaffected as she claimed.

As if in answer, Eve continued. 'But I regret not coming sooner. I was always going to and then life got in the way.'

'What about Sienna?'

'Sienna says she vaguely remembers him. I nursed my mum when she was dying and one thing she said stuck in my brain: fall in love, enjoy, but don't get married if there is a voice in your head saying "run".'

The more Callie heard about Eve's mum the less she understood her father following her. 'Funny advice for a mother to give her daughter.'

'Maybe. But I see some of my friends unhappy a few years down the track and wonder. I'm thirty now and if I don't find a soulmate I'm not getting married.'

'So she didn't regret not marrying him?'

Eve shrugged. 'So she said, but she never denied she fancied him from the first moment she saw him. She gave Sienna his name and then she had to do the same for me or it would have been odd at school. But maybe it was lust and not love, though apparently they tried to work it out for Sienna. I think I was an accident that delayed his return.'

'So you spent your whole childhood without a father figure?'

'Not really. My grandfather was there. He understood me the best and we used to go fishing, just him and me, every now and then. I loved that. He worked a sixty-hour week in business but that paid for Sienna to go away to boarding school. I refused to go. Kept running away until Mum let me stay home. I think the phone calls from the school wore her down.'

Callie looked at her and smiled. 'I can see the determined little girl.'

Eve laughed. 'I didn't fit at home but I certainly didn't fit at boarding school. Sienna thrived and went on to med school, where she found her niche.' She looked at Callie. 'Funny. You seem almost the total opposite of Sienna. Did *you* enjoy med school?'

Callie thought about that. 'Some parts. I loved the knowledge. The riddle of medicine. But I was lonely. Missed Red Sand. Missed my mum and dad. And Bennet. Until I started to go out with Kurt.'

'So why did you marry Kurt and not Bennet? Bennet's gorgeous.'

Her belly flipped again. Yes, he was. Why the heck had she married Kurt? 'Kurt courted me. Made me feel like a princess. I'd never felt that before.'

'So what about Bennet?'

Callie looked away. Blushed in the darkness. 'There's nothing to tell about Bennet. He was my friend and sweetheart when we went through school. I idolised him a bit because he'd stick up for me if someone teased me.'

Eve mumbled a disbelieving swear word and Callie had to smile.

'Come on. The room gets cloudy when you two share space. He makes your mum laugh. He makes you laugh.'

'Yeah, well, I might have blown that. But I think that's why I couldn't settle down with Bennet. I was terrified the same thing that happened to my mum would happen to me if I married my childhood sweetheart. So I went for someone totally different to my dad, and look where that got me.'

'Yeah. Don't start me on the Kurt I'd like to hurt and I haven't even met him.'

'No.' Callie laughed. 'I don't think I'd let you.'

'Well, anyway. I want to know about Bennet.'

Callie could feel the heat getting higher in her cheeks. She was feeling very silly about Bennet and there was Eve, watching her with that perceptive smile, knowing Callie wasn't immune to Mr Kearney's charms.

'Bennet is a friend. I hope he becomes a good friend, like he was when we were kids, but there's a lot of water under the bridge for both of us and a lot of grief for his wife on his side.' *And now some history down by the creek.*

Eve's eyes brightened. 'Still waters run deep. I think you should dive in and let Bennet have his wicked way with you.'

'Good grief.' *Again?* She didn't say it but her belly fluttered. 'I'm a married woman.'

'No. You're permanently separated prior to divorce from a nasty little man who has already thrown away his wedding vows.'

God bless new sisters. 'You certainly have a way with words.' Callie shook her head. 'But this is a small town. We don't do affairs unless we want everyone to know about them.'

Eve shrugged. 'I do get that. But how about mutual healing in secret?'

'Seriously, Eve, stop it! Or I'm going to blush like crazy when I see him next. But yes, okay, I do fancy Bennet a bit. We'll just have to see what happens.'

'I'm pretty sure he fancies you too.'

'Enough about me.' Callie looked at Eve. 'You said you were going to talk about you. What about you and Henry? He seems to head straight for you every time he sees you.'

'Henry? No way.' Eve rolled her eyes. 'They'd call me Cougar Eve. But he came in this morning and I'm going for a fly with him tomorrow. Some errand that needs doing in Charleville for his mother and he asked if I wanted to come.'

'Ooh, helicopter love.'

'Don't even think about it. But he'll give me a laugh. I'm meeting him down at the airstrip at 7 a.m. so I'd better not drink any more or Sergeant McCabe will have me for DUI.'

They both looked and mimicked the other's expression.

'I have to admit,' Callie murmured, tongue in cheek, 'crime has dropped to zero since that particular law-enforcement officer has arrived. He even makes Blanche nervous.' They both grinned again.

'What's his story?'

'Not common knowledge. I think Mum knows something that he told Dad but I haven't got around to asking.' Callie swirled the remains of her drink in her glass and tossed it over the verandah. 'I don't suppose he'll stay long.'

FOURTEEN

Eve was cold. It was a different winter to Brisbane. Stinking hot through the day and chilly at night. She huddled into her scarf and watched the sky lighten. The sunrise painted its pastel path across the barren paddocks as she waited for Hotshot Henry. This had been a bad idea. But it was only her second weekend off and the prospect of her first helicopter ride had seemed like fun.

Then she heard it.

The helicopter approached faster than she expected and within thirty seconds it had created a mini dust storm as it landed in the paddock a hundred metres away.

She'd have thought Henry was the type of guy to land right beside her like a show-off.

She walked towards the rotors and a hand appeared where the door should have been and gestured her across. She bent her head like she'd seen people do on TV, but seriously, it was also out of a natural instinct to avoid being decapitated. Her hair whipped around like a windmill as she stretched her hand out to hold onto the edge of the door frame so she could she look across at . . . Lex?

'Where's Henry?' She couldn't hear his voice so there was no way he could hear the stupid little tremor in hers.

She saw his mouth move. Looked like he said, 'Jump in.' She

contemplated running. The guy had serious hunkability but there was not a lot of welcome in the hand that beckoned. The last thing she wanted to do was spend the morning trying not to drool over Lex McKay while he ignored her.

But she didn't get up at this ungodly hour on one of her only two sleep-in days just to freeze – physically or metaphorically.

By the time she'd struggled inelegantly into the seat she already regretted the decision, thanks to the cheeky glimpse of humour in Lex's eyes. He gestured to the bulky headphones and microphone set hooked on the central support in front of her, and she pulled it on.

'Good morning.'

She jumped. It was louder than she'd expected, even though Lex's voice came through tinnily in the headphones, but the background thumping of the rotors was blessedly reduced to a hum.

'The headphones are automatically switched to receive so if you want to say something, just push this button here.'

She eased out her breath and nodded. Took another one in and breathed out slowly, forcing the tension from her shoulders. She pushed the button.

'Good morning, Lex.'

'Henry sends his apologies. Something came up. Hope you don't mind me stepping in?'

So Lex had grounded him? 'The attraction was the helicopter, Lex.'

Crikey – did she just say 'was'? She'd meant 'is'. Though now she sat in it she didn't feel particularly reassured. The aircraft was smaller, less sturdy than she'd expected, and doorless. Only the seat-belt that she was hastily pulling across her chest would save her from hurtling to death through the open door.

'We still going to Charleville?' she asked.

'Yep. Errand for Blanche. Shouldn't take long. About 400 kilo-metres.'

'At how fast?' She could work that out. How long till she could get away?

'About 80 knots.'

Like she knew what that was. 'In kilometres per hour?'

'About 150.'

That was a lot of time sitting next to Lex. She shivered.

He didn't miss much. 'You cold?'

'It was freezing out there.'

'Not quite. Two degrees.' His teeth showed white. Eve was glad someone was amused.

'Thanks, weatherman.'

She thought he said something, but he didn't put his microphone on.

Then his voice came through again. 'Blanche thought you might like to go out to the sandhills on the way back. Have you climbed one yet?'

Did Blanche? 'No. Saw them from the road. They weren't as big as I thought they would be.'

He spread his fingers each side of his ears to show he hadn't heard her. *Geez.* She pushed the button and said it again.

'You'll see. She sent a basket for lunch.'

He leaned across and she tried not to lean away to avoid him or blush but he just checked her seatbelt was tight enough before set-tling back in his seat.

'Right then. Let's go.'

The craft vibrated and then the tail swished first one way and then the other as they started to rise. The butterflies swayed back-wards and forwards in her stomach as well. The sparse grass of the airstrip flattened as they rose swiftly into the morning air. Red dust ballooned under them.

She looked down to where her feet were pushing hard into the transparent floor and saw the ground receding. Eve eased off the pressure. She wasn't sure whether she liked the view or not, but either way she didn't want to push through the perspex.

Lex's voice startled her. 'Good view of the pub from here.'

She looked across to where Sylvia's house sat in its little patch of green, one of two double-storeyed buildings in town, and nodded.

'How is Sylvia?'

She remembered to press the button. 'Thinner. And she has a pain in her hip that Callie and I are worried about but Sylvia plays down.'

'Sounds like Sylvia.' There was definitely sympathy in his voice, and she was glad he could see she really did care about Callie's mother.

She looked again at the long, low building of the pub and the trellised beer garden that lay behind it, green from the pump Sylvia used from the creek. Eve saw the little thread of brown river that ran along the back of the town.

He must have seen the direction of her gaze. 'Have you been down to the river?'

'No.' She remembered to use the mic. 'Haven't had a lot of practice climbing through fences. Maybe Callie will take me down.' She paused. 'I hadn't realised it chewed so many hollows through the land. There are quite a few erosion runs that look like dry creek beds?'

'When the Cooper runs it spreads out like ribbons. That's why they call it the Channel Country. Last proper rain was a year ago. Last flood two years.'

A year? She nodded. 'And that's when you get the wildflowers?'

He frowned at her. 'That's when the cattle put on condition.

Ground goes green overnight.' He shrugged. 'Most roads are impass-able and if it's storming you can't fly.'

My mistake. Cattle, not flowers.

He gestured with his hand towards the front and side windows. 'So what do you think?'

It was vast. Empty. 'Amazing.'

Lex was staring straight out the front windscreen, his large hands confidently directing the little craft like he was holding the reins of a very familiar horse. She could feel the muscles in her neck relax. She was safe in his hands.

It was a shame there were muscles elsewhere she could feel limbering up. An ignition switch in her belly she hadn't used for a while lit up and glowed. In an understated way, unlike his exuberant brother, Lex McKay was a very sexy guy.

Then he smiled directly at her so that his teeth shone white in the early morning sunlight and his eyes glinted with a sudden joy.

'God, I love this.'

It was totally unexpected and gave Eve a bigger kick because of that. A great big glad-to-be-alive grin that had her blinking and blushing. The heat of it rushed under her skin. *Good grief.*

She jammed her tongue against the roof of her mouth to make some saliva but still her voice squeaked when she got it to work. 'I can see you love it.'

He couldn't hear her. She pressed the stupid button and repeated it. Then decided the comment had been lame. *Sheesh.* She nudged herself back into normality.

The smile had gone but the moment lingered in his eyes as he narrowed them at her. 'Yeah. Wouldn't be anywhere else.'

Lex pointed out landmarks. There weren't that many of them, but she had to admit that the incredible ribbons of colour were growing on her. The way the pale-blue sky met the orange and brown and downright red of the earth was surreal, and the chocolates and yellows explained the colours used in a lot of Aboriginal art.

A while later they flew over the township of Quilpie, and below, the thin strip of bitumen road glowed from the shimmering brick-orange soil around it.

The flight showed, more than anything, the remoteness of the homesteads, the tracks that curled around scrub, and the lack of water. Lex offered more commentary than she'd expected and her questions were answered thoughtfully. Once she even found herself the recipient of an approving nod.

After the longish flight they landed at the airport, and were in and out of Charleville in less than an hour.

Fifteen minutes after that Lex had a brief discussion with the control tower and they took off again. Eve decided she could get used to the perspex floor window as she watched the airfield recede further beneath them.

Her headphones crackled as Lex spoke. 'Flying doctor service down there.' He pointed to a pair of houses on the outskirts of Charleville. 'They take the calls there, and the other one is the museum.'

She remembered to push her own button. 'They do an amazing job.'

He nodded. 'Blanche had toxaemia when she was in labour with Henry. They flew in, scooped her up, and she delivered twenty minutes after they landed in Longreach.'

'Bloody hell,' Eve muttered. The memory of a young woman she'd nursed who almost died flashed vividly in her mind. 'I've seen that too.'

He nodded with unexpected understanding in his eyes. 'Of course you have.'

For a ridiculous moment she felt like crying because she wasn't used to people getting her. But she forced herself to look away and concentrate on the line of black tar slicing across the red earth below. Both ends were hidden by scrub so there was just one little straight stretch.

Eve switched on her mic and pointed to the road. 'It looks like a burnt match on a plate of oranges.'

He grinned and she was happy.

The sun shone from behind the helicopter, and the expanse of ochre and brown land disappeared into the horizon.

Two and a half hour hours later they landed beside a brick-red sandhill shaped liked a low pyramid.

The wind-carved side angled steeply and had been rippled in perfectly symmetrical corrugations by the wind. The other side lay smooth, as if waiting for the brush of an outback artist on its unpainted red canvas.

Up close, fascinated, Eve kept shaking her head. 'It's beautiful.'

'Yes.'

Man of few words. She glanced at him. 'Can we climb it?'

'Sure.'

She bent down and picked up a handful of the glittering red particles of sand and the tough crystals ran through her fingers like tiny jewels. 'I can't believe the colour.'

'That's why they called the town Red Sand. This is the start of the big sandhills that stretch across the Simpson Desert all the way to Uluru and beyond.'

They started to climb, feet sinking deeply into the coarse sand, and Eve was conscious of marring the previously untrodden perfection of the surface with their footprints. It was like they were the first people to walk on the moon.

To her left she saw a thin pattern of imprinted diamonds in a line across the surface. Something had been here before them. The tracks were sharply defined and precise, like an artist had stick-drawn them in a slight arc with care. She turned to Lex, who was climbing behind her.

'Snake,' he said laconically.

She blinked. Glanced around cautiously.

'Gone.'

She shook her head with a wry smile. 'And if it wasn't gone?'

'Stop. Wait. He might just forget you're there. Back away slowly.'

'How could he forget I was there?'

'Snakes have short memories. I was told about forty seconds. So don't move. Don't frighten him.'

'So if I moved after forty seconds I could frighten him twice, you mean.' Who'd frighten whom twice?

A little later on, she pointed out a spot with a thin line followed by another.

'Beetle,' he said.

The next one was easy. Tiny Ys in the sand.

Eve glanced at Lex and imitated his voice. 'Bird.'

He didn't smile but she was looking for the change of expression in his eyes and hugged the flash to herself when she saw it.

A brilliant lime-green desert bush with hard, shiny leaves sprouted in isolation halfway up the side of the first hill, framed by the luscious red sand, and she wished she had her phone to take a picture of the contrast.

When they reached the first rise, the majestic sweep of the next sandhill drew her on, and when she got to that one the next beckoned. She turned back to survey the way they'd come, their helicopter a flash of reflective metal out in the paddock. Now that she looked she could see the cattle spread out in all directions.

'How many cattle do you have, Lex?'

'On Diamond Lake Station we have 28 400. In the Kimberleys we have another 6000.' His face softened at her round eyes. 'But there are bigger companies with bigger stations.'

She gazed into the distance and there wasn't a dwelling in sight. 'It's a long way from Brisbane.'

He gave her a hard look and then glanced away. 'You finished here?'

She'd lost him. Eve sighed and was going to follow him when he turned to go back, but then changed her mind.

'I'll be a few minutes. I want to sit.'

'You're lucky it's not summer or you'd be boiling by now. I'll open the esky under the tree.'

She heard the swish of sand for the first few steps as he began the descent, and then it was quiet again, with just the wind gently blowing and the birds cawing overhead.

She sat down with her knees under her chin, digging her hands into the sand again and twisted them so that the warm particles massaged her fingers as she let the peace envelop her. Out in the distance a windmill was turning. She could imagine the creaking noise she'd come to recognise as the shaft moving when the blades turned.

Up above the flat world on her little red castle she could feel the magic soak into her like chalk soaking up red ink. She'd missed her quiet times, and vowed to make the time to renew each day before she was caught up in the slower but still relentless pace of Red Sand township.

Peace. Strangely, unexpectedly, she didn't want to leave this spot, didn't want to walk back down the hill, wanted to stay in the embrace of the red sandhills she'd fallen in tune with today.

But she was thirsty and hungry, and Lex was waiting. All good reasons to come down off the hill.

FIFTEEN

Lex had set up the food under the shade of the lone spotted gum, about 50 metres away from the helicopter. Some time in the past someone had rolled a couple of logs under the shady branches to sit on and the scene was peaceful – as well as promising to settle the embarrassing rumbling of Eve's stomach.

She eased down on the log and sighed as she glanced around. Bare paddocks, galahs in the distance, a few white Brahman cattle grazing.

'So you have a lot of lives to look after.'

He frowned. 'Working families, you mean?'

'No. Cattle. I'm thinking of your birth rate compared to my hospital's. It's lucky cows don't need midwives.'

He laughed and shook his head like he couldn't believe she'd said that, then he sent her an apologetic glance. 'Fair enough.'

She watched the tiny calf under a smaller spotted gun. 'I've never seen a calf being born.'

'They come the same way. Have to find you a birth to watch then.'

She grinned at him. 'Likewise.'

'God, no.'

She frowned. 'But you'll be there when your child is born.'

Mocking grey eyes met hers. 'Which child would that be?' he drawled.

She shrugged. 'The one who takes over your thousands of cattle from you.'

He raised his brows and glanced around at the deceptively barren landscape. 'If we still have a station after my mother finishes blowing money on a pipe dream.'

The crux. *Finally, he talks.* 'So you don't think the centre is useful?'

'Some will benefit. But most people should have definitive care in a larger centre or phone the flying doctor.'

Well, now she knew what Lex thought. 'They'll still do that. It's just antenatal care well before they're due. And we still refer calls to the RFDS.'

He looked up and his eyes had hardened. 'It's the babies I worry about.'

Thanks for the vote of confidence. 'That's my problem. I'll worry.'

'If the centre wasn't here we wouldn't have to worry. It might make women stay home longer. But my mother doesn't think that.' He looked away and then back, and she could see he was genuinely regretting his outburst. 'Sorry.'

'Your sister?'

His voice dropped and he wasn't talking to Eve any more; he was talking to himself. 'If her baby had lived my sister would have lived. But the baby died.' His face tightened with grief and she understood now why he'd seemed so cold on the idea of the centre. It wasn't money at all, though she'd never really thought it was.

He was adamant. 'No way do I want women to think they can birth here or stay around longer into their pregnancies because the centre becomes the backup plan.'

'I can see how you could think that. But I don't see it that way. I think the access means people will ask for help sooner if problems arise. Come and get checked more often. Maybe we'll save babies that way. And even mums.'

He shook his head and she could see the wall. She guessed he had the right but she felt sad he wasn't 100 per cent behind them. She was beginning to see how much having Lex as an ally could mean.

'Well, your mother thinks so too. But everyone's entitled to their opinion.' She gestured to the open expanse in front of them, changing the subject. 'And I used to think lunch at the Botanic Gardens was good.'

He nodded. 'This land is me. My life. But I see why women who aren't used to it wouldn't want to stay. Why they could be tempted to run as fast as they can, back to the city.'

Lex put a tin mug in front of her and poured tea from the thermos. He passed across a huge slice of thick-crusted spinach quiche on a metal plate and one of two small bowls of salad and some cutlery.

Eve fell on it with passion. 'This is so good.' She spied a semi-unwrapped tea towel exposing date scones and a round plastic tub of butter.

He laughed as she unwrapped the scones and put one at the side of her plate. 'You love your food. I like that in a woman.'

'Lucky.' She rolled her eyes and groaned as the last of the quiche went down. 'This food is almost as good as in the best restaurant in Brisbane,' she teased.

'But not as good?' He shook his head. Let his breath out with exasperation. 'Of course it's not.'

That was a bite. She frowned at him. 'Boy, do you have baggage.' She shrugged, picking up her knife and the butter with relish. 'Your problem, not mine. See,' she paused thoughtfully, 'I'm more of a live-for-the-moment sort of girl. So what's here and now is the best.'

She could feel his scrutiny but was determined not to let him spoil the moment.

'I'm sorry if I find it hard to believe you're not comparing the facilities here to where you are from.'

'My fault for mentioning Brisbane.' *Sheesh.* 'Why on earth would I ruin this moment by lusting after something I haven't got?' She shook her head at such stupidity. 'Is this real butter? It tastes divine.'

He glanced down at the little plastic tub. 'Blanche makes her own butter.'

Eve wanted to lick her fingers but guessed she shouldn't. 'The woman is a marvel.'

'She can be a pain.'

Eve laughed and took a bite of the scone. 'All great people can be.'

He sighed again. 'I'm sorry.'

She chewed the piece of scone in her mouth – she should not have taken such a big mouthful – and looked at him as she tried to keep her mouth shut. Finally, she swallowed.

'Sorry for what?'

'Being anti-Brisbane. It's not your fault my ex-wife lives there.'

Darn. Ex-wife and hang-ups. No one had told her Lex had been married. What a mood killer. It looked like she wasn't going to snuggle up to that white R. M. shirt and have a nice little cuddle. She looked away and ground her lips together to stop herself from grinning.

'Something funny about that story?'

Oh, Lord. When you've dug a deep enough hole, the truth was the only way out. 'No. Was thinking I'd better not imagine myself plastered to your chest, then, seeing as how I'm from the city too.'

She could tell he was struggling not to laugh. Nice pastime, Eve decided, watching that mouth.

'Be careful.' He stood up and tipped out his tea. 'I might decide I'm up for a little short-term plastering.'

She could feel the heat in her cheeks so she was glad he was walking towards the helicopter. She called after him. 'You can't be finished. I haven't had another scone yet.'

'Take your time. I need to make a call on the satellite phone. Then we'll head.'

Wednesday morning saw Eve close the back door of the big house quietly behind her, as she stepped out to where the cockatoos were raucous on the telephone wires. Sylvia and Callie had been up in the night with Sylvia's upset stomach, so getting out a bit early seemed a good idea. With Sylvia unwell today Callie wouldn't come in to the clinic; Eve was happy to deal with whatever came through the doors.

As she stepped with a leisurely pace along the street a young ringer in his dusty ute waved at her as he drove past and she remembered his grinning face from her first emergency suture experience on Monday.

Callie had been called up to the big house with sudden visitors and Troy had walked into the clinic, clutching a disgustingly dirty handkerchief soaked in blood.

She'd told him the only things she'd stitched up were ladies' bottoms, and he'd nearly choked laughing. Which was pretty good, as the sizable chunk he'd taken out of his finger needed a fair repair job. The skin had come together well but she'd had to listen to a host of teasing remarks about what he didn't want it to look like when she'd finished.

She was still smiling as his ute disappeared into the distance when she heard her name.

'Eve. Wait.' The voice came from the post office she'd just passed. Mrs Saul, panting a little from her chase, stepped out into the street to stop her. 'I hear June wants to start a tai chi class.'

Eve stopped. 'Morning. You interested? We thought we could hold it at the medical centre.'

'I am. If you'd like to make a sign I could put it up in the window and maybe we'd get enough starters. Fran wants to come too.'

Fran hadn't said anything at work but she must have talked to her mother. That was great. Eve could feel the pleasure expanding.

'We'll get onto it today. I was thinking Saturday mornings. That suit you?'

'Whenever.' The older lady waved the problem of timing away. 'As long as I don't do my back in. I've always fancied the slow, gentle stuff. I'll see you later then.'

'Sure.' If she could whistle Eve would have broken into a tune.

As she opened the clinic door she was preceded by a wild-haired cherub in a disposable nappy who tore into the room and ricocheted off the walls like a rubber squash ball.

Eve followed him around, righting the spilled paper waste and disentangling him from an electrical cord before she caught him up and sat him on her hip, where he squirmed and grumbled and waited for his mother.

Colleen, the remarkably unstressed blonde with the baby in the breech position, followed soon after with a tiny version of herself clinging like a limpet to her neck. Eve could see again where the children had acquired their looks. She'd thought last week that Mum was a stunner.

'Johnny. You be good.'

Eve smiled. 'Thanks for coming back, Colleen. I know it's a big drive from the station. It's just a check to make sure you're still breech before we make the arrangements.'

Johnny squirmed and Eve reached down and pulled a chunky plastic truck and some blocks from her drawer. She put Johnny and the toys down on the floor beside his mother's feet and he was instantly diverted. Colleen shook her head indulgently as Johnny proceeded to remove all the wheels.

Eve readied her blood-pressure cuff. 'I'd better get this done quickly before he gets bored.'

Colleen smiled and put her arm out and Eve rapidly wrapped the cuff around it. 'You're a busy woman.'

'You bet.'

'I think you're amazing. You look well.' Eve pumped up the cuff and then let it down again before writing the result on the card Colleen had handed over.

'Any worries, apart from the chance you might have to go in to Brisbane early?'

Colleen frowned and shook her head. 'No. That's enough worry.'

Eve could see she was still not happy. 'Baby moving well?'

'It's kicking,' she replied.

Something was up. Eve glanced down at the history in front of her. This was only the young woman's fourth visit to an antenatal clinic in thirty-four weeks. 'Was it hard for you to get here today?'

She shook her beautiful hair. 'Easier today. Sometimes it's hard.'

'I see both your babies came a little early?'

'Went to Brisbane both times even though I was supposed to go north. It wasn't fun. I don't like leaving my husband.'

She remembered something about Colleen's station being one of the hardest hit with the drought. 'No way you could take your whole family and stay with someone in Brisbane?'

'Nope.'

'Okay.' Eve waved towards the couch. 'How about I have a feel and check the position, then we'll have a listen to your next gorgeous baby?' She grinned at Johnny, who was getting cross with the truck. It looked like the toy was going to fly across the room any minute now.

Colleen climbed awkwardly up onto the couch. There was a lot of unspoken conversation going on here, Eve thought, as Colleen lay down with her little white-haired limpet still stuck to her side.

Johnny stopped what he was doing and glared at Eve as she palpated the smooth oval of his mother's belly.

She smiled at him reassuringly. 'It's okay, mate. I'm just feeling for the baby.' Her hands glided in a circular fashion around the mound. 'You have any aches up here?' She gently massaged a round baby part that shifted under her hand just above Colleen's rib cage.

Colleen grimaced. 'All the time.'

'I still think your baby is breech, or bottom-first, at the moment, but there's still a little time for him or her to turn the right way up.'

'Yep.'

'I'll take blood today to check you aren't anaemic, but as your baby is still breech you'll have to decide if you will have a caesarean up at Longreach or if we'll send you to Brisbane to try for a normal birth. Have you talked to your husband about it?'

Colleen's eyes slid away. 'I'll go Brisbane. Don't have much choice, do I? Rather not have a big scar with these two.'

Eve could certainly understand that. 'That would be my choice too. I'll turn the ultrasound on and when it's warmed up and confirms the baby's position, I'll write it on the card again. You'll need to mention that if you go into labour before you get there. Like I said last week, sometimes a bottom-first baby can be a little trickier at birth and sometimes it's not. But it's good to be with people who are skilled at birth in that position. Okay?'

'Hmm.' She looked at Eve. 'So you've delivered babies that are breech?'

Uh oh. 'Three. But I had specialists not far away so it was very different to here.' She could just imagine Callie's face, or Lex's for that matter, if Colleen ended up here to birth. 'So you'll go next week?'

'Guess I'll have to.'

Eve smiled but a flicker of unease remained as she watched Colleen leave.

SIXTEEN

Early on a leisurely Sunday morning Eve watched Callie help Sylvia into the room. The older woman's hair was bundled up in a towel, and she could hear Callie saying, 'Well, you washed my hair enough when I was kid, it's your turn now. And tell me, my mother – if it was me who was sick, would you mind drying my legs?'

Eve smiled as she picked up the ringing phone. 'Hello? Wilson household.' It still felt strange to say that.

She listened. Frowned. Looked up at Callie and held her eye. 'Sure. Come in. About an hour is fine. I'll be down at the clinic.' She hung up.

Sylvia sat down and Callie began to rub her mother's hair dry. 'Who was that?'

'Molly Hollis. Irish Molly. Baby seems unnaturally quiet, has been all night, and the lack of little kicks and prods has scared her. She's wondering if maybe she had a leak in her waters that she thought was something else.'

Callie's hands stilled. 'That scares me too.' She started rubbing her mother's hair again but her hands were shaking. Callie glanced at the clock. 'Might just be sleeping.'

Eve gulped down her tea and checked her watch. 'I sincerely hope so. We saw her last week. She was due to go to Toowoomba in the next day or so.'

Callie rubbed more slowly. 'Maybe she should go there now instead of driving back this way.'

'It's a fifteen-hour drive to Toowoomba and only an hour to here,' Sylvia said.

Eve agreed. 'We can check her out here and get her there quicker if need be.'

Callie still wasn't sure. 'Maybe she should have rung the flying doctor instead of us?'

'She's on her way now, Callie. We'll sort out the best thing to do when she comes. It might be nothing but we can check.'

Callie nodded and fluffed up Sylvia's damp hair with her fingers, but her eyes were focused on something else. 'We have the baby monitor and the ultrasound.'

'Yeah.' Eve shrugged. 'I might even be pleased to use the damn CTG in this case – as long as we find a heartbeat.'

Callie sighed deeply. 'It's moments like this when maternity care freaks me out. After I lost Bethany —' she glanced at Eve and her mother, and Eve wondered if this was the first time she'd mentioned Bethany in a conversation '— I had this fear I would miss something and the mother would be as heartbroken as I was. I'll be praying until she comes in.'

An hour later Eve found Molly Hollis's baby's heartbeat. But it was fast. And there was none of the spiky pattern she wanted to see on the paper recording, so quite possibly baby was conserving energy for the essentials of clinging to life. Not a good sign.

If she'd been in Brisbane Eve would have called an obstetrician, and booked the theatres for a caesarean while she waited for the doctor to come in. They didn't have that option. There was no way for a caesarean here, and the flying obstetrician was all the way out at Roma, but they could call the flying doctor and get Molly transferred as fast as they could.

Eve's fingers shook as she picked up the phone to call the RFDS. The doctor on the end of the phone was calm and methodical. 'She's stable? Observations good? No pain? No contractions? No loss of fluid?'

'No. Everything else is negative. But no foetal movements noticed since last night and I'm not reassured by the foetal heart rate on the trace.'

'Decelerations?' The unspoken query was for any signs of a last-gasp effort by baby to hang on.

'Not on this graph.' Eve didn't like to say, 'Not yet'.

'We'll arrange the transfer to Charleville ASAP. I'll ring you back with a landing time.' The RFDS woman murmured something and then came back on the line. 'Put a cannula in. Give her a stat dose of Benzylpenicillin and run some fluids. Hold on.' Eve could hear her talking again in the background. 'We'll be about an hour.'

'Great. I've got saline up now. I'll give the ABs as soon as I get off the phone. Confirming with my colleague.' She repeated the dose and type of antibiotic so Callie could check them with her in a moment.

'Fine. See you soon.' Then the woman on the phone added hesitantly, 'I don't need to tell you to keep her on her side and keep monitoring until we get there.'

'Nope. Will do, right until I take her out to the strip. We'll be ready to go when you get here. And thank you.'

Simon, Molly's husband, sat white-knuckled on the arm of the couch as Eve hung up the phone. He said the words Eve didn't want to hear. 'I should have rung the flying doctor.'

Both of Molly's hands slid protectively to cup her silent belly and Eve could see frightened tears as she squeezed and then let go to clutch Simon's hand again.

'You guys have done everything right,' Eve said.

She watched Simon grip his wife's fingers and couldn't imagine how he felt. It had been a tough year with the drought, watching the condition fall off the cattle. Eventually the rain would come back, but tiny babies – tiny babies who didn't make it – they never came back.

She shook off the horrible thought and watched the pattern of the baby's struggling heartbeat for improvement as the antibiotics were injected into Molly's vein.

It was Callie who reassured them. 'We don't know what's wrong but the most likely reason is infection. So Molly will get the antibiotics at the same time as if she'd been in the plane now. Same time, Simon. It would have taken them more than an hour to get to you as well, and we'll give them now. You couldn't have done it any quicker.'

Eve agreed. 'And the IV fluids going in now will often improve a baby's heart rate.' She looked at them both. 'The big thing is that you picked up the reduced movements. All we can do now is get you ready to fly as soon as they land.'

She glanced with worry across at Callie, writing the orders down and documenting the time of the call. Eve glanced again at the CTG and tried to remain reassuring. This was not a happy baby. But at least there were still no decelerations, and maybe there had been a slight increase in beat-to-beat variation with the fluids running in. She hoped so.

Less than an hour later the RFDS sent a message to say they were fifteen minutes out and Eve and Callie began to prepare for the shift into the ambulance. By the time the RFDS landed on the airstrip beside the cemetery Eve had the ambulance backed up, waiting to pull in beside the aircraft as soon as the engines were off.

When Eve and Callie watched the plane take off with Molly

and Simon on board a while later, their faces were drawn and tense. They'd all hung around the open cockpit door to hear the rapid beating of the handheld Doppler the flight nurse had used after she settled Molly into the seat. So far their baby was being a tenacious little cowboy or cowgirl, determined to survive, but no one would relax until they knew it had arrived safely.

Sunday lunch was subdued in the Wilson household as they waited for the call from Charleville.

Bennet, who was staying on the farm next door to the Hollises', had driven in to see Callie when he'd heard, and even Sergeant McCabe, a friend of Molly's husband, had been to see if they had any news. After he left, Callie remembered Eve's question and Sylvia explained that the policeman's sister had apparently died in a car accident while he was overseas. She was pregnant at the time, and he was always concerned around pregnant women.

Callie twisted her hands. 'This is why I didn't want to be responsible for babies.'

Eve could see the shadowed fear in Callie's eyes but didn't know what she could do to help. 'There was nothing to see last week. You have to remember, most women have normal pregnancies and healthy babies. Maybe she did rupture her membranes and somehow they got infected.'

Callie's teacup rattled as she placed it back onto the saucer. 'I can't even read the trace on the foetal monitoring properly to explain the situation to the receiving hospital.'

'I can.' Eve reached across and squeezed her sister's hand. 'I don't feel as confident as I should with adult ECGs when someone with chest pain comes in. But you can read them easily. And without us nobody has any medical care until a plane arrives.' She let go and sank back into her own chair. 'We did a good job.'

Finally the phone rang and Eve jumped up to get it. She glanced apologetically at Callie, who waved her on with trepidation.

'Wilson residence, Eve here. Simon! It is you. What's happening?' She listened and then broke into a smile. 'She did? Congratulations. How is she?'

Eve put her hand over the phone and whispered. 'A girl, 2 kilos. Tiffany. In NICU but stable.' She took her hand away. 'That's great. And Molly?' She put her hand over the mouthpiece again. 'A caesarean at 11 a.m. Give her our love, Simon. No, that's fine. We're just glad everything is looking better.' She glanced at Callie and smiled. 'Sure. I'll pass it on.'

She listened some more. 'They'll do swabs,' she told him. 'To find out which bug caused the infection, make sure they're using the right antibiotics. Okay. Go sit with your new daughter. Thanks so much for ringing. Bye.'

Eve put the phone down and then collapsed into the chair and closed her eyes as she let out a pent-up breath. 'Intra-uterine infection. Tiffany is septic. They put a drip in her and will give her broad-spectrum antibiotics until they get the swabs back, but the paediatrician is cautiously hopeful.'

Callie was frowning. 'But Molly wasn't sick, was she?'

'She said she didn't feel sick. And she looked well.'

Sylvia's quiet voice drifted from her chair. 'Whatever it was, it sounds like that was too close. I wonder what Blanche will say when she hears.'

They didn't have to wait long. Blanche had Lex fly her into Red Sand on Monday morning. She strode into the clinic, her riding boots clacking in time with the hand she was tapping against her leg.

'I hear the Hollis baby is stable.'

'Yes, thankfully. It's good news, isn't it,' Callie said cautiously.

'In one way it is and in another it was too close for comfort.' She put her soft leather bag down on Eve's desk and pointed her nose in Callie's direction. Eve was glad she wasn't looking at her.

'Can you do research, Callie?'

Eve saw Callie blink at the question and shrink a little more – trying to hide.

'The basics, but it helps if the researcher has a passion for it,' she said dryly. Callie glanced at Eve. 'The only time I was analytical I married Kurt, and look where that landed me.' Nobody commented, and she sighed. 'I guess I could try, do a refresher course.'

Blanche turned Eve's way with a glance that said she already assumed that the likelihood of Eve being analytical was slim. 'What about you, Eve?'

'Lord, no. All those numbers and cross-referenced notations. That was always Sienna's forte.'

Blanche pounced on the comment like one of those black-eyed carrion birds eating roadkill. Eve wished the words unsaid because no good would come of this. But it was too late.

'Of course. Your sister. Where did I put that card?'

Eve felt her stomach sink. Blanche had that look on her face. But there was no help for it. 'She won't come. She's an obstetrician in Melbourne.'

Blanche cocked her head. 'Does she do research?'

Eve nodded cautiously. 'She's at the Greater Melbourne Research Hospital. Just finished a thesis and a paper on diabetes in pregnancy among older women. But she's up for the director's role, been work-ing towards it for five years.' Eve shook her head. 'She wouldn't come out here just to look at all the baby statistics, not for a million bucks.' Eve saw the look Blanche cast Callie: triumph.

Eve shook her head again, this time at Callie. *Don't support that idea*, she vibed silently, but Blanche didn't need any encouragement.

'Not for a million, then.' Blanche didn't even blink. 'Perhaps her hospital would send her for two?'

Holy crap. Now she was getting scared of this woman. Eve tried to keep the picture of a Sienna-tirade out of her mind but it wasn't easy.

'Please don't do that. I'm not keen on living with an angry Sienna.' *Been there. Done that.*

Blanche was supremely uninterested. 'Babies are dying, or almost dying, out here and we still don't know why.'

Callie watched helplessly as Blanche steamrolled them both. Bravely she tried to maintain some semblance of having a say. 'It could have nothing to do with why the other babies died.'

Blanche ignored that and glanced around the room, almost grinding her teeth with frustration. 'Let's make sure, shall we. I'd hoped setting up the clinic would stop this from happening. We still need someone to find out if there is a reason behind it that we can do something about. You two do an excellent job but we can't have another stillbirth.'

'We've only been here a month,' Callie said, her face pale.

Eve straightened. *Whoa, there.* She stared straight at Blanche. 'Don't you start apologising, Callie. We did an amazing job ensuring Molly's baby got out of here in as good a condition as possible.'

Then to Eve's dismay Blanche's eyes misted with emotion. 'I know you did. And everyone appreciates it. But I won't let it happen again. You have a sister who is an experienced obstetrician with research qualifications. In the brief time I spoke to her she struck me as a very efficient woman. I like efficient women, and I don't have time to search for another one. If I have to drag your Sienna screaming all the way to Red Sand to work this out, I will. I don't care how much it costs or how upset she is, as long as she can tell me we are doing all we can for our babies. I need that to happen.'

Eve spared a brief thought for what Lex would say to another two million dollars. Actually, she wondered where Lex was hiding, considering Blanche had said he'd flown her in.

'I have a friend in Melbourne,' Blanche muttered darkly as she too glanced around. 'Where's Lex?'

Eve closed her eyes. Sienna would not be happy.

SEVENTEEN

That afternoon in Melbourne, Sienna was definitely not happy. 'You're sending me *where*?'

Sienna Wilson had never been a trusting soul, but recently, painfully, she'd become more sensitive to the aroma of rodent. To detecting when Sienna was being royally screwed. The idea of remaining calm got lost in the rush between her ears and the immaculately French-polished tips of her fingernails dug into Wallace Waters' solid cedar desk, as if holding onto it would keep the dream alive. They couldn't do this to her. It had to be about Mark.

'Red Sand. Evocative, isn't it?' Wallace mused. Was he actually laughing at her? 'And apparently there's a Diamond Lake.' Wallace, skin gloriously tanned from celebrating his seventieth birthday in the penthouse at the Waikiki Sheraton, smoothed the grey hair that had been combed skilfully over his balding scalp. He dropped the words with a certain satisfaction, because first and foremost he savoured the power.

No surprises there.

He followed with a measured pronouncement of her fate. 'Very small town. In the corner of Channel Country, far west Queensland.'

'I know the place. I was there earlier in the year,' said Sienna through gritted teeth. She had every reason to hate the name of it.

The first man to let her and her sister down had come from there. School of hard knocks. *Don't trust men. Use them.*

Be seconded to a small town in the outback, stuck in a dust bowl full of rangy cattle and cowboys, while some male jerk with less experience spun in her Melbourne office chair? *God, no.* Sienna loved the city lifestyle. She abhorred the idea of everyone knowing her business, interfering in her life, talking about her behind her back.

She shook her head. 'I don't think so.'

Wallace looked up at her then turned away, walking a few paces to even their heights out. She knew what he was doing because his son did it. Small man syndrome.

'Population 200,' he said, ignoring her, 'and there's been a recent establishment of an antenatal-care centre that's available to townsfolk —' he rolled the word around his mouth as if it amused him '— plus families on cattle stations in a huge radius, though seeing patients is not your problem. Why their inhabitants have had a two times greater than state average premature birth rate over the past twenty-four months is your problem. It's a fact-finding mission.'

She didn't want to accept this mission. Couldn't she burn the tape before listening, like Tom Cruise?

She could see a scaly patch of old sunburn on the top of Wallace's scalp and glared at it from her extra inches. She wished she'd worn shoes twice as high. *Little worm.* She could barely look at him through the slits of her eyes, she was so wild. *He'd promised.*

Finally Wallace looked blandly at her and inclined his head for her comment.

'I've finished my thesis and you led me to believe I had the director's job here. We agreed.'

She paused, counted to three. She'd slaved for this job, everyone expected the announcement, but the moment called for big-girl pants, not a whining voice. She didn't consider tears, not that she could remember the last time she'd cried. She had to win this. *Would* win this.

'I'm scheduled to start next week,' she went on calmly, trying to instil a subliminal sense of fait accompli.

Wallace walked back to his desk, framed by the skyscrapers of Melbourne out the window. 'Your appointment is still viable, just put back for three months.'

And that was where it all really sucked. Because she knew then that he was lying. This was the first step of the plan to give her job to someone else. She'd seen him do it before but stupidly she'd thought she was safe. He looked past her shoulder and she wanted to scream, 'Look at me!'

Then came the death knell. 'It's Blanche McKay's hometown, and her family is our new *major* benefactor in research grants. It's you she wants.'

'I've only met the woman once.'

'Our hospital has been offered a two-million-dollar research grant.' He stopped and whistled incredulously. 'Two million,' he repeated, in case she hadn't heard him. 'If – *if* – you stay for the three months. Not bad at all. If you actually discover a way they can improve care, the amount goes to five million.' He looked at her. 'Do try for that.'

It was a double whammy: distance from Mark, and money. She had no hope.

She took her fingers from the desk, noted with disappointment the fine wood had been impervious to her horror, and straightened.

'So you sold me for a donation.'

He stood, came around the desk towards her and stopped a foot away, his hands held out in supplication. What a con this guy was.

'Twenty-four months of research funding in return for your esteemed presence in an outback town for three months.' He flashed his fingers like a game-show host with a winning number. 'I think that's reasonable. Did I mention this town is reeling from a sudden increase in birth incidents they can't explain?'

He said it as if it were her fault. 'Yes. You did.'

Wallace rubbed his hands together: to his mind the matter was settled, and he was so glad she could see his reasoning. 'So they need someone who can review the documentation of women's pregnancies and gather enough stats to point them in the right direction. They need an obstetrician who is an experienced researcher with a nose for anything suspicious.'

Well, obviously she didn't have that last requirement. She hadn't been suspicious enough of either of the Waters men. But Sienna could inhale the powder of betrayal and it choked her like that thick red dust she dreaded.

'Are you sure this is just about the money? Nothing about my relationship with Mark?'

Wallace replied blandly. 'Nothing at all. I'm sure Mark will wait for you.'

Sienna turned away because she couldn't stand the look of insincere sympathy on Wallace's face. 'It sounds like a demotion if you ask me. I'm a city girl. What the hell would I do in the outback?'

'Learn to ride a horse? Or if you hate it that much, come back on weekends.' The lack of interest stung. 'You could fly in and out from Longreach. It's four and a half hours' drive from Red Sand, I believe. Brisbane is a two-hour flight from Longreach.' He looked briefly amused. 'Though you might want to leave your pretty little red sports car at home and get a four-wheel drive. Should be fun.'

His face changed, hardened. 'Get over it, Sienna. You'll be well paid and the hospital will be too. The decision has been made. Unless you wish to resign?' He'd like that. He must have already chosen her successor. Wallace waved the problem away. He was finished. The discussion was over.

Sienna gazed past him out the window. She could see the trams, the shops, the restaurants below them, and the big ships steaming across Port Phillip Bay far out to the south. God, she loved all that. She loved her town's streets, lined with cafes, designer clothes shops and Italian shoes – not scrubby trees and feral animals.

But the sinking feeling in the pit of her stomach said there wasn't a lot she could do about it unless she wanted to burn her bridges here. She stared at the grain in Wallace's desk. Maybe she did. But she'd calm down before she decided to do that.

She would drive from Melbourne to Brisbane and out to Red Sand. It would take her at the very least a couple of days but no way was she going to be stuck without wheels in the back of beyond. And no way was she driving four and a half hours to an airport in some clunky off-road vehicle like the one Eve had made her travel in. She'd drive her own car. And she'd take a small suitcase so she had an excuse to come home.

'When do I leave?'

Sienna threw open her office door, making her secretary jump. 'Get my sister on the line, please.'

The phone rang while she was still staring out of her city-view window. 'Eve?'

'Sienna?'

'What the hell happened? Are you responsible for my being seconded to Red Sand?'

'God, no. You gave Blanche your card.' Sienna could hear the vehemence in her sister's voice and her ire settled a little.

Eve went on. 'I told Blanche the last thing I wanted was an angry Sienna in a small town.'

To her own surprise, Sienna laughed. You could rely on Eve to call a spade a spade. 'Okay. I believe you. Damn that woman and her money.'

'Callie and I are not experienced at multi-level analysis.'

Sienna could feel the rise in her blood pressure. 'Callie? Did she say bringing me in would be a good idea?'

'Seriously not Callie's fault. All Blanche. The woman is funding the whole health centre. She's like an express train on steroids. You met her.'

'Apparently she's very rich.'

'Owns half a diamond mine. And two stations.'

Sienna could well believe it. Five million dollars to a hospital over 2000 kilometres away was ridiculous. And it would be five million because of course she'd find a reason. That was her job. 'Got a son?'

'Two. Both good-looking.'

Something in Eve's voice was intriguing. 'Fancy them, do you?'

'One's a pretty playboy, and the other is way out of my league.' Eve laughed but there was an unusual bitterness in her voice. Eve didn't do bitter; that was Sienna's forte.

Poor Eve. Sienna didn't like the idea of some stupid man upsetting her sister. 'Well, if he doesn't like you, he'll hate me.' Her fury at being banished to the outback returned with full force. 'Three months, Eve. You reckon I'll last?'

'Of course you will,' Eve said heartily. Too heartily, maybe. But Eve went on before she could question it. 'It's a good cause. If anyone can solve this, you can, Sienna. All angst aside, I do believe that.'

Hell and damnation. 'Well, I don't have much choice.' The sooner she started the sooner she'd be finished. 'See if you can get permission from all the affected women to email their medical records through. I'll look them over between now and the drive up.'

'You're driving?' Eve squeaked. 'In your car?'

That just made Sienna more determined. 'I'll take a few days. And Eve?'

'Yes?'

She tapped her fingers on her desk. 'See if you can find someone to wash it when I get there.'

Eve laughed. 'I don't think they wash cars out here, Sienna. Wouldn't waste the water.'

Sienna's fingers stilled. 'We'll see about that.'

'What about accommodation? Did they say where you were staying? You could probably stay with Callie and Sylvia.'

'Not a hope in Hades. I'll look for a B&B.'

'Oh.' Sienna heard the hiccup of laughter and didn't like the amusement in her sister's voice but there was nothing she could do about it now.

'See you next week.'

EIGHTEEN

Callie sat quietly behind her office desk and listened to the battle of wills. Every now and then she smiled as Eve directed Blanche back to reality regarding what Sienna would do and what she wouldn't. The two other women were facing up to each other like two tall hens, though Eve leaned against the wall and watched Blanche pace.

It was Tuesday afternoon and Lex had flown Blanche back into town to discuss the new developments, but Callie was more interested in the fact that he'd asked Eve for a coffee afterwards. She would have been terrified but Eve seemed quite excited by the idea.

Blanche paused in her conversation as Lex entered, and even let the door close behind him before she spoke again.

'Lex?' She looked him up and down. 'You're very pale.'

He massaged the back of his head with some obvious distress. Eve must have agreed with Blanche because she went straight to the sink to pour him a glass of water. He seemed a little calmer once he'd taken a sip, whether it was from the water or just Eve's being there Callie didn't know. But she didn't miss the look on Eve's face as she spoke gently to Lex.

'Are you all right?'

He blinked and looked at her vaguely as if through a mist. 'No. I don't think so. I've had some disturbing news.'

Blanche paled. 'Is Henry all right?'

'Henry's fine.' He looked around as if not sure this was the place to share the information. He must have decided they were safe. 'It's Kareena.' He glanced at Eve. 'My ex-wife.' Looked back at his mother. 'Kareena and her parents were all killed in a car crash this morning on the Gateway Bridge.'

Callie gasped. Blanche had gone a pasty white. Before Callie could stand, Eve had filled another glass with water.

'Sit down, Blanche,' Eve said as she pushed a chair over.

There was rare obedience from Blanche as she sank into the chair. 'That's dreadful.' She took the glass with shaking fingers. 'So much tragedy in the last few months. What is the world coming to?' Belatedly she remembered Lex's distress. 'Are you okay?'

'That's terrible news,' Callie said quietly, but looking at Lex's face she realised there was more. She could have done with Bennet as support if it was going to get worse. Her own reserves for dealing with bad news were pretty low.

Lex was watching his mother. 'There was a girl in the back of the car who survived. She's seventeen. Her name is Lily.' He took another sip of the water so that he could enunciate clearly. 'Sergeant McCabe tells me I'm listed as her father.'

'What?' Blanche squeaked, and then coughed. 'You're what?'

'You heard me, Mother. Lily is your granddaughter.' He sighed. 'Kareena has kept it a secret so I can only imagine she didn't want Lily to grow up here.'

Callie heard the sudden surge of bitterness in his voice for those stolen years, and winced for the dead Kareena. Lex glanced apologetically at Eve and Callie for embroiling them in this, but something in his face said he was glad for their presence.

Before anyone could say anything else Blanche's head came up and there was a glint of new purpose in her eyes. 'Well. You'll have to go and fetch her.'

'If she'll come,' Lex said, a shadow of insecurity in his voice that wasn't like him.

'Don't be ridiculous. Of course she'll come. Where else would she go?'

'It's better to be prepared.' Eve spoke slowly, gently, as if to Lex's frightened daughter, and Callie looked at her. Eve had that knack of picking up on people's needs. She constantly amazed Callie with her perception. 'She might be too heartbroken to leave everything she knows just yet. I imagine there must be some family left?'

Callie wasn't really surprised Eve would come to the rescue. She'd begun to realise Eve was fearless when in protection mode and she could see Lex appreciated her input. He wasn't a man who usually needed champions. But Lily would need champions as well.

'Don't be silly.' Blanche wasn't budging. 'I assume you want to leave now? Go home so you can get to Brisbane!'

Lex was looking at Eve thoughtfully and then he nodded. He seemed to take her insight on board, and Callie wondered for the first time if perhaps these two were suited. 'Lily is in hospital, not physically injured but apparently she hasn't spoken since the accident,' Lex said.

His mother stood up and nodded at Eve. 'I haven't finished this conversation. We'll discuss it on the phone later this week.'

'I look forward to it,' Eve said dryly, and Callie wondered if she could see a small smile lurking at the back of Blanche's penetrating look at Eve.

'Hm.' She glanced at her son. 'Are we ready to go then, Lex?'

No coffee then, Callie thought, but there was no disappointment on Eve's face, just concern for Lex.

Three days later, Henry appeared at the clinic. He hung around until the last patient left and then leaned on Eve's office door.

'Fancy a wine and maybe even a dinner for two at the pub?'

Eve smiled. Stretched the kink out of her shoulders. 'I don't do dates with you, Henry. You know that. Plus I think Sylvia's had a casserole cooking all day for tonight. But I'll have a drink.'

'Why don't you do dates with me?' He spread his hands wide. 'You do dates with Lex. I'm a good-looking guy.'

'I don't do dates with Lex either. Just a coffee now and then.' She looked him up and down. 'And of course you're gorgeous.' She grinned at him. 'I like you, Henry, I really do. But it's never, ever going to be more than that.' She put her finger to her lips and whispered loudly, 'And I'm never going to sleep with you.'

Callie came in at the end of the sentence and her mouth twitched as she pretended she hadn't heard.

Henry blushed and stood up. 'Well, I'll see you at the pub then.'

Eve looked at her sister and closed her eyes in silent communication: *Forget you heard that.* 'I'll come now. Callie, can you tell Sylvia I'll be about an hour?'

Callie nodded but her lips remained compressed as her eyes danced.

Eve took Henry's arm and squeezed it once as they walked out onto the street. She leaned into him. 'I'm sorry. I was teasing. I didn't mean to embarrass you.'

'I'll use your remorse for my own ends.' Henry had rallied. 'I'll forgive you if you sleep with me.'

Eve laughed. 'Well, I think we've covered that one. So tell me, how's Lex and his new daughter?' Henry didn't answer and Eve raised her brows. 'That bad, eh?'

'Lex is pretty worried about Lily. Said he was coming in to talk to you tomorrow. I hear he's asking you out to lunch at Diamond Lake?'

'I didn't hear that.'

'Bet you won't tell him you don't do dates.'

'Green-eyed Henry. And it's not a date if he's worried about his daughter.'

'Hmm. Well. So I guess I'll leave it to him.'

Eve blinked and then nodded. 'So what have you been doing this week?'

'Boundary fences.' He groaned. 'Which is why I needed your company. It's been a long, boring week.'

She patted his arm. 'Poor baby. But tonight you're here in town. It's a Friday. There are lots of chicky babes here waiting for you.'

They'd arrived at the pub and she followed him to the bar. She nodded to Mick, the old bushman who lived here most afternoons. She'd often hear his horse clopping away at ten at night when the pub doors shut, and she'd heard he slept all the way until his horse stopped at the farm verandah post and he slid off. Apparently he managed to undo the girth and lift the saddle off before he stumbled to bed. Sergeant McCabe let the Riding Under the Influence go because it had been happening for more years than anyone could remember.

The new backpacker barmaid was leaning her gloriously rounded cleavage towards Henry and, to Eve's amusement, his eyes glazed. It reminded Eve they needed to advertise the new women's health clinic hours. That had been Callie's brainwave and not a bad idea.

'What will you have, Eve?' Henry said, dragging his attention back to his companion.

'I might buy a bottle of nice shiraz. It's the end of the week and there's that casserole waiting. I'll take the rest of the bottle home with me.' There was a lot to be said for living next door to a country pub. 'I'm happy to share if you'd like a glass?'

He glanced around the room and smiled at the hopefuls trying not to look in his direction. 'Nope. Was going to stay the night but think I'll just head home after this. Mother will be happy to get the supplies tonight.' He smiled at the barmaid. 'A squash, thanks.'

Eve hoped Henry wasn't really crushed by her silly statement in the medical centre. She suspected his skin was thicker than the solid leather of old Mick's hat. They took their drinks to a little round table in the corner and perched on the high stools, looking out the window across the street. A dust-coated LandCruiser utility, complete with a red cattle dog asleep in the back, was situated nicely to block the glare of the afternoon sun.

Eve sighed as she sat down in the stripe of shade it offered from the burning ball in the sky. 'Nice to stop.'

Henry tilted his head. 'Would you have rather I hadn't asked you? Maybe you'd prefer to just put your feet up at the house?'

Eve looked at him over the top of her glass. 'No. I do thank you for asking me, Henry. I can't live in Callie's pocket the whole time and it's nice to have my own friends.'

He sniffed into his drink. 'At least I'm a friend.'

'If you start that again I will be sorry you asked me.'

'Fine. I've been meaning to ask you. How did you go with Lex in the helicopter the other week?'

It was Eve's turn to blush and Henry's eyes narrowed. She ignored the look. 'The flight was fine. We saw the red sandhills on the way back. Your mother sent a basket of food and I loved it.' She paused. 'He told me about his ex-wife.'

'Seriously?' Henry couldn't hide his surprise. 'That's a bit eerie, considering what happened this week.'

Eve shuddered. 'She was very young to die.'

'Yeah.' He seemed to shake himself into a better mood. 'I don't remember much about her, except that Lex treated her like she'd break. And she didn't ride. Main basis for my disbelief that he'd married her.'

Eve smothered a laugh. 'I don't ride either.'

He lifted his head. Considered her. Put his head down again. 'You wouldn't be afraid to learn.'

'I'll take that as a compliment.'

'It is.' He grinned at her. 'I hear Simon and Molly's baby is doing well.'

'Yep. Brilliantly. They hope to come home next week. I'm driving out as soon as they get back to see them.' She couldn't wait. That had been a darn near thing.

'Used to have a thing for Molly.' Henry shook his head and then looked at Eve. 'You love your job, don't you?'

'Yep. Love catching babies too. That's something I miss.' She looked at him: a well-dressed, leanly muscular man in the prime of his life, who was tragically wasting it. 'What do you love, Henry? What's your dream job?'

He shrugged and she caught the eye of the barmaid, who sighed languorously. Eve tried not to laugh as she brought her attention back to her companion.

'Apart from the chicky babes? Don't have one.'

Eve concentrated. *Be in the moment*, she admonished herself. This was important for Henry. 'Yes, you do. I'm interested.'

He shrugged. 'I love horses. Always have done. Would love to breed racing stock.'

That sounded very Henry. 'Why don't you? I could see you at the mounting yards at Eagle Farm. Last-minute instructions to the jockey. Pink shirt and coat at the Melbourne Cup.'

'Not a pink shirt. Please.' He smiled ruefully at her fantasy but she could see he was right there in it in his own mind. 'It's too frivolous for the board.'

'Have you fought hard enough for it?'

He shrugged again. 'Why bother? I'll lose.'

Eve raised her brows. 'Lose? With that extremely positive attitude? Nah.'

He laughed. 'See why I love you?' He drained his squash, and Eve picked up her own glass.

'You don't love me, Henry. You just hate not getting what you want. Why don't you show the same tenacity for what you really want to do? Something really important to you.'

He glanced around. 'I'd have to leave here for that. Be a little fish in a big pond. Not the other way around.'

She took a sip. Watched the red liquid swirl in the glass. 'I hear it's a good year in the diamond mines. Why not start with something modest and make a go of it?' She put her glass down and looked at him. Saw the yearning he tried to hide.

'You just want me to get out of your hair.'

'Now, why would I want that when you're my only friend who's not related to me?'

'I thought Lex was your friend.'

She wished she could be sure of that.

*

Lex did phone the next morning. 'I need some advice with Lily, and Blanche suggested you. Are you up for a helicopter trip out to Diamond Lake Station for lunch? I'd bring you home before dark.'

It was a less-than-romantic invitation from Lex but an unexpected compliment from Blanche. And strangely depressing that Lex hadn't thought of it himself. 'Sure. I didn't have any plans for today.' Apart from washing her hair.

'Sorry. Should have asked.' She could almost imagine him rubbing the back of his neck. 'Appreciate it.'

When she thought about what his family was doing for the district it was a small ask. Very small. 'What time do you want me at the airstrip?'

'An hour?'

She looked down at her pyjamas. 'No problem.' Wet hair wouldn't matter.

Callie watched from across the table. 'That Henry?'

'Lex. I think the new daughter is causing concern.'

Callie nodded. 'I imagine she'd be heartbroken. So what are you supposed to do?'

'He said he wanted some advice.'

'Lex McKay? I didn't think anything rattled that guy.'

'We all have our weaknesses.' She just hoped Lex wasn't one of hers.

Callie winked. 'I'll look forward to hearing about Lex's weaknesses when you come home.'

They both laughed. 'I could tell you but then I'd have to kill you.' Eve gulped her tea and put the cup in the sink. 'What are you two doing today?'

'Mum and I are going to have a quiet day. She's got some photos she wants to show me.'

Sylvia had started planning the slide show for her own funeral. Eve was finding it reminiscently morbid. Sylvia's take was they'd all been in too much shock when Duncan died to really celebrate the man he was, and she wanted a memorial service for her husband more than herself.

Eve was glad she was going out today. She'd done all this for her own mother. Sometimes she worried she was encroaching on Callie's time with Sylvia, even though both women often told her they appreciated her company.

Eve hurried through her shower and stood, wrapped in a towel, surveying her meagre wardrobe. What did you wear to meet a grieving seventeen-year-old who didn't feel like she had a friend in the world? Eve shrugged. She'd wear what she always wore. Colour.

NINETEEN

Lex had already landed when she got there and the engine was off. He didn't start up right away. He glanced across at her as she did up her safety harness.

'You look like a very pretty budgerigar.'

'Cool.' She grinned at Lex. 'And you look like the Marlboro Man. Very R. M. Williams.'

Except that he appeared unusually tired. The man could ride and brand cattle from dawn to dark seven days a week so it wasn't physical labour that had exhausted him.

'You okay?'

He shrugged. 'I'll survive.'

Well, she'd need more information before they arrived if she wasn't going to put her foot in it. 'Don't start the engine yet. How's Lily?'

He didn't answer directly. 'Thank you for coming, Eve.'

'You're welcome, Lex.' She prodded. 'So?'

'Before we get onto Lily I want to talk to you about something else, though it's not the main reason I asked you to come.'

'I thought Blanche asked me to come?'

'She did but I wanted to see you anyway.'

Eve supressed the little jump in her belly.

'I've been trying to catch up with you for days. I want to apologise.'

That was a turn-up for the books but she couldn't think of one thing he'd done wrong. 'What for?'

'For judging you, and to a lesser extent Callie, for helping my mother achieve the concept of the medical centre.'

'You didn't judge us, Lex. You had an opinion, which is your right, and it was obviously coloured by the loss of your sister. I understood that.'

The look he cast warmed her all the way down to her toes. 'You understand a lot, Eve.'

Sometimes. She shrugged. 'I understand women better than men.' And wasn't that the truth.

'As long as you know I do appreciate the work you do. You and Callie. And what you did for Molly's baby.'

'We were all very lucky.' She sincerely thought that, but it was a bonus if he was warming to the centre. 'Though I admit to being nervous that Sienna will blame me for Blanche hijacking her.'

Lex's scrutiny made her feel that he was interested. 'It's a worthy cause. I'm sure she'll be fine.'

'You don't know Sienna.' Eve guessed she didn't know Sienna very well either. It looked like she was going to get the chance to remedy that. But Lex didn't need her family stuff. She was here for his.

'So tell me about Lily. How is she?'

'Hard to tell. She's still not speaking.' He stared out the windshield with his lips compressed.

'Sulking, or not at all?'

Shook his head. 'Not at all.'

Eve's mind raced. 'Has she spoken since the accident?'

'Nope. The doctor said it would just take time. But it worries me.

If you could just check her out, blood pressure and stuff, to make sure she's okay? She refuses to travel to town and I don't like to ask Callie to come out with Sylvia unwell.'

'Sure.' It was tough for all concerned. 'No wonder you're worried. You know she mightn't want to see me?'

'I know.' Now he turned to look at her, putting his hand up to his hairline and rubbing it. 'And if you can't help, then that's okay too. I just have to believe time will make her feel more comfortable with us.'

Time would help. But that reminded her that Lex had lost a lot of years. 'How's Blanche coping?'

His hand fell away and he leaned back. 'Kareena's death knocked her about. She started mumbling about how the old ones should go first. I was getting worried, but she's bounced back surprisingly well since Lily arrived.'

'I thought she might.'

Lex turned to look at her, a small smile on his lips. 'You admire my mother, don't you?'

'Very much.'

He shook his head. 'But you're not intimidated by her?'

Eve shrugged. 'I think she's awesome. But no, I'm not scared of her – she's a lot like a very good friend I have in Brisbane.' But this wasn't about Blanche. 'So, what is it you want me to do, Lex?'

She saw the sigh go through him and he reached for the ignition again. 'I guess be a friend for Lily if she's looking for one. I know she's a lot younger than you but I thought that as you were from Brisbane you might be able to connect with her. I don't know.' He looked as distraught as a laconic he-man could. 'And Blanche is worried. She's had enough worries. She's terrified something's going to happen to Lily, because of Victoria taking her own life.'

Eve could understand that. 'Hence me.' *No pressure.*

He grinned and she felt that warmth again. 'Don't know why.' As if he could read her mind. 'You just help.'

She wasn't quite sure if that was compliment but of course she would do what she could.

He glanced at his watch. 'You right if we go?' he asked.

She nodded and he began his pre-flight preparation.

Soon afterwards they took off and Eve barely registered the shudder of the aircraft as she looked across at Lex. His face was calm as he flew and she remembered the last time he'd been the pilot. His sudden joy in the moment. Well, he wasn't getting that with the worries he was carrying but she could see he had regained some peace by the relaxed way he maneuvered the little craft. She hoped their talk had had something to do with that. She was glad for him, and settled back to enjoy the changing scenery.

They flew for the next thirty minutes in a companionable silence that neither was in a hurry to break.

Finally Lex pressed the speaker button and gestured with his hand. 'That's the start of Diamond Lake Station.'

Eve looked down. A winding ochre creek bed lay below them near a few greenish waterholes under shady river gums. The wide empty banks wound away like a lost snake for as far as the eye could see.

In the other direction a mountain range formed a natural amphitheatre, and to the north, the way they were flying, was a collection of buildings. On the other side of those she could see dry scattered washes that stretched like thin veins towards the large expanse of water.

'Diamond Lake,' Lex said, and it glittered in the bright sunlight.

*

Lily Campbell was tall. Not as tall as Eve but way over Callie's height, and she had her father's grey eyes. The good news was that she didn't have her grandmother's nose.

'Hello, Lily. I'm Eve.'

Eve held out her hand and tentatively Lily took it. Eve shook, let go, and stepped back. 'I can't imagine how hard it's been for you. I'm so sorry to hear about your mum and grandparents.'

Lily breathed in heavily through her nose and nodded.

Blanche, worry creasing her face, gestured to the cane furniture out on the back verandah and wrung her hands. Eve sat down with Lily.

'I'll go and get some cold lemonade, shall I?'

Lily didn't answer and Eve smiled. 'Thank you, Blanche.' She looked around. The view stretched for miles, and except for the house yard, which was lush and green and dotted with little islands of rockeries and flowering shrubs, the rest was flat, orange and brown, with grey-green stumpy trees disappearing into the distance.

'Wow. It's brown.'

The girl made a *pff*ing sound with her lips that could have been a sarcastic laugh.

Eve scanned some more. 'I've never been to the station before, but I haven't been in the area long. So I don't know the McKays too well, either.'

Lily stared down at her hands.

'I'm guessing the lake I saw is on the other side of the house?'

Lily nodded without looking up.

Tough gig. Never one to waste energy on an unequal battle, Eve went with instinct. Her voice was gentle. 'Lex tells me you're not up to conversation yet?'

This time Lily's head came up and her chin jutted out: a silent *So?*, with emphasis.

'Did your father tell you I'm a nurse?' Eve grinned. 'Actually I'm a midwife, but I'm a nurse too.'

Lily nodded and started to fiddle with a loose thread on the cushion of the chair.

'So while you're here I'd like to check your blood pressure and stuff. Lex and Blanche want you to feel at home but they also want to make sure you're okay. You fine with that?'

The girl sighed and shrugged but she did nod, so Eve felt that at least she wasn't forcing herself on Lily. But she was over doing all the work and wasn't sure it was even helping.

'I don't know about you, but this is pretty awkward. You want to go for a walk and maybe show me around before we think medically? I'd like to see the lake.'

Surprise flared briefly in eyes very similar to Lily's father's, and Eve resisted the impulse to smile. She made a show of gathering her sunglasses and preparing for a walk while Lily digested that bit of straight-talking.

They descended the verandah steps together and Eve trailed her finger over a bougainvillea petal. 'I love gardens. But I've got a black thumb. Every pot plant I've tried withers and dies. I feel so guilty but I either give them too much or not enough water or light or conversation. I don't know.'

No response from Lily.

'I understand it might be easier to retreat, not get into conversations. No way could I do that. My mouth runs on wheels and I'm pretty sure I talk in my sleep. "Monkey chatter", my older sister used to say.'

When Lily spoke, her voice was a little hoarse from lack of use. 'I don't have a sister. Or a mother.'

For once, Eve didn't rush into speech in case Lily had bottled up a whole lot more. They just walked along the gravel-strewn path around the side of the big Queenslander, sticking close to the house so that nobody could watch them from the verandahs above.

Finally she whispered forlornly, 'My gran and grandpa are gone too.'

'I know. It must be horrible for you.' The face that turned towards her gave a clue to just how horrible it was. Eve winced. 'Everything must be very different here.' That was the understatement of the year, she bet.

'Yes.'

'So what about your friends?'

Lily shrugged. 'Boarding school. They're scattered.'

'You could phone them. Or text. Email?'

'I don't want to do anything.'

Eve could understand that. 'Okay. But I'm happy to listen any time. And I understand confidential.' It was Eve's turn to shrug. 'I have to in my job.'

Lily paused, turned to face her and narrowed her eyes at Eve. 'I'll remember that.'

Eve wasn't sure if Lily meant she would remember Eve was there to talk or that Eve was bound to confidentiality. That could be problematic.

'I guess I need to clarify – confidentiality is conditional on everyone being safe.'

The girl pulled a face but Eve liked the way Lily thought about it before she answered. A lot of seventeen-year-olds would have fired up; maybe this girl had a lot of her father in her, despite the distance between them.

'I'd want to know before anything was passed on.'

This can of worms was getting wormier. 'That's fair enough.'

'Okay.'

'Um, can I tell your dad that you're talking? Not that I have vast experience of this, but I imagine that's the sort of thing fathers want to know.'

'If you want to, I guess.'

'Only if it's okay with you. I won't if you prefer I didn't.'

A long sigh. 'If you think he needs to know.'

'I think he does. Thank you. I'll stop there. Your dad wants to be here for you. You know that?'

'So he said.' Lily looked unconvinced but Eve understood these were early days yet. She didn't see how even a broken-hearted Lily could miss that her father was honest and reliable.

Lily glanced across at the house and grimaced. 'And then there's the grandmother from hell!'

Eve laughed, tried to stop, shaking her head in apology, but it was a little while before she could speak. 'I'm sorry. I've got a boss just like her in Brisbane.'

Lily rolled her eyes.

'Seriously, Blanche is good people, but different. I predict one day you'll be so proud of that woman it will blow you away, but there's no hurry. She's a lot to get used to and you've got enough on your plate.'

Lily stopped and balled her hands into fists, which she dug into her sides. Her lips flattened as if she wasn't going to say anything, and then they burst like a dam breaking.

'Why did I have to lose my family? Why me? Why couldn't I have died too?'

Eve guessed it was good that she was getting it out, but there were no answers. 'I don't know, Lily. Why anyone?'

They walked on and Lily's steps were more rushed as the girl battled with her emotions.

Eve had a stab at verbalising what Lily wasn't. 'It's not fair. It's horrible. But maybe you didn't die because you have your life to live.'

No comment from the girl beside her.

'Tell me to shut up any time, but you do have relatives who can be there for you. You're not an orphan and you could have been. Maybe the McKays can help your sadness. And you can help your dad's sadness over how much he missed of your growing up.'

'I don't care about him. I care about me. I've lost my mother. I've lost my grandparents and it sucks.'

Yep, it did. Big time. 'Of course.'

They walked on for another ten minutes before they said anything more. Eve realised that if Lily could not talk for four days, then keeping silent for an hour in Eve's company would be easy for the girl. But Eve couldn't do it. So she did what she always did. Talked.

'At least when I lost my mum I knew it was coming,' she said eventually. 'I nursed her at home until she died. My dad died a couple of months ago, here, and, like you, I didn't know him. But I can't imagine how hard it would be for your whole life to change so suddenly. Nobody can.'

She'd said nearly enough. Just one more thing. 'But everyone wants to be there for you if you need them.' Goodness knows how much Lily was actually hearing and how much was just the noise of Eve talking. She decided to shut up.

'You didn't know your dad either?'

Eve guessed it was always the unexpected that people heard. 'I wanted to, but it never happened. I feel pretty guilty about that, and now it's too late.'

'My mum said my dad was dead. I thought he was.'

'Of course. No way you could think anything else. She must have had her reasons.'

There was a pause. Lily didn't comment and Eve couldn't help continuing. 'When I was younger Mum said my dad was too busy for me to see him. But before she died she told me she hadn't let him come.'

Lily snorted. 'I don't want to talk to them.' She inclined her head towards the house.

Eve shrugged. 'No one can make you. Just try to remember that Lex and Blanche and Henry haven't done anything wrong. And it's easier for them if you talk.'

She sighed. 'I suppose.' A lost little voice, floating out from under a waterfall of dark hair. It was hard to remember that this young woman was in a totally different world last week.

'Are you having bad dreams about the accident?'

Lily gave a quick hard shake of the head. 'I wish I did. I don't remember anything. The doctor kept saying it was good that I was asleep when it happened. But I don't think so.'

It was a tough call either way but Eve leaned towards agreeing with the doctor. 'You'll never know if it was better or not.'

They walked on a little further before turning back towards the house.

'I like the thought that people you love were protecting you while you were asleep,' Eve mused. 'That's why you're still here.'

Lily stopped to look at Eve. 'That's the kindest thing I've heard all week. Thank you.'

'So how did you really go, talking to Lily?' They were in the helicopter, safely landed again at Red Sand's airstrip after an awkward lunch where Blanche tried too hard, Lily tried too little, and Lex watched on helplessly. Eve had indigestion for all of them.

'Fine. And lunch wasn't too bad. At least Lily is answering in monosyllabic grunts. She's not so different to her dad after all.'

He almost smiled. 'I know. Thank you for that. It is a start. I just feel so ill-equipped to deal with a teenage girl, that's all.'

'You don't have to deal with her, Lex. She's a young woman. You have to remember, where I worked it wasn't uncommon for women her age to have babies.'

Lex shuddered. 'Heaven forbid.'

Eve laughed. 'I can see you with a shotgun, watching the boys she dates. But she's tough and capable. I think she has a lot of her father in her. Just love her and the rest will work.'

He looked at her and shook his head. 'How did you get to be so wise?'

'Ha. That's a laugh. I'm the one who *didn't* go to med school. Wise people have "doctor" in front of their names. My mother and sister have added "poor" in front of mine, as in, "Poor Eve can't get her life in order."'

The look he cast her way was long and considering, and a small smile played around his lips. 'I think Poor Eve is richer in life experience and wisdom than the lot of us.'

Eve's eyes prickled and stung and she looked away quickly. It was a pretty tall compliment from someone who managed a million-acre station and juggled a strong-willed family. She chewed her lip furiously to hold back the ridiculous dampness in her eyes, even if it did take the skin off her mouth. It had to be the nicest thing anyone had ever said to her. She swallowed the lump in her throat, took a deep breath and got on with it. Professionally, at least.

'Anyway, apart from massive, understandable grief, Lily checks out perfectly health-wise. Her blood pressure and pupils don't show any signs of underlying neurological damage.' She shot him a cheeky smile. 'Not so bad having a medical clinic closer to home, is it?'

He undid his seatbelt, and then, in slow motion, reached across and undid hers. Instead of sitting back he leaned in and pulled her towards him.

'Thank you, Eve. I owe you,' he said as he brought his face closer to hers.

She realised what he was going to do just before he kissed her. His mouth was warm and solid and incredibly commanding – just like he was.

Yum. She felt like she was tumbling down the red, red sandhills right into his arms. Her hands unconsciously reached up to his neck as she opened to him.

He pulled back and then, as if changing his mind, leaned in again and she was lost. It felt like her heart wanted to burst from her chest, like the birds at the edge of a waterhole exploding into flight. But that euphoria settled as he let her go. The sudden knowledge she'd fallen for the unobtainable brought her back to earth. An outback cattle baron and a midwife from Brisbane? The dream was a long way from reality.

But as 'thank you's went, she should be more than happy with the kiss.

He eased back further, and so did she, right after she remembered to open her eyes. *Okay, then.* It was over.

His eyes were teasing but his face was deadpan. 'I just felt like a little short-term plastering.'

It was pretty cool that he remembered her words from their picnic. But not a good idea to make too much of it.

'Hmm. Well.' *Come on, brain.* She opened her door. Babbled some more. 'Thanks for showing me Diamond Lake, Lex.'

At least she hadn't said thanks for the kiss.

TWENTY

Colleen, the mother with the breech baby, went into labour not long after Eve had left for Diamond Lake Station.

Callie had just seen out her last patient before lunch, and shown in Bennet to share her sandwiches, when Colleen's husband, eyes creased with worry, hurried across the wooden floor.

'She's gonna have this baby,' the tall man said, and Callie looked at his concerned face and then at Colleen's strained one as she eased into the room.

Callie, whose heart rate was probably as high as Colleen's, steered the couple through to Eve's room, where the ultrasound and baby monitor were. 'Get the flying doctor on the line, please, Bennet.' Why couldn't this have happened when Eve was around?

Colleen groaned and muttered almost inaudibly, 'It's coming.'

Cripes, Callie thought, considering helplessly the options of trying to listen to the baby's heartbeat or getting ready to listen to the baby on the outside. Where was Eve when she needed her? 'It's okay, Colleen. The flying doctor will be here soon and they'll take you to Charleville.'

The young woman crossed the room hurriedly to the examination couch as if she had a date with the table, but instead of climbing up she squatted beside it and held onto the deck above her head. And pushed.

Cripes, cripes. Callie stuck her head out the door and spoke in a deceptively calm voice. 'Bennet. I need you. Now.' Bennet was a vet. He knew about birth and could help if she got into trouble. It might have been worse.

Colleen's husband paled and Callie glanced at him. 'Sit. Now.' The man did what he was told and stumbled into the nearest chair.

There was no time to think negative thoughts. All positive thoughts. *Everything will be fine. Just don't touch the baby unless you have to.* How the heck would she know if she had to? Where was Eve?

She pulled herself together. Eve had said the mother would position herself where she wanted, she would do all the work. *Have faith.*

Faith was a little hard to come by at the moment.

Bennet reappeared. 'Plane's on its way.'

'Great.' She met Bennet's eyes and he nodded reassuringly. Well, he had faith in her, anyway. Her mind was clearing. 'Can you grab me a towel and pop a couple more in the tumble dryer to heat up, please? And a bunny rug?'

Bennet nodded and returned quickly with two towels that he placed gently on the desk. 'I'll try and reach Eve. Holler if you need me.'

As he disappeared from view Colleen made a grunting noise. Callie refocused, casting her eyes towards the suction tubing and oxygen that Eve had intuitively prepared for such an event.

'I think you might need to take your pants off, Colleen.'

There was a flick of a towel for Colleen to stand on, another quick shuffle and it was done. 'I haven't lost the water yet,' Colleen gasped before she grunted again, but she didn't look scared now she was here.

The calm that eased over Callie was something she hadn't expected. She sank onto the little stool Eve used when she was talking to children and pulled her gloves on slowly. *Well, then. Let's just do that normal thing.* She opened the little pack of disposable instruments, two metal clamps for the umbilical cord, a pair of scissors for separating mother and baby, and the little plastic peg that stayed on the umbilical stump afterwards. She hadn't expected to be looking at those.

She reassured herself again. In the old days breech babies were normal. *Just don't interfere.* She put another one of the towels down to catch the flood when it came.

As if on cue, the waters broke, and it happened just as Eve had said.

A little bottom appeared in a curve like a fat banana and then one leg flopped down, quickly followed by the other. Colleen was squatting not far off the floor so pretty soon the little feet were touching it on tiptoes. Now Callie could see the stretched umbilical cord and an extended tummy.

Callie reached across and very briefly felt the thick cord. Eve had said she didn't need to, but she *needed* to, and sighed with relief at the steady heartbeat of the baby as it pulsed in the cord. She pulled her hands away, lest she was tempted to touch anything else.

Bennet crouched reassuringly behind her. Callie reached out her hands as the chest, shoulders and arms appeared slowly. With the extra length of body the baby folded into a sitting position, then baby's face and finally all of its head eased out until it fell forwards into Callie's outstretched hands.

The baby cried. So did Callie, but no one noticed. She wiped baby shakily with a towel Bennet had handed her, sorted the tangle of cord to clamp and cut it, and handed baby to Bennet so she could help Colleen. The placenta plopped out with very little blood as Colleen stood up, and it was done.

Then there was a soft thud as Colleen's husband fainted and slid out of the chair.

Four hours later, Colleen had safely landed in Charleville so the paediatrician could check out her baby, Bennet had driven her husband home, and Eve was back from Diamond Lake Station.

Eve was clapping her hands. 'I am so jealous. Go you, Dr Callie!'

'I would not have survived if you hadn't talked me through it beforehand.' Callie shook her head and Bennet squeezed her shoulder. Her hands had finally stopped their St Vitus dance and Bennet had only just stopped saying how proud he was of her.

'Sure you would have.' Eve's face was filled with delighted excitement.

'Thank you, Eve.'

'What for? I wasn't even here.'

Callie looked under her brows at Eve. 'Somehow, over the last couple of months, insidiously, you restored my faith in birth. In women. And in trusting that good things can happen.'

Eve waved that away. 'It was all in your head. I knew you would be amazing.' She glanced at Bennet, who wore a bemused expression every time he looked at Callie. 'She's amazing.'

'I've always known that,' he said quietly.

'Let's go tell Sylvia. She'll love it.'

TWENTY-ONE

Sienna knew the drive to Brisbane would be a long one. By the time she'd reached the Darling Downs and hit the Warrego Highway she was over it.

Then there was Western Downs, Dalby, Roma . . . if she saw another old farm machinery museum advertised she'd scream.

She stayed overnight in Roma for a prearranged interview with the flying obstetrician and gynaecologist, Phillip Willis, a man she'd done some training with a long time ago in Melbourne. He had been grappling with the district's losses as well, and his thin face was serious as he shared his own theories.

He'd been incredulous at Sienna's travelling from Melbourne to Red Sand in her tiny car, and amused by the fact she would be staying there for three months. He angled for Sienna to give him a day off every now and then as the emergency obstetrician while she was staying in town.

'Not a hope. I don't like to fly in large planes, let alone the sardine cans you fly around in.'

'It's a very safe aircraft.' Phillip wasn't ruling it out. 'We'll see. I know you're out there.'

As if. 'Don't count on it. This is a fact-finding mission only.'

This time he roared with laughter. 'Not the way it works out here. Everyone pitches in because when it happens – you're it!'

She hadn't been told that. What the hell had Wallace put her in for?

The next morning, another 268 kilometres down the road, Sienna drove through Charleville, where a billboard tried to point her to the flying doctor base. *Visitors welcome.* She smiled tartly.

'Not on your Nellie,' she growled, passing the old pubs and courthouse, until she found the sign that directed her to Quilpie. She passed a billboard assuring her she was now on Australia's longest road. The Diamantina Development Road. Well, it had better be developed because she wasn't bashing her baby around. Ahead lay a long thin strip of black tar slashing through the orange dust swathe. Every now and then she saw an emu – which even she had to admit lightened her mood.

She encountered a few four-wheel drives and a couple of intrepid caravaners – she refused to leave the bitumen, so the passing traffic had to – and the occasional lean cow and calf grazing hopefully in the scrubby mulga forests. And of course there were the ghastly birds feeding on the relentless roadkill. But mostly she had the 200 kilometres of red ribbon–edged tar to herself.

She slowed to avoid a road train that took up most of the bitumen, dug her heels in at hitting the dust – but then, so did he, so that was interesting because she nearly lost paint – and finally, over another dry creek bed bridge, she hit Quilpie.

The scrub had been cleared and there was a pile of red boulders with a sign poking out of it. Surely there would be coffee here.

As she drove in it wasn't as sparse as she'd feared. Wide bitumen streets with a green median strip housing tables and chairs gave it a welcoming demeanour. *Okay.* If Red Sand was as pleasant as this she'd possibly survive, but what she'd seen last time hadn't enthused her. She lifted her brows at the flat wrought-iron emus and sheep sharing the grass strip with the caravaners drinking thermos coffee.

She passed a two-storey pub and a row of surprisingly diverse retail outlets. And a coffee shop! She stopped and climbed stiffly out of her car and stretched her hands over her head to pull out the kinks.

So this was the nearest town. At least it had a 'hairdresser'. She smiled wryly to herself. Mark had said she wouldn't find one.

After the surprisingly good coffee and a last glance around the arty little outpost she flexed her shoulders and put her hands back on the wheel for the last 400 kilometres to Red Sand. The sun had a few hours to go. Eve had warned she should stop driving before sunset because of the wildlife on the roads, but Sienna wasn't quitting now.

It was almost dark as she hit the '10 kilometres to go' sign. And that was when the approaching vehicle's lights veered off the thin strip of tar and stopped suddenly.

Sienna frowned. Either there was a farm entrance up ahead and the person had got out to open the gate, or something had made them run off the road.

She slowed as she drew closer. An older model Holden, like something from a sixties sitcom, had spun off the road and finished driver's side door up against a fence.

Sienna's heart rate sped up as she pulled over and climbed out. She crossed her fingers superstitiously as she approached the passenger side of the vehicle. It didn't look too bad, except that the vehicle was tilted into the culvert gouged out of the dirt at the side of the road. The angle didn't allow her to see the driver easily.

'Hello? You okay?' Sienna stepped onto the downward slide of loosely packed red dust at the side of the road. She slid the last few feet and stopped as her hip hit the passenger door and she flattened against the side of the car. Not elegant, but at least she could look in.

When she peered through the window she could see a young woman jammed up against the door on the far side. Sienna's eyes widened at the big bulge of pregnant belly just in front of the steering wheel. This wasn't good. She'd need to go to hospital regardless.

'Hi. I'm Dr Sienna Wilson. What's your name?'

'Gracie.' A young, shaky voice drifted across.

'Are you hurt, Gracie?'

'*Noooo*. But my waters broke and I hit the kangaroo. At least, I think that's what it was. Is it okay?'

Sienna gave a cursory glance around the area. 'I can't see it anywhere so it probably hopped away.' Suicidal wildlife was not high on her list of interests.

Then the pale face winced and screwed up as a contraction followed her words. It looked suspiciously long and strong to Sienna and she reached into her pocket to pull out her mobile phone. She glanced at the bars and thanked God the service was coming back in.

'Well, it's your lucky day. I specialise in babies. Can you get out?'

'I want to, but the door won't open.'

'It's okay. The car's against the fence. We need help. I'll just phone for an ambulance and then I'll try to get you out this way.' Which was going to be a mission when gravity was pulling Gracie the other way. 'At least we'll see what we can do to make you more comfortable.'

There was a whimper in reply and then a sigh so big Sienna expected the girl to deflate like a balloon. Brows raised, Sienna remembered to be reassuring.

'So you know your deep breathing. Clever girl.'

The phone finally connected and she gave her name, their position and the problem. Ten kilometres out of town shouldn't take them too long but as Sienna hung up Gracie moaned.

Oh no, you don't, Sienna thought, *we're not having this baby here*. She yanked the door open – thank goodness she'd been going to the gym because it wasn't easy – and peered in.

Definitely a puddle of water. She saw a ripple of movement through the thin material of the girl's dress and her relief expanded. At least baby was okay for the moment. A birth she could cope with, but a flat baby would not be fun.

'So, Gracie, when this next pain is finished, can you take your seatbelt off and slide along the seat towards me? We'll see how we go.' It had been a long time since she was at a birth away from the high-tech world, with paediatricians seconds away. This baby better have read the rule book about breathing.

Gracie got halfway along the seat before the next contraction started. There was a pause as she breathed and then gave a big sigh.

'Something's happening.'

'That's okay. I thought it might be. If we have to we can take your pants off, have a baby, and maybe even get them back on before someone comes.' If the pants came off they weren't going back on, but it sounded reassuring.

'I think it's *comiiiiing*.'

Shit. Sienna had hoped a bit of calming would slow things down, but bloody Eve would probably say it was the opposite.

Despite the increase in her heart rate, Sienna's voice was calm and quiet. 'Let it happen. Can you manage to wriggle out of your underwear and move so you're not sitting so upright on your bottom?'

It wasn't easy but the girl managed to get one leg free of her bikini bottoms.

Gracie moaned; Sienna was on tiptoes, leaning in and then up on her knees on the seat beside her, backside in the air for passing traffic – if there'd been any. Thank God for the old Holden's bench seat. Life certainly promised to be different out here.

In a rush it happened; it was bloody lucky she'd climbed up there to reach for the jumble of limbs or baby would have been floating in the pink water around the accelerator pedal. She scooped the new-born from between the mother's legs and unwound a tangle of cord from around a plump little shoulder as the sound of a siren whooped over them, drowned out by the gasp and cry of an indignant baby.

'I'm going to push baby up under your dress until —' Sienna peered between the baby's legs to establish the sex, '— she —' they grinned at each other '— pops out the top. She'll stay warmest against your skin. Okay?'

'Holy cow! I guess.' Gracie sank back in shock as Sienna wiped the baby with a cardigan on the seat, and then, still joined by the long umbilical cord, she was settled between her mother's breasts, jammed into place by the thin material of the baggy dress. The baby blinked.

Sienna stared down at the perfect fingers that had popped out with the little scrunched face, and eased back a little.

She felt the exultant laugh bubble up in her chest, a buzz that seemed to have been lost over the last couple of years of high-risk care, and she smiled with astonished pride at the new mum.

'Gracie! Congratulations. I have to admit, you are one incredible young woman!'

'Excuse me. I need to get to this pregnant woman urgently!'

Sienna wiggled her backside to retreat along the seat so she could glance backwards. She brushed her hair from her forehead with the back of a bloody hand and looked up, a long way, into the angled face of a ruggedly macho policeman. They bred them bigger out here, apparently.

'Actually, Officer, she's not pregnant any more.'

The man's face paled but before he could say anything the baby cried again and the sound was undeniably healthy.

He turned into a sergeant-major. 'Move!'

Sienna kept the smile on her face as she winked at the new young mother with the wide-eyed baby glued stickily under her dress. She took one last assessing glance at the little pink face gazing owlishly at the world before she wriggled completely out of the car. She had the idea the cop would pick her up and remove her none too gently if she didn't.

There was a certain primordial attraction in the thought.

Gracie and the baby would be fine. The rest could wait; she didn't want to wrestle with afterbirth if she didn't have to, and her knees were killing her.

'Thank you,' the officer growled as his way cleared to see in, and after one long look back, which said he hadn't missed much of her dishevelled appearance, he turned away.

Tsk tsk, Sienna thought with a certain grim satisfaction. *Don't like waiting, do you?* She didn't feel it was unreasonable that there was a touch of tartness in her voice as she spoke to his back. 'You're welcome, Officer.'

She had noticed he was big and rangy and importantly cross as he'd pushed past her, but now she could hear his voice had softened as he spoke to her new friend.

'You okay, Gracie?' It was totally unlike his tone to Sienna. Fatherly. Concerned.

Sienna arched slowly as she backed away from the car and eased the kinks out of her spine.

His exasperation with Sienna should have been approval but approval was a little hard to come by this week. Mark hadn't cared that she was shipped out here and that Blanche woman was treating her like a pawn to be shifted where she chose. All she needed was a wise-arsed pin-up policeman to give her a hard time and her week would be complete.

Lucky young Gracie had been driving an ancient, roomy sedan, and not some tiny Japanese whiz car, or they'd both still be stuck in there like corks in a bottle.

Sienna glanced down at her messy hands and edged carefully back over the uneven rocks to her car. Her heel wobbled. She should have packed the runners. She grabbed her water bottle from the car and poured it over her hands. Then she crouched and rinsed her nails until there was a puddle of red water in the dirt at the side of the bitumen. She watched the swirls of blood spin like the pattern on a cappuccino until they sank into the ground.

The sky rumbled and a flash of lightning in the distance warned of a storm coming. God, she'd kill for another coffee.

Sienna straightened again, shook the droplets from her hands, then scooped out the emergency hand sanitiser from her car, one of those things a woman just couldn't live without, and chewed the last of the red lipstick off her lips. There might be a lot of things she'd be living without now. But it was only three months.

The sound of the approaching ambulance drifted in and out through the evening shadows. Sienna glanced at the taut rear end of the law and decided he would find her even if she left as soon as the ambulance arrived. It'd be any second now. She massaged the evaporative gel into her palms and between her fingers. There hadn't been time for protective gloves, and she'd have to scrub her nails when she got to the B&B, but her first in-car delivery was special enough to put up with the mess. It had been a long time since she'd delivered a baby without the hordes in labour ward around her.

The ambulance pulled up and the policeman retreated and waved reassuringly to the alighting person.

He loomed over Sienna in the cool evening air. 'Gracie seems as comfortable as possible.' He spoke almost as if it would have been her fault if she wasn't.

Sienna struggled to keep the irritation from her face. 'Then I can go?'

Cool grey eyes brushed over her as if she were on trial, though she did wonder if there was a tinge of appreciation in that glance. But the unspoken message was an order. 'We need to get her safely into the ambulance. If you could spare another few minutes in your rush to get somewhere, then I'll take your name and contact details before you leave.'

'Sienna!' Eve strode across the road and hugged her. 'You okay?'

'Fine. You're an ambulance driver, now? No end to your talents. I was just passing. Your patient's in there.'

The policeman looked at both faces and saw the resemblance. Then he scowled. 'Gracie's in the car.'

Two hours later, back in Red Sand, Sienna had checked into Fran's B&B, and now she was back at the medical centre to see Gracie.

The storm had prevented the flying doctor from coming in, and she'd agreed to take over Gracie's care until the young woman went home the next day. Eve would do the night shift and Callie would run the clinic in the morning, so they had sorted out the logistics of staffing a place that didn't cater to overnight stays. Already they were breaking the rules.

Eve was busy assembling some inpatient notes for record-keeping when Sienna went in to see her patient.

'And here's Sergeant McCabe, come to visit,' said Carol, Gracie's mum. That made Sienna glance up as that hunky policeman strode down the corridor of the tiny medical centre. He stopped at the sight of a packed room and Sienna's eyes were drawn to the bunch of desert flowers gripped in his large hand. He seemed totally unaware he'd choked the life out of them.

TWENTY-TWO

'You have quite a fan club, Gracie.' Sienna's voice was low but carried confidently as she looked up at Sergeant McCabe and raised her brows. She saw the policeman give her the once-over and then hastily lay the flowers down and shake Gracie's dad's hand before excusing himself. All in the space of a few seconds. What a strange man . . . The thought floated briefly across Sienna's mind before she concentrated on her patient.

Young Gracie seemed to glow at the unexpected pleasure of being the centre of attention. Eve had said Gracie was the eldest child of six. Sienna couldn't imagine growing up like that. The proud mum beamed from her hospital bed like a little red sunflower, her appreciative audience arrayed like one of the floral arrangements resting on the metal chest of drawers – tall Dad at the back, little thin Carol in the middle, younger brothers and sisters leaning on the bed at the front so they could all see Gracie's gorgeous daughter, Tilly, in their sister's arms.

To Sienna's relief, Eve, who'd arrived with a patient chart, asked Gracie's mother to gather up her mob, and tucked Gracie's baby in the crib. Within seconds, apart from herself and Eve, only Gracie and her baby remained.

It seemed that respect for the patient's privacy lingered in this backwater; Sienna could be thankful at least for that.

Gracie wasn't technically anybody's patient. Or was she Callie's? Or Eve's? Whichever way, Sienna wasn't here to do rounds of a medical centre that wasn't supposed to have overnight patients, but she wanted to check on Gracie before she went to bed.

She noted the bruised-looking eyes, luminous skin and pale lips of the mother and wondered what her red-cell count had been before she'd had her baby.

'Her Hb was normal last week.'

As if her sister had read her mind. 'But the new results won't be in till tomorrow lunchtime,' Eve went on. 'The bloods won't go until morning.'

Sienna sighed for the speed and effortless computerised system she was used to. 'Fine. Thanks.' She looked at Gracie. 'Can you lie back? I'd like to feel your tummy again, just to make sure it's still going down and everything is normal with your uterus after such a quick birth.' She palpated. *Well down. Good.* 'Not bleeding too much?'

Gracie blushed. 'Like a period.'

Sienna glanced around the little hospital room: there were real boards halfway up the wall, even a picture rail with paintings. And was that pressed metal on the roof? How quaint. It made her think of the bed and breakfast that had turned out to be better than she expected, though she'd been surprised that its owner worked with Eve too.

She looked back at her patient. 'Your baby is perfect and you didn't break anything, so you were very lucky.'

'Except my waters.' Gracie grinned.

The three women shared a smile and Sienna wondered why she felt such a rapport with this slip of a girl. Maybe she liked Gracie because she didn't seem fazed about the idea of having a baby on the roadside.

But Gracie didn't need Sienna. She had a supportive family and a town that cared, if the phone conversations she'd overheard at the B&B said anything.

And she had Eve.

Sienna and Eve had never been close. So it was normal that working with her sister would feel weird. She hadn't even seen Eve in her role as midwife before. She had tolerated but never understood her at home on the brief leave weekends and holidays away from boarding school, and had always felt vaguely sorry for her. 'Not enough drive in the girl,' their mother had always said.

But as a professional, even Sienna could see, Eve was a force to be reckoned with. There was a light that shone in her when she was caring for people.

Then Sienna frowned at herself – she wasn't here to reunite with and appreciate her sister. Just to do a job and get out, ASAP.

'So how are you feeling in yourself, Gracie?' Eve asked, bringing Sienna back to her patient.

'Great.' Gracie lifted her shoulders and winced. 'Tired, but very happy.'

Anaemia, shock from the accident and a newborn. Exhausted, more likely. 'That's good. Hope you're not expecting a lot of visitors tonight?'

Gracie's eyes lit up. 'Depends on the weather. Mum will come back later 'cause she's staying in town, but my friends home on school holidays will probably come in if they can.'

'I prescribe rest before you go home.'

Eve smiled. 'Gracie is going to do her midwifery as soon as Tilly goes to school.'

'Just born and already talking school?' *Life on hold.* Tragic, but she didn't say it. Apparently she may as well have.

Eve's eyes glittered. 'Not at all. Gracie is going to be the most amazing mum first. She started uni before she fell pregnant. It will all work out.'

Sienna nodded to placate Eve, unsure what had happened. She glanced at the dresser crowded with homemade posies of desert flowers and hardy foliage and tried a change of subject.

'You're a bit of a star around town, from what I've been told.' She picked up the bunch of mangled stems in a wilting posy on the bedside table and they wobbled drunkenly in her hand. 'Looks like they've been squeezed in a vice.'

'They're from Sergeant McCabe.'

'I know.' Hence the vice. The man looked like he didn't know the meaning of the word gentle. He'd seemed very uncomfortable standing in the doorway when he'd arrived. And when he departed, Sienna remembered with amusement. Indeed, he didn't strike Sienna as the sociable type. But then she remembered his voice as he spoke to Gracie in the ditched car. Surprisingly, she could also remember his well-muscled thighs. She frowned at herself for the thighs.

'Lots of good wishes going your way. So, home in the morning if all goes well overnight?'

Gracie shrugged and her hair flopped into her face. 'We'll be fine. And Eve said she'll come out and visit.'

Sienna blinked and glanced at Eve. 'I thought you lived 150 kilometres out of town?'

'Yep. Not too far, luckily.'

A home visit would remove a staff member for half a day. Novel idea. The upkeep would bleed like a severed artery.

'Sure, if that's normal around here.'

'We don't have a normal.' Eve smiled at Gracie. 'Not even supposed to have patients staying here but the electrical storm sorted that, and by the time the RFDS can land, Gracie will be ready to go home if you say she's fine.'

Sienna bent over Tilly and stroked her tiny hand. Baby fingers never failed to fascinate her, especially these ones that could have been such a tragedy if things had turned out differently.

'I'll be back to see you tomorrow morning.'

Gracie's big eyes stared up at her. 'Thank you, Doctor.'

Sienna had never had anyone hero-worship her before. She'd had respect, but not hero worship. She didn't do warm and fuzzy; it made her uncomfortable. Or that's what she'd always told herself. She'd decided early on not to expect people to love her. Her mother had been one driven woman, and not given to praise. Sienna had respected her enormously.

'Well, thank *you*,' she gestured to the baby bassinet, 'for making my first night here memorable, and for introducing me to Tilly.'

She needed to get out of here. Get her stuff unpacked. Be efficient somewhere.

TWENTY-THREE

The next morning, after she'd dropped in on Gracie and assured herself mother and baby were both fine, Sienna headed to the hole of an office they'd given her to get ready for her first day of trawling through that mountain of medical records.

It was very quiet. Almost sleepy after the excitement of lightning and thunder through the night. She wasn't used to waiting for things to happen. Normally she was juggling research, emergency caesareans, long clinic days and board meetings.

She'd be wishing someone had a crisis soon because she had too much time to think.

The secretary – and her landlady – appeared at her door. 'Dr Wilson? Dr Callie asked if you were okay for drinks at her house tonight?'

God, no. 'Look, Fran. I don't do chatting to people. I don't socialise much. I work. That's what I do.'

'But . . .' Fran blinked at her through heavy, plain-framed glasses. 'What do you do on your days off?'

'When I have them? Drink coffee in coffee shops. Get my hair and nails done.' She looked at the woman beside her. 'What do you do?' *Obviously not your hair and nails.* But the really funny thing was, she was actually interested.

Fran ran her hand nervously over her own hair. 'I guess I clean the B&B. Catch up on the housework. I have four grown sons and you've met the one who lives at home. My husband,' she hesitated, 'died during the last drought.'

They hadn't got into family history when Sienna arrived last night. 'I'm sorry to hear that.' She glanced out the tiny window of the ex-storeroom. She wasn't complaining about the space because the air-conditioner was big and she needed get started. 'Better get back to work.'

Fran nodded and disappeared.

They had a meeting later that day to discuss the project outline, the medical records she'd read before she came, and the chance of finding a common factor. Sienna would give it a good run for their money. Callie could have asked her then about drinks instead of passing the message on. Eve still raved about her so she probably was as nice as she'd seemed before. But Sienna still couldn't believe Eve was actually living with their father's widow. Talk about disloyalty to Mum.

Sienna had seen the B&B advertised online and jumped on it. Apparently Fran was the local information service in emergencies and the locals got their updates through her. So she had two phone lines and good internet service. Thank God she could use her internet. That had been a huge relief.

She put her laptop down on the desk and spun in the chair. The sooner she started, the sooner she'd be out of here. Her mind drifted back to the night before and it was surprising how clear the snapshot was.

So why was she thinking about the surly man who'd visited Gracie last night with a posy of crushed wildflowers?

She shrugged and switched on her laptop. It had been a while since she'd spent the night with Mark. She'd finished that relationship last week in disgust after his lack of support in regards to her secondment. Diversion was not a good idea.

Work! So how was she going to collate the data? Who and what was involved when a woman became pregnant around 2000 kilometres from Brisbane? *Logic.* The woman needed to confirm her pregnancy. She needed tests and antenatal screens, bloods taken and transported, results returned. So Sienna would check those.

The woman might be exposed to fertilisers, cattle disease, earthborne infections – she'd check them too.

The woman needed more frequent observation towards the end of pregnancy. She'd need access to good transport in the last weeks, and seamless storage and retrieval of the information so a woman was admitted for delivery with all documentation present.

Then Sienna would need to plot the data for the stillbirths and premature labours over the past two years. When the increase happened. At what stage of pregnancy and who discovered and dealt with it.

Had any of those women delivered a healthy infant since?

These were all questions that needed answers, and there were about a thousand more. But she would get there. Already, despite herself and the situation she was in, the questions gnawed at her. *Was there a reason or was it all just coincidence?*

Fran knocked timidly at the door. 'Eve asked if you could come through, please.'

She sighed, distracted from her purpose. She was the researcher, not the handy consultant obstetrician, and she'd make sure her sister knew it.

'You wanted me, Eve?'

Eve stepped closer to the sun-browned woman with the unmistakable pregnant belly as if to shield her, and Sienna felt her little sister's censure.

She hadn't meant to be abrupt with the patient but she'd been busy.

Eve was smiling but her eyes suggested she was less impressed. 'This is Hattie Ironfield. Hattie lost her baby last year at thirty weeks. She's twenty-nine weeks and her husband is asking if she should go to Brisbane for the birth of their baby now.'

Sienna's mind focused with a slap. She needed to remember that the numbers weren't just numbers. They were women like the one in front of her with big sad eyes and rough-skinned hands from manual labour. She guessed she'd needed the reminder.

'I'm sorry to hear of your loss, Hattie. I'm Dr Wilson, Eve's sister, and I'm here to go through all the information to see if we can come up with a way to keep other babies safe.'

She sat down on the spare chair. 'So it's a good question and if I was in your shoes I'd be asking it too.' Sienna repeated the point. 'Can it happen again?' She looked Hattie in the eye. 'To be honest, anything can happen. But we'll be doing some extra tests this time, keeping a closer eye on everyone here. I wish I could tell you that going to Brisbane would guarantee your baby being well.' She watched Hattie's face. 'But I can't.'

The woman's voice was strained. 'I know that, Doctor.'

Eve quietly asked, 'What happens if you do go away? Can they manage on the station without you?'

Hattie shrugged. 'They'd have to. The kids would miss me.'

'Do you have people you could stay with for a couple of months in Brisbane?'

'Not really. I'd have to go to a hotel but there is one we stay in if we have to go to Brisbane. So at least I know it a little. And I'd do that if it would make my baby safer.'

Here was a dilemma. It was no use her making a decision to

uproot a woman for an extended time, Sienna thought, if the people in Brisbane don't think it's necessary.

'How about I have a chat to the obstetrician you'd be referred to in Brisbane? See what they say about the service here now and whether it still means you'd be better off going to the city.'

Hattie's shy smile peeped out like a little ray of sunshine. 'That would be good.'

'Okay.' She glanced at Eve. 'Pass me the antenatal card. I'll recheck Hattie's medical records and then I'll have a chat with the director of obstetrics in Brisbane. No use just talking to the one on call.'

'Guess not.' Eve was dry but there was a glint of approval in her eye. Sienna found herself grinning back. Since when did she need approval from her little sister?

Eve handed over the notes and Sienna nodded to Hattie. 'Give me a good fifteen minutes. I need to know what I'm talking about before I ring. If I have any questions I'll come out and find you so don't go too far away.'

Hattie nodded. 'Okay.'

Sienna looked at Eve and then at the portable ultrasound parked in the corner like a computer on wheels. 'Maybe you could do a quick ultrasound, if you like. Practise your umbilical flow assessment.' She shook her head. 'I can't believe the toys you have here.'

Eve grinned. 'More than I was allowed to play with in Brisbane. You haven't spent much time with Blanche yet.'

Four hours later Sienna met up with Callie, who'd been with Sylvia for her doctor's appointment. She was just the same as she'd been before, quietly pleasant and calm, but Sienna still didn't like to think of her as a half-sister.

If she was honest, she could see why Eve liked her; she probably had more in common with this new sister than she had with Sienna. And there was nothing wrong with Callie's brain.

She'd cast her eyes over the notes for Hattie, picked out the two grey areas that Sienna had noticed, and agreed with the obstetrician in Brisbane that nothing could be changed by a higher level of care. So, happily, Hattie would stay home until four weeks before her due date.

They finished discussing the cases. Sienna outlined how she planned to structure the review and her initial feel for the grey areas.

Callie broached the subject when Sienna was least expecting it. 'So are you up for any O&G consultations while you're here?'

I knew it. 'You have the FOG to do that. I had a chat with Phillip up in Roma as I came through.'

'I'm not talking about cancelling Phillip, just the days when he gets called away to emergencies and can't make it. Eve and I can do the women's health stuff like pap smears and breast checks and contraception. But the women who need to see a specialist have often travelled hundreds of kilometres and they shouldn't have to wait another month for something that might need more rapid assessment.'

'You mean one-offs, here and there? Fine.' *God!* She was such a softie.

'What about things like diathermies, removal of polyps, problems that only need a local anaesthetic to fix before the patient can go home? Save another trip rather than referring them on for admission at Longreach?'

She was getting needy here. 'Fine. Anything under a local. But I don't have colposcopy instruments so anything that needs a good look I can't do.'

'Sure.'

Sienna didn't like the way Callie said that: there wasn't a lot of sympathy there. 'I've got work to do as well, and work to get back to in Melbourne, so as soon as I've done what needs doing here I'm off.'

Callie nodded politely.

Sienna was starting to suspect this Ms-Nice-Lady act was a front for a very determined woman. 'Okay, then. Of course if there's a last-minute cancellation I could do a couple of hours of catch-up.'

Callie carefully avoided her eye. 'That's great.'

As the day came to an end, Callie and Eve were back on the veran-dah of the big house and Sylvia was propped up comfortably on cushions, enjoying the company and the spectacle of the receding electrical storm, even if there'd been little rain to go with it. She looked thinner, frailer, but more serene, as if happy just to fade away quietly in the background.

Every time Callie's gaze travelled over to her mother Eve saw a flicker of pain cross her sister's face and she wanted to weep for both of them. But that was the last thing Sylvia wanted. In fact, she'd for-bidden them to.

Eve had her own familial cross to bear. 'I'm sorry Sienna wasn't more helpful.'

'I thought she was very helpful.' Callie smiled gently at Eve. 'Stop worrying. She was fine. I've met a lot of specialists like her. They always seem more driven and focused, which is reasonable given the meaning of the word "specialist". And she's here, isn't she?'

'Thanks to Blanche.' Eve could feel the tension seep away from her shoulders. She really did feel responsible for her sister, yet she hated the thought that she was being disloyal to Sienna. 'And she'll get the job done. I've never seen her not complete something once she's started.' She shrugged. 'But she's not a warm and fuzzy person.'

Callie smiled. 'Maybe she hasn't met her warm and fuzzy other half?'

Eve ran her mind over a few of Sienna's past boyfriends and winced. Mentally rolled her eyes. Again, disloyal to Sienna.

TWENTY-FOUR

The storm had stopped and as she walked down the slippery road to her B&B Sienna wondered if she should have stayed for that drink she'd knocked back. Suddenly she felt the need for company.

Up ahead a broad-shouldered, erectly postured man in a pale-blue shirt and dark trousers backed out of a door and locked it.

Ah. She'd know those thighs anywhere. Sergeant McCabe securing the premises. All safe in the police station. The thought made her smile in the dimness.

Sienna walked on until she was level and strangely the whole world seemed to slow right down, until her feet had carried her close enough to smell the tinge of clean sweat. It was not something she'd had a fetish for before, but this was just enough to know he was a man's man. She wondered if he was a ladies' man as well.

She lifted her chin and glanced over at his back and shoulders. Either way, he was a fine dude to have beside you in a dark alley. Which suddenly made her think of other things. *Good grief.* She fancied a new man, and here of all places. Now that was amusing.

She heard the jingle of keys as they slid into his pocket, noticed the raucous cries of the cockatoos in the big gum across the road and could suddenly feel the warm breeze on her skin. What was with the sensory overload?

He turned around, unsurprised to see her there; in fact he'd probably known she was there before she'd recognised him.

He looked down at her. He was one tall guy. There was not a lot of men she could say that about.

'Evening.' He spared her a nod and turned to walk away.

She'd better say something or she'd be on her own again. 'You're an interesting man, Sergeant McCabe. What's your problem with women?'

He stopped, turned back and glanced at her coolly. The guy was vibrating aversion. He looked up and down the street as if searching for someone or something to rescue him. An armed hold-up? A break and enter?

There was nothing to save him. 'I don't have a problem with women. I avoid them.'

He had carved-from-rock facial features and hard grey eyes to match the evening sky. He didn't look gay.

'No little boyfriend hiding away?'

His brows went up and then back down to expressionless. Implacable. *Hmm*. She leaned a little closer. 'What happens when a woman doesn't ignore you back?'

'Nothing. Because I don't notice.'

She raised her brows and smiled. 'Nasty.'

'Reality.'

The devil came out to play and Sienna wondered idly if it was her way of saying to a town that had forced her to live in it that she did things her way.

She stepped up really close and rested her hand on the solid front of his shirt. Felt the muscles bunch under her fingers, enjoyed the thrill of that. The intensity of her own response surprised her. He was a very good-looking man.

He glanced up and down the empty street again and she lowered her voice.

'You and I know that's just a theory. A smokescreen for the masses.'

He reached out and his big fingers curled around and gripped her biceps. Lifted her body easily out of his space so there was a good foot of air between them and put her down.

'What are you after, Dr Wilson?'

She shrugged away his hands and resisted the urge to rub the fingermarks she'd bet were on her arms. But her belly was kicking like a mule. He'd shocked her with the movement, but she reckoned she could shock him too.

'A night. Nothing more.'

She could see the struggle. *Phew*. At least he was having one – she'd worried she was losing it for a moment there. This whole unexpected confrontation amused her. And inflamed her. He was a powerful man at the mercy of his uptight scruples. Not a lot of those around, and as far as she was concerned it was an aphrodisiac with a capital A.

And he was so different from the polished and perfumed boys like Mark. What was there to lose? She'd be gone in a couple of months. Less than three, to be exact. She was a woman, footloose and fancy-free. And just a little lonely – and so, it seemed, was Sergeant McCabe.

'An affair?' His impersonal gaze travelled from the top of her hair to her high-heeled shoes and back again with a leisurely thoroughness that unexpectedly made her skin hot. 'With you?' Still no expression.

She licked her suddenly dry lips. 'Where would a policeman go to have a torrid little affair in this dust bowl?'

This time he smiled but it was still at her – not with her. She wasn't sure she liked being amusing to someone.

'That's not going to happen, though, because the whole town would know.'

'I could slip into the police residence through the back door.'

'I don't do lying to people.'

'Really? How do you get along?'

'With celibacy. You should try it.'

She shook her head. 'Not interested in that.'

'We're very old-fashioned around here.' He held her gaze. 'But I've got an idea.'

'What?' She tried to read his expression, she really did, but he was giving nothing away. It was like trying to read a big rock wall and you kept looking because there were interesting hand-holds. Really interesting hand-holds.

Then he said the unexpected. 'How about you seduce me?'

Goody. She stepped back in closer and he held up his hand.

'Not with your body. With you.' That amused but dismissive glance that infuriated her. 'You could try to make me like you.'

'I don't care whether you like me.'

The smile said that didn't wash. She wasn't sure how he conveyed the message that she had to play by his rules, but again – intriguing.

'Well, I have to care. Or it's not on.'

Sienna sighed, thought about it and didn't say no. 'I've got nothing else to do after dark.' They began to walk down the street towards her B&B. She could get to know him a little and her sideways look measured him. 'So tell me about you. Who is Sergeant McCabe?'

'I don't talk about myself.'

'Try it. I am actually interested.' She shrugged as if to say she could hardly believe it herself. 'You're bitter, misogynistic, and buried in this sweaty armpit of the world. Alone. Why?'

He looked down at her coolly. 'I like this sweaty armpit of the world. I enjoy the harshness, the serenity, the primitive order of basic survival. Perhaps if you gave Red Sand a chance without expecting the worst the town might grow on you too.'

She shook her head and scanned the immediate vicinity. 'I am here as a means to an end. As soon as my job is done I am out of here.'

'I'm not liking you.'

'Tough.' She batted her eyelashes at him. They'd come up to her gate. She should exit while she was still ahead. If she was ahead. How the hell did you make someone like you? She had no idea. It wasn't something she'd ever wasted time on before. 'Interesting talking to you. Maybe I'll try harder tomorrow.' She turned to go and glanced back over her shoulder. 'Or not.'

The next morning at breakfast she cornered Fran. 'So where do the young people go to flirt and grope each other in the dark out here, Fran? It feels like everyone is watching everyone in this town.'

Fran smiled and it was singularly sweet. She was too nice to be true, Sienna decided.

'It only feels like that if you're contemplating doing something you don't want to advertise.'

Sienna had always been impatient if the answer was coming too slowly. She gave up on Fran being any help.

Fran picked up on it. She was nice, but not slow. 'There's the creek out the back of the pub, down by the river. Or the lake.' Fran sighed. 'I loved going out to the lake when my husband was courting me.'

'A lake? Out here?' Well, she guessed there must be a couple – seeing as how the damn people who had all the money owned Diamond Lake Station! 'So how do I get to the lake?'

'Just go back out to the edge of town, the Brisbane side, and you'll see the sign.' She looked a little dubious. 'Not sure your car would make it, though – there's a lot of ruts and sand.'

Well, that was fine then. Sergeant McCabe could take her to the lake. Maybe she could go for a wander around lunchtime and tee up this afternoon's sunset. She thanked Fran, picked up her bag and let herself out.

At work a few minutes later, Eve knocked at the door and Sienna glanced up.

'Well, I'm not interrupting because you haven't started yet.'

'Was that one of those "attack is the best form of defence" openers?'

'Probably. Just letting you know Callie won't be in today because Sylvia isn't feeling well.'

'Okay.'

'And I'll be out all day as I'm doing home visits in the ambulance.'

'So I'll be able to get lots done.'

Eve smiled. 'That you will, big sister. Bet you miss me.' With that she was gone and Sienna assured herself she wasn't that needy.

At lunchtime Sienna glanced around the empty rooms as she left. Funny old day at work. Maybe it was more fun when Eve was there but she got a heck of a lot more work done when she wasn't.

She would finish this and get herself back to Melbourne where she belonged.

Sienna spied Sergeant McCabe heading back to his little police station as she stepped out onto the street. She could just go home to her B&B and Fran would have cold pie waiting for her in the fridge (it seriously was not a B&B in the true sense of the term) or she could harass the good sergeant. She knew which promised to be more fun.

She came up behind him. Though he didn't turn, she knew he knew who was there. He had awareness all around. The thought made her smile.

'I hear you have a nice little lake around here?'

He turned to look at her. There was nothing to read in his face, as usual. 'So?'

'Apparently my toy car wouldn't make it.'

'No. Road's very rough.'

'Man of few words. That could get old.'

There was a tiny hint of a smile lurking at the corner of that stern mouth and she'd bet it was against his better judgement. Sienna felt a ridiculous surge of satisfaction. *Gotcha.*

'Excuse me, Sergeant. Would you have a vehicle that would make it an easy drive?'

'Could have. Why?'

'Apparently the sunset is very beautiful out there and I'm keen to find something beautiful in this place.'

A little tinge of sarcasm. 'I'd have thought that was the last thing you were looking for.'

'I think you're pretty.'

'Don't talk nonsense. Doesn't suit you.' Then he shrugged. 'Guess I could. Around five. I haven't been out there for a while. Save me having to open the gates.'

'Gee, thanks.'

'You don't have to come.'

'But that was the whole point of asking.'

Four hours later Sienna bounced along beside Sergeant McCabe in the cab of a very 'hardy' four-wheel drive. What the hell was this guy's name?

'What is your first name?'

'Thor.'

She laughed out loud. 'I can't believe you said that!'

'Lucius?'

'Nup.'

'Colin.'

'Please, no.'

He laughed this time. It was the first time she'd heard the sound. It was very short but incredibly satisfying to hear – a strange feeling for Sienna. 'You surprise me . . . whatever your name is.'

'Douglas.'

'Douglas.' She thought about that. Strong. Manly. Understated. Yep. That suited him.

'I can do Douglas.'

'Only if I let you.'

It was her turn to laugh again. He amused her. Big time. And he turned her on something wicked.

Then the lake came into view. Out of nowhere.

'Now that's unexpected.' Everything was unexpected out here.

She could hear the disbelief in his voice. 'How is that unexpected? You knew there was a lake out here. Asked me to show you, in fact.'

She refused to bite. 'Smart alec. I meant I didn't expect *this*.' She pointed. It was huge. And gorgeous.

He slowed as they pulled up at a picnic area complete with descriptive signage and rustic picnic table. She opened her door and climbed out as soon as he stopped. Sienna spread her arms out. She ignored whether he was getting out as she was drawn to the edge of the still water, where the roots of a huge white and brown spotted gum reached into the water like fingernails dipped in nail polish. She smiled at herself. She'd bet he wouldn't get that image.

Overhanging branches shadowed the foliage in the water with an echoed semicircle of tiny water succulents, and where the sun struck, the bronzed water lay still and silent, not telling tales yet redolent with history.

He came up to stand beside her, raising his nicely muscled arm to point. 'Normally this place is full of grey nomads camping in their vans. But the track is too rough for them at the moment, until the council grader comes in and fixes it.'

'My little car would not have made it.'

'No. Can you see the emus and black swans across the other side?'

'Emus.' She looked in the direction he'd indicated and saw a herd of grey-flecked fluffy emus treading with stately precision through the water. She flashed him a genuine smile. 'I like emus.'

'You would. The females are not maternal.'

'Career emus, you mean?'

That almost got a smile. He looked down at her and she was sure there was a twitch. 'Hmm. Babies are brought up by the father emu for the first two years. Did you know that?'

'Makes a lot of sense. I'm all for that. Probably the only way I'd ever have kids.'

'You didn't look like you had a maternal bone.'

'None that I can find personally.'

She'd made him smile but she didn't feel warmed by it.

'Then why are you an obstetrician?'

Unexpectedly the truth came out. 'My friend died having a baby. I wanted to stop that happening. Only way I could say sorry that I wasn't there for her.'

'I get that.'

She looked at him, Mr 'I feel guilty about something I'm not sharing with you'.

'I guess you do,' she said thoughtfully, then glanced back at the birds. 'So I like emus.'

'Nice to have found something you like from around here.'

She batted her eyelashes at him. 'Oh, come on. I like the lake.' She glanced up at the giant gum. 'I like this tree.' She saw his mouth soften.

She teased him. 'You couldn't call it a smile, but nearly. Admit it. I just scored a point.'

The softening disappeared and she laughed at him, then turned and walked away along the edge of the lake. She could feel his gaze resting on her. Sienna not so innocently bent over and picked up a shiny leaf to show off her rear end. She heard him laugh and wandered back to him at the table. He just watched her.

She smiled. 'Let's have a glass of wine.'

'I'm driving.'

'You're allowed one glass. That won't put you over the limit.'

'No,' he said, implacable. 'Go ahead. I'll watch.'

'As always,' she said coyly, making her way back to the car.

He reached in behind her and his muscles bulged as he lifted out the basket she'd packed. It was almost worth the weight she'd struggled with back from the shop just to see that.

'What the hell have you got in here?'

'I had much difficulty stocking it from the local store. They seriously need a deli here.'

Exasperated, he put it on the old wooden picnic table that had seen a lot of extreme weather down here by the lake. 'Why would you possibly need a delicatessen out here?'

'Choices. Just because we're out in the armpit of the world doesn't mean we shouldn't have access to the choices those in the city have.'

'Yes, it does – if you owned the shop you'd have to wait for some passing tourist to buy your stuff because nobody in town would touch it with a barge pole.'

She started laying out the picnic basket. Tablecloth. Glasses. Bottle of white wine and some biscuits. Cheese. She unscrewed the lid and poured herself a wine. Sienna looked at him as she hovered over the second glass she'd put out. 'You sure?'

He looked at her as if he didn't get it and shook his head. 'Do you have to do something all the time? Can't you just sit?'

She glanced over her shoulder at him. 'If you sit, you die. Or life passes you by.'

'Not in my experience.' As if he wished it would.

She tilted her head at him with full attention before taking a sip. 'And what is your experience, Sergeant McCabe?'

'This and that.'

She turned to face him fully and studied his lean features. The harsh lines at the side of his mouth. The saving wrinkles around his eyes that said sometimes he found life comical, though she'd seen precious little of that in him.

'So I would say the army.' She looked harder. 'Inscrutable special forces or medic?' He watched her, deadpan, as she went on. 'Some tragedy that you blame yourself for has soured your life and you came out here in penance.'

'That's enough.' He stood up, then abruptly turned back to her. 'What about you?' There was a bite to his response. 'Lost your dad very young, did you? A couple of failed relationships? Decided to use men from there on in so they didn't use you?'

She shrugged, immune to this sort of response. 'Pretty much. But then, I'm achieving what I want in life. Are you?'

'Wouldn't have picked you for a woman who wanted to do research in the outback.'

She waved her hand dismissively. 'This is temporary.'

'I'm thinking everything is temporary for you.'

She frowned at him. 'Nothing wrong with temporary.' She glanced around at the deserted lake. They were fencing when it seriously wasn't necessary, but she had to admit it was amusing.

'Listen. Why don't we just slip in there behind those bushes and go at it hammer and tongs? Get this ridiculous attraction thing out of the way and then we can go our separate ways. I really don't think this "friends first" thing is going to work.'

'I'm not that kind of guy.'

She sighed. 'Pity.' She'd tried and now she was just a little over it. Sienna turned back to the picnic basket she'd brought and peered inside. Held up a piece of cheese. 'Cheddar? Would you like a biscuit with your water?'

TWENTY-FIVE

Callie looked at the two lines on the pregnancy test strip and sank onto the edge of the bath. It couldn't be. With Kurt it had taken years to fall pregnant with Bethany; she'd been told it was unlikely she'd ever fall again. No wonder she hadn't thought of it.

The specialist had said it was her lack of eggs that had been the problem, and now one mad moment with Bennet and she was pregnant. The crazy idea had come to her last night when she'd been lying in bed and her belly had fluttered.

Her father had been gone five months, so she was almost that far along. It seemed medical centres weren't all Bennet could build.

'Whoa. Whoa.' She bent forwards as she puffed out the words.

She was forty. It had to be something else. She dropped the stick in the bin and felt her breasts. Tender. But they'd been tender a couple of times a month for a few years now.

Periods. Well, she was so irregular it had never really been a surprise if they were late or absent.

Her hand slid down to her belly. There was a definite roundness she'd previously attributed to Eve's love of after-dinner chocolate. Her mind flew to the young pregnant women who streamed in and out of the clinic. That was her now! Except she wasn't young. And she didn't have a husband.

Whoa. The nausea came out of nowhere like a road train in the night as it whooshed up her throat and left her shuddering over the bowl. She really was pregnant. Or in shock. Or both.

She had to talk to Bennet. Tell him it was okay. That she understood they weren't together. Explain about the risks.

The risks!

She closed her eyes and felt the pain tear at her. The ghastly fear of this baby growing and wriggling and communicating through her belly just like Bethany had . . . and then dying as well.

Would she survive such a tragedy a second time?

Well, she knew what she wouldn't survive: she wouldn't survive not giving this baby a chance. So she wasn't doing anything about it, no matter if she or he wasn't perfect.

Which meant she'd prefer not to have any tests to check, because there was no need. That at least was clear, even in the first five minutes of knowing. She would love her growing baby with all her heart for as little or as long as she could. And she'd certainly know the due date because she'd only had sex once. Roughly 266 days from conception. That gave her a date to work out as exact as any ultrasound could give her.

She rinsed her mouth out, wiped her face and neck and felt better, then remembered her occasional half a glass of wine and felt worse. Thank goodness she'd never been a big drinker, or the guilt would be a hundred times worse. It'd be abstinence from today. Bennet was coming for lunch with her mum. Goodness knows how she would tell him.

Callie opened the bathroom door and went through to the kitchen. Her mother was sitting at the table with her hand on the teapot. Her eyes were closed.

'You okay, Mum?'

Sylvia opened her eyes and smiled, a smile that stroked her daughter's face and brought new tears to her eyes. God, she would miss that smile. She wanted to catch it and hold the love in it in her hand so she could pull it out and look at it. Be healed by it.

Sylvia studied her face. 'I'm fine. Good morning, my daughter.'

'Good morning, my mother.' Callie breathed out a long, slow sigh and vowed again to savour every moment.

After lunch Callie and Bennet watered Sylvia's garden while she rested.

'There's something I have to tell you, Bennet.'

'What?'

God. How did you tell a man you were having his baby when it was the last thing he expected? 'You know that time down at the river?'

Bennet took a breath, glanced around to make sure nobody could hear them, and held up his hand.

'No. I thought you didn't want to talk about it, so I haven't. I know what you're going to say. It should never have happened.' It all poured out like a gully rusher down the creek, now that he had permission to speak. 'I don't know what came over me. At least you had the excuse that you were beside yourself with grief; your father had just died and your husband had left you.' He shook his head in disbelief. 'I don't know what happened.'

Callie winced. 'Well, thanks for that, I think, but that wasn't what I was going to say.'

Her voice trailed off and Bennet looked at her. He bent his head and furrowed his brow. Blinked. Straightened and stepped back as his mouth opened.

'You're on the pill, right?'

'No. I had fertility problems.'

He was flooding a bush with the hose as he listened. 'Had?'

There was nothing slow about Bennet. That was a good thing, she decided. But now she really did have his full attention.

'You said "had". So what are you saying?'

But she could see he'd guessed. So she needed to get it out in the open. She was trying. Really. But it was hard in the face of his shock and disbelief. Even though it shouldn't be hard because she'd decided she expected nothing from him.

'I'm pregnant.' There. It was out, but dancing in the air between them like a swirling little whirly wind, sucking the breath from both of them. 'It's your child – but not your responsibility.'

His voice was very soft as he bent the hose to kink it off so he could concentrate. 'How is a child we both made not my responsibility?'

'It's my fault.' She spread out her hands. Of course it was her fault; she'd practically seduced the poor man.

Bennet crossed to the tap and turned off the hose before facing her. 'I'm pretty sure there were two of us there.'

He wasn't saying the things she expected. But then again, this was Bennet, not Kurt. Kurt would have left her in no doubt as to whose fault it was. She needed to stop thinking like that but it was hard after fifteen years of keeping the peace. Maybe she and Bennet could have a civil, grown-up conversation.

His voice was calm. Calmer than hers. 'When are you due?'

She'd only just worked that out for herself. 'Twentieth of December. I'm twenty-one weeks now. So I'm due before I can file for divorce.' She looked away. Now for the even harder part.

'There's more?'

'Bethany.' She licked her lips, swallowed the pain. 'My daughter had Down syndrome and died at birth. I'm not having an ultrasound. Or any tests for Down syndrome. I'm not getting rid of this baby, even if there is something wrong with him or her.'

She couldn't bear to see the shock in his face so she didn't look up, but she sensed him step closer. Callie felt his finger on her chin, lifting her face so she had to look at him.

'Okay. I can understand that. That's your choice and I appreciate your honesty.' Then he smiled at her and it was that Bennet smile from a hundred years ago. The one that said she was the best thing that had happened to him all day. Today had to be 'amazing smile' day.

His voice dropped, enveloping her in a warm blanket the way only Bennet could. 'Who have you told?'

She shook her head. 'No one. Just you.' She watched his eyes widen. Then came a rueful smile that couldn't quite hide his delight.

'Thank you. I appreciate that.' He looked at her and sighed. 'So can I be involved?'

She thought she was going to faint, and had to put her hand out and rest it on the fence for support. 'In what way?'

'I don't know. Go to the doctor's with you. I won't get to see any ultrasounds.' He could even tease her. This was turning out so differently to what she'd imagined.

'I probably won't go to the doctor's. Eve will look after me until she goes as long as I stay healthy.' She didn't want to think about Eve going. Or her mother, who was leaving much more irrevocably.

But Bennet was stuck on her previous statement. 'Why wouldn't you stay healthy?'

'I had quite severe toxaemia of pregnancy last time.'

'So that means you'll have it again this time?'

'Not necessarily.' She had to smile. 'A different father of the child can make a big difference.'

Then he smiled too. 'I'm sure I have much better DNA than your husband's.'

'I don't doubt that.' Though it would be a shock for her mother.

'What about Sylvia?' he asked, as if he'd read her mind. 'Can I come with you when you tell her?'

She hadn't imagined he would offer. But in that moment she could see how much that would help. Even if she and Bennet didn't end up together, Sylvia would see they both wanted what was best for the baby. It would relieve her mum's mind a lot, which was all Callie wanted in these last few months. Her mum might even be excited at the thought of a grandchild.

'I'd like that. If you don't mind.'

'Silly. So what if I did mind? I'm sure it's not a conversation you look forward to.' He tilted his head and examined her. 'Though you're getting used to this, aren't you?' He took another step back and examined her face from a distance, then smiled at her. 'You're glowing.'

She wouldn't be surprised if she was. Callie's hand crept to cover her stomach. 'I will always grieve for my lost baby, but the idea that I might finally have a child of my own,' she looked at this man who was everything Kurt was not, 'with a man I can respect, is a gift. And I'm a little excited.'

'Only a little?'

She looked down, trying to hide the fear that had been growing as she became accustomed to the news. 'It's further along than I can believe but if there is anything wrong with my baby there's a big chance of miscarriage. When I feel movements I'll be more excited. I think I can but I'm not sure yet.'

'Okay. So when should we tell your mother?'

She looked up and his strong features were so calm, so empathetic. She was incredibly lucky. 'Today? But if you want a couple of days to get used to the idea, then I can wait.'

His voice lowered, as he picked up on what she hadn't said. 'Time is short?'

Callie swallowed. 'I don't know. She could be here for months or her heart might give way. I just want her to know.'

He held out his hand and she felt his strong fingers curl around hers and squeeze. 'Then let's go tell Sylvia the good news.'

Sylvia was asleep when they entered the house, lying back in the easy chair with a light blanket covering her knees. The dim room was kind to her sunken cheeks, and the yellow of her skin seemed less pronounced.

She opened her eyes and smiled as Callie and Bennet sat down on the lounge together. 'Hello, darlings.'

Her voice was soft, still a little dreamy with whatever pleasant cloud she'd been on, and Callie waited for her to wake properly. She watched her sit up, wince and look tense for a moment before the collection of pains and discomfort she seemed to be able to push into another part of her mind went away.

'What?' Her faded blue eyes began to twinkle. 'You're both bursting with news.'

Callie drew a big breath. Got it out as fast as she could after the slow start with Bennet. 'Bennet and I are going to have a baby.'

Callie looked at Bennet and he smiled reassuringly back. She went on. 'It's very unexpected and early days yet, Mum, so anything could happen, but we wanted to tell you.'

Sylvia beamed at them. 'I think that's lovely news. I've always wanted you as a son, Bennet.'

Callie put her hand on her mother's and softly patted it. She wasn't going to start lying now. 'We're pregnant – not engaged, Mum.'

Bennet eased the awkwardness. 'Plenty of time for thinking about that when she's rid of the other fellow.'

Callie could have kissed him – and she just might later on, once she'd stopped blushing.

'Indeed.' Sylvia gave him a wink. 'And when is your baby due?'

Callie pretended she didn't see the interplay between them. Her mother hadn't been upset. Any embarrassment over Bennet was minor in the scheme of things. 'Before Christmas.'

Sylvia sighed. 'I won't be here.'

Callie shook her head. 'Of course you will. It'll be something for you to look forward to.'

Sylvia didn't say anything. Then she turned to Bennet and smiled. 'I'm glad.' She considered them. 'A bit of a shock for both of you, I'm thinking?'

'We're not telling anyone for a few weeks. In case anything happens. I want to feel our baby move more before people start talking about it.'

'Of course. Thank you for telling me. Are you going to tell Eve straight away?'

Callie glanced at Bennet. 'I'd like to. She'll keep an eye on both of us. I'm really hoping she'll stay until after baby is born.'

'Ask her. She's a good girl.'

The 'good girl' blinked a couple of times, scrutinised her sister's shyly excited face and then whooped. 'You're kidding me! That's awesome. You naughty girl! When are you due?'

'Around the twentieth of December.' Callie blushed and Eve laughed.

'All those hints of mine and you'd already seduced the local vet. I'd better tell Chippie I won't be back till after Christmas. I'm not missing out. I am so going to tease you about this.'

'Well, not for a couple of weeks, please. I'm trying hard not to count my chicken until the baby is definitely growing.'

The smile fell off Eve's face. *Poor Callie.* She nodded. Then her grin broke out again. She couldn't help herself. 'And what about the rooster in the henhouse? What did Bennet say?'

Callie blushed again. 'He wants to be a part of the pregnancy. I think he wants to be a part of more than that.'

Bless Bennet. 'And . . .?'

'I was shocked.' Callie spread her hands wide. 'Considering I still have a husband.'

'No, you don't. You have a creep who is living with someone else and you're just waiting to get your name back legally.'

Callie looked away and Eve guessed she was still doing the guilt trip. Not worth pushing, then.

'Well, Bennet took it well.' She looked back. 'I'm still shocked that he became invested so quickly.'

Eve wasn't sure what that meant but she could see how fragile Callie was. 'I think it's lovely.'

She thought about the whole abnormality-testing issue and let it lie. Callie would talk about all that when she was ready. She knew the risks as much as if not more than anyone else. Nobody knew her history better. Except maybe the sleaze she'd married.

'Okay. So, mum for a few weeks.' They both grinned at the pun. 'What did Sylvia say?'

'She's happy for me, I think. She was lovely to Bennet and Bennet was lovely to everyone.'

Obviously. ''Cause he's a nice guy. So how are you feeling? Are you sick? Boobs hurt? Got any silly cravings?'

'You know cravings are an old wives' tale.'

'Disagree. Metallic taste in the mouth, gone off anything you usually love, extra tired?'

'That's me.' Callie joined in, raising her hand. 'Tired with frequent trips to the ladies'. The nausea was never noticeable. If it had been maybe I would have thought of this sooner. I feel such an idiot.'

They both giggled.

'How about we go for a little wander down to the clinic today to take some blood, check your blood pressure and work out some dates. It's probably too late to take supplements but we can check your iron.'

'I guess I'll get the ultimate pregnancy refresher.'

'Nothing makes it sink in faster than putting yourself in that position. But I don't think even Blanche expected you to put so much into your study.'

'Blanche.' Callie grimaced. 'Everyone is going to say I'm too old to have a baby.'

Piffle, Eve thought. 'Everybody can go hang. You are the perfect age for Callie Wilson to have a baby because for you it's the right time. Imagine having one with the ex instead of Bennet. I know who I'd prefer as my dad.'

They both stopped to look at each other, speaking of dads. Eve sighed and squeezed Callie's arm and Callie chewed her lip and looked away.

It had been a very intense five months since that fateful morning when Duncan Wilson had brought them together. And there was more heartbreak to come.

TWENTY-SIX

Two weeks later, on a day when the mailman was suffering from a nasty bout of kidney stones, the local policeman offered to do the mail run. Douglas McCabe arrived at the medical centre to pick up an extra supply of prescriptions and medications to take with him.

Instead of 'hello', as he came through the door he said, 'Your sister is insane.'

Eve looked at Sergeant McCabe as he leaned into the doorframe with his shoulder. 'Callie?' She couldn't imagine how Callie had offended him. Callie didn't offend anyone.

'Sienna.'

'Oh.' *That* she could imagine. Eve tilted her head and studied the tall man in front of her. She'd picked him as a private man, slightly forbidding, and Eve hadn't noticed him offer something personal about himself or anyone else until recently.

She had actually seen him around more than usual, now that she thought about it. He'd even turned up at Callie's to see Sylvia last Friday night, when the three girls had been there for their weekly debrief about Sienna's research progress.

Eve had thought then that it had been the closest they'd been to a family.

Now it seemed Sienna had managed to penetrate the thick hide of Sergeant McCabe and set up a nasty little skin irritation. That was pretty funny.

She tilted her head and looked at him. 'She's my sister but I'm not sure I understand her.'

His brows lowered even further. 'I don't think anyone understands that woman.'

Even more interesting. 'Do you want to?'

He glared out the door. 'I don't think so.' He didn't sound sure about that.

Eve was silent for a minute. 'Okay.' Best leave it all alone, then. She handed him the pack of medications she'd put in the bag for Aggie O'Malley. Callie had written the scripts out earlier for the widowed station owner, who lived by herself 150 kilometres from Red Sand township.

'I heard the full run takes eight hours of driving?'

'I have Saturdays off.' He shrugged. 'I like to check the outlying roads every now and then for trouble.'

Eve poked the scripts in after the medications. 'Is this the last thing you need to pick up before you leave?'

'Just some cheese and milk for Bellbird Station. I was leaving that till last.'

'Molly's doing well with her new baby.'

'So I hear. Jill at the store mentioned Molly had ordered her food for yesterday because the mail wouldn't be out again till Wednesday next week. She was out of dairy.' He shrugged, embarrassed. 'She might want milk – keep her own up for the baby.'

Eve didn't like to tell him milk didn't make breastmilk. But the thought was very sweet. 'A good all-round diet does help. So do you ring her when you're at the gate?

He looked surprised. 'Sometimes she runs stuff out for Simon in one of the paddocks so she might not even be home. I've got some feed for her horses as well. Bennet's been driving out but he's tied up today. I'll just leave it in the fridge in the kitchen.'

Eve laughed. She couldn't believe this place. Or the people. She'd miss it like a limb when she went. 'Can't get service like that in Brisbane. Service straight to fridge. That is so cool.'

'Well, it is a fridge,' he drawled, deadpan.

'Don't tell me there's a sense of humour under *your* mask as well?'

He raised his brows. 'As well as who?'

'Lex McKay cracked a joke the other day. I nearly fell over.'

He almost laughed. 'Seems you Wilson girls bring out hidden depths in us.'

He glanced at his watch. 'Well, better go pick up the madwoman.'

Eve blinked in shock. Madwoman? There was only one person he'd talk about like that. 'Sienna wants to go on the mail run with you?'

He shrugged and picked up his parcels. 'I told her it wasn't a joy ride but she said she may as well see what all the fuss was about.'

He saluted as he went out the door and Eve shook her head with a wry smile on her face. Wonders never ceased, though Sienna may get a shock associating with a real man for a change.

And then her thoughts flew like a homing pigeon straight back to Lex. She hadn't seen him this week. *How was he going with Lily?*

Sienna saw Douglas pull up at the store across the road and grabbed her bag. This had been a dumb idea but she was out of others. She'd been chipping away at him every time she had a chance for two weeks but hadn't got anywhere.

Eight hours in an outback refrigeration truck just for the thrill of a grumpy man's company. But what else was she going to do on a Saturday?

Well, work would have been a good option. She'd never been a Monday-to-Friday girl, so why start now? Didn't she want to get back to Melbourne before they stopped missing her?

Nah. Not today. Douglas was driving her mad. She'd give this man one more chance and if she couldn't seduce him sitting next to him for a day then he was a lost cause. Or she was.

He looked up as she opened her door. 'You know you'll have to open the gates?'

He could have said hello. 'I'm sure I'll survive.'

'Will I?'

'Within an inch of your life. Looking wary there, Sergeant McCabe.' She smiled, feeling immensely better. *So you should be wary.*

'You realise I know karate.' There might have been a twitch of humour as he said that.

Sienna replied sweetly. 'I know Kama Sutra.'

He leaned forwards and started the car. 'This should be interesting.'

They drove out past the lake and three black and brown emus began to run beside them.

Sienna's nose was glued to her window. The emus' incredible long legs stretched out in front of them in enormous strides, their fluffy bodies of feathers puffing and shimmering.

She laughed out loud as one glanced across and she could see his beady eyes as he ran faster, pulling away; she wanted to reach her hand out the window and touch him but Douglas slowed and the emu pulled further away. Before she could urge Douglas to drive faster she saw why he'd slowed, as suddenly the old man emu veered in her direction and dashed in front of the vehicle.

'If you hadn't slowed we would have hit them, wouldn't we?'

'Maybe.'

'Why would they do that? Why wouldn't they go the other way?'

'Sheer contrariness. Like someone else I know.' He went on before she could comment. 'See the wedge-tailed eagle there?'

She looked. 'Ugh. Saw dozens on the way here. Eating the roadkill.'

He slowed again. 'Plenty of food at the side of the road for them. Rather it got eaten than rotted and stank. But they take off in a straight trajectory if you startle them; you think they'll lift but they end up in through your front windscreen.'

She tried to imagine that huge wingspan inside the car. 'Wouldn't fancy one of those in the seat beside me.'

'No. So watch out when you drive past.'

Any excuse for a lecture. 'You can't help yourself, can you?'

He looked at her. 'Try not to complain in the first hour.'

Ohhh. 'I cannot believe I chose to come with you.'

He raised his brows, then slowed the vehicle some more. 'You want me to stop? We're not too far out. You could walk back in an hour.'

She glared at him and then suddenly laughed. Laughed until the tears ran down her face. 'You'd bloody well do it. Drive away and leave me out here to walk back.'

'It wouldn't kill you.'

'But I'd kill you.'

He grinned at her. Admitted he'd been baiting her to blow her top. 'Yeah, well. Worse ways to die.'

By the time they pulled up at their first mail stop two hours later they'd even had a couple of normal conversations.

An old rusty fridge stood forlornly at the entrance to a dirt driveway that disappeared into the distance. There was no sign of a house or cattle yards or even a windmill in the distance.

'So where's the house?'

'Five kilometres that way.'

He got out and so did Sienna to stretch her legs. The day had warmed from the chill of the morning to a dry heat that wasn't unpleasant after the cool of the air-conditioning in the truck.

She glanced around at the barren landscape hiding the light brush of barely visible grass around the edges of the dirt track. A distant steer wrestled with the grey-green tufts of some low, wiry-looking bush. There were no tall trees – not enough sustained water for that, but plenty of medium-height bushes. A lovely spotted gum beside Douglas reached its multi-coloured limbs to the sky; it was not the tallest she'd seen, but still a sight you'd never see in the city.

Douglas was grappling with the door of the 'mailbox'. She tried to imagine a rusting fridge on her kerb back in Melbourne. If she painted her house number on a dead appliance in her upmarket street she could imagine the horror from her neighbours. It might be almost worth the effort.

Douglas collected two stamped envelopes to post in town and lifted a brown-wrapped box from the back of the truck and jammed it into the fridge. Then he put several letters on top of the box and glanced at her.

'Ready?'

She sighed elaborately. 'Are we there yet?'

He laughed, strode over and pulled her to him. Stared into her eyes. Kissed her long and thoroughly.

'No. And you get one of those every time you ask.'

Holy crap. Sienna opened her eyes when it was over and didn't even try to resist the urge to grab his shirt and pull him back for more.

When that was over she could barely feel her feet. But Douglas was steering her backwards to the truck. He opened her door and pushed her firmly up into her seat. 'We have places to go.'

'And don't I know it,' she muttered happily. She glanced across at him as he climbed in. Sienna loved the way his shirt strained as he pulled himself into the seat. *Ooh ah*.

She grabbed the map he'd given her of their route for the day. Even that made her smile now. Couldn't hide her impatience. 'So where's the next mailbox?'

TWENTY-SEVEN

With the news of Callie's baby they all hoped that Sylvia had rallied and decided that she had to live to see her grandchild. And for the next two months she seemed to be holding her own. But after that each week seemed to tire her more.

By the time Callie was thirty-five weeks they all knew Sylvia had given herself permission to stop fighting the disease.

By mid November she could barely stand and needed help with nearly everything. Callie and Eve shared the constant supervision to prevent her dodgy sense of balance from letting her down, which it did often and none too gently.

Callie had stopped going to the medical centre unless someone was on hand to keep Sylvia safe.

Each day Callie reminded herself she was lucky she was home. 'You have no idea how much I regret wasting my time in Sydney when I could have been here with you earlier,' she said to Sylvia one day. They were in the bathroom and Callie was awkwardly drying her mother's frail legs after a shower. It was much more difficult with a pregnant belly.

'Everything is perfect. The only thing I regret is that I'll never see your baby, my darling.'

'Maybe you will.' But they both knew that wasn't going to

happen. Callie reached down to wipe her mother's feet.

Sylvia shook her head. 'You shouldn't have to do this.'

'And why not?'

'It's not right.'

Callie sat back on her heels and looked up at the dear face above her. 'And I was just thinking how right this was. I'm pretty sure I've said this before, but tell me, my mother – if it were me who was sick, would you mind drying my legs?'

Sylvia's mouth twitched. 'Of course not.'

'Thank you. I rest my case.'

'But I am sorry you've had to look after me so much. I'm the child now and you're the parent.'

Callie slipped the soft cotton nightie over her mother's head, and for a moment she could see the young woman she remembered from when she was a child. 'It's a gift. This time we have is precious.'

'I'm very tired, Callie.'

'I know.' She kissed her mother's forehead. 'I love you so much.'

'I will always be here.'

'I keep telling myself that.'

'And I want to see your father.'

'I know.' Callie brushed the tears from her face. 'Say hi for me.'

Sylvia sank onto the chair to rest before walking further. 'Eve's a lovely girl.'

'Sienna's not too bad.' They both smiled but it was hard to find amusement when they knew their time for conversation was so limited.

They shuffled through to the little bed Callie had dragged into the big dining area off the kitchen so her mother could stay a part of the heart of the house. She tucked the light cover around Sylvia's legs as the day warmed.

'Rest now. I'll go and make a little milkshake for you. Eve should be home soon.'

'I'm so pleased she's here for you.' Sylvia's dark lashes sank onto her cheeks as she closed her eyes.

'Don't worry about me. I'll be fine,' Callie whispered.

But her mother heard her and she whispered back, still with her eyes closed, 'I know, my darling. But it helps me.'

Callie swallowed the huge jagged lump in her throat and walked through to the kitchen. She paused at the big kitchen table and rested her hands on it. How many times had her mother sat here? Presided over the family. Given comfort and wise advice. How many times had they all laughed at something outrageous her father had said, been hosts to friends and visiting dignitaries. Her family would soon be all gone and there was nothing she could do about it.

Even Eve would leave. Sienna couldn't wait to, and Callie suspected she might even miss her more abrasive half-sister when the dust settled.

But she would have Bennet. And her baby. And Bennet's son, Adam, who would hopefully grow to love her as she would grow to love him. And it was true her mother would always be with her in spirit. But she didn't want her human form to leave.

Eve found her sister with tears streaming down her face as she stood at the table and for a horrible moment she thought Sylvia had gone.

'Callie? What's happened? Sylvia?'

Callie sniffed and straightened. 'I'm fine.' She glanced across to the corner of the room where her mother slept. She wiped her cheeks with the back of her hand and then took a tissue from the box Eve pushed into her hand.

'Boy, have we gone through a few of these.'

'And more to come,' Callie said as she blew her nose.

'How is Sylvia?'

'Very weak. I don't think —' her voice broke. 'I don't think it will be long now.'

Eve saw the pain and wanted to draw Callie's head against her shoulder but could see her diminutive sister had her I'm-being-strong coat on. She remembered her own resistance to letting go at this time and reached out and drew Callie against her chest.

'Poor Callie. It's so hard.' She stepped back and looked into her face. 'But it's beautiful too, that you can be here to help your mum at this time.'

'You did this with your mum?'

'Yeah. Tough times but I don't regret them. Though I think I'd be happy to go from a hospice myself. It's hard to be the one waiting for the moment without the break of responsibility you get in a hospice.'

'That's what I think it is. The responsibility of making sure she has enough pain relief, not too much that she sleeps all the time, but is comfortable, coherent.'

'Sylvia is a dream compared to my mum. Denise kicked and screamed all the way to the pearly gates.'

Callie smiled. 'Tough, like you and Sienna.'

'Ornery like us.'

The words hung with nowhere to go until finally Callie changed the subject. 'So how was the clinic?' They'd shut down the GP side of the centre temporarily so it was only offering basic nursing and ante-natal care.

'Sienna talked to the FOG about a gynae clinic. He's going to lend her his equipment for the day and it means those on the waiting list get seen three months earlier.

Callie couldn't hide her surprise. 'Maybe when she goes home she could still come out here once a month.'

They looked at each other and smiled at that unlikely scenario. 'We could ask her,' said Callie.

'Yeah, well. Dreaming. Though I do think she's seeing the need. She may surprise us yet.' But this was about Callie and her impending loss.

Eve glanced across at Sylvia. 'So is she sleeping much?'

Callie blinked. 'Yes. We'd just got out of the shower and it exhausted her.' She opened the fridge. 'I was getting her a milkshake before I faded out.'

Eve touched Callie's arm. 'I saw Bennet in town today. He said he was coming over soon. Why don't you go for a drive with him and I'll sit with your mum. Maybe go out and watch the sunset at the lake or something? There's mobile coverage out there. I could ring if I needed you. Have a little break before you can't leave.'

When Bennet came he was persuasive too. 'Just for an hour.' And then Sylvia joined in. 'Take a photograph on your phone and bring me the sunset. It's been a long time since I was out there and I'd like to see that.'

Callie put up her hands. 'Fine. We'll go. I'll take the lemonade we made today and make an occasion of it.' She glanced at Sylvia and Eve as if to reassure herself they'd still be here when she came back. 'Be back before dark.'

Eve watched them go. Then looked across to where Sylvia had drifted off to sleep again. She went out to the verandah to phone Sienna and warn her it was getting close.

To her surprise, Sienna offered to come over. 'You want company while Callie's away?'

'Sure. If you can spare the time away from your research.'

'I'm a bit stumped anyway. Maybe talking it through will help. I keep thinking it's something so simple we're missing it.'

'That would be good. Simple we can fix. See you soon.'

Eve opened the door ten minutes later and Sienna stepped into the kitchen with a bottle of white wine. Even leaned forwards and kissed her cheek. It was probably just a sympathy peck because Sienna knew how much Eve had grown to love their father's wife, but it was comforting that she cared enough to do something so out of character.

Sienna stepped back. 'What time is Callie coming home?' Her voice was brisk. *Regretting it already*, Eve thought with a wry inner smile.

'Just after sunset. She won't stay away long. Just getting a breath of outside before it's time.' They both glanced through the door to the lounge.

'Go through. Sylvia wants to say hello to you.'

Sienna hesitated then nodded. 'Sure.' She put the bottle of wine on the kitchen table. 'Thought we both might need a glass later?' She crossed to the little bed and pulled a chair over. 'Hello there, Sylvia.'

'Hello, darling. It's nice of you to come to keep Eve company.'

Sienna shifted closer. Eve stood behind her. 'How are you?'

They could see her face was becoming more thin and drawn every day. 'I'm ready.'

Sienna nodded. 'Are you in pain?'

She brushed the concept away with a frail hand. 'The only thing that bothers me is that I won't be here to see my grandchild.' She wiped a tiny silver tear from her cheek and *tsk tsk*ed herself for the weakness. She sighed and closed her eyes. Talking more to herself than Sienna, she said, 'I so would have liked to see the baby at least once, but . . .'

Sylvia drifted off to sleep again and Sienna eased out of the chair quietly as she looked down at the luminous woman in front of her. She crossed the room with Eve and their eyes met in silent acknowledgement of the impending moment. They both moved out onto the verandah to watch the sky darken and so they wouldn't disturb Sylvia.

'She looks like an angel already. She won't be here for Callie's baby.'

'I know.'

'It's the only thing holding her back, I think.'

Eve had been toying with an idea but had hesitated to bring it up with Callie. Maybe Sienna's input would help. 'I wondered if we could bring the ultrasound up here? It's portable, really just like a bigger laptop computer.'

Sienna's eyes brightened and then she shook her head. 'Great idea but Callie might not want that. She said she didn't want any tests.'

'We could run it by her. And you're so good at ultrasounds you could choose what she sees. Not like us.'

'We can ask when they come back.'

An hour later they heard Bennet's truck pull up, then the sound of Callie and Bennet climbing the steps. 'That's them now. You ask her.'

'Hello, Sienna,' Callie said, searching Eve's face for reassurance.

'She's fine. Sleeping.' Eve glanced at Sienna. 'We've got an idea.'

Callie raised her brows in question and Sienna inclined her head in Sylvia's direction.

'Your mother wants to see your baby. We wondered if you'd consider showing her an ultrasound. We don't have to do anything diagnostic. Maybe facial features, baby fingers, stuff like that?' She shrugged. 'But it's just an idea and only if you want to.'

Callie blinked a few times and bit her lip. She glanced at Bennet, who Eve decided was trying to keep his face expressionless. But the unconscious yearning in his eyes gave him away.

Callie sighed and shook her head at her own obtuseness. 'That's a beautiful idea. Thank you, Sienna. Don't know why I didn't think of it sooner.'

Sienna shrugged as if to say, it was just an idea anyone could have thought of, then looked at Eve and smiled. 'Actually, it was Eve's idea. Anyway, the later in pregnancy the better for seeing things to recognise. So don't go to the loo,' she reminded Callie as if she didn't know. 'Hold that thought and everything else while I scoot down to get it.'

Callie turned to Bennet. 'Will you go? Carry it for Sienna. It's not light.'

He jumped up with alacrity. 'I'd love to.' He practically dragged Sienna off the verandah. Eve and Callie watched them go. 'I think Bennet's keen.'

Callie sighed. 'I hadn't realised he was missing out on so much. Of course he wants to see the ultrasound. I've been selfish.'

Eve laughed and put her arm around her sister's shoulder. 'Yeah. Such a selfish witch of a woman. Maybe you've just been a little busy while caring twenty-four seven for your mum, being town GP, as well as dealing with all the discomforts of pregnancy.' She gestured to Callie's belly. 'I think this is a lovely way for your mum to see your peanut.'

Callie clutched Eve's arm. 'What if we see something that proves my baby has problems?' she whispered.

'I have no doubt it will mean you will love your baby even more – if that's possible. True?'

Callie sagged. A smile trembled on her lips and she nodded. 'You are so right. And wise. Thank you, Eve. I love having you as a sister.'

'You're the best present our dad gave me, that's for sure. He just left it a little too late before we all got together.' Eve was going to burst into tears if she talked much more about it. 'Let's clear the side table.'

Bennet and Sienna returned a few minutes later. He carried the ultrasound case carefully up the stairs and deposited it gently on the table.

Eve grinned. 'Bags not telling Lex if you break it. He and Blanche had a big fight over that piece of equipment.'

Bennet lifted it even more gingerly when Sienna pointed to the small table beside Sylvia's bed. Eve dragged the lounge as close as she could get it to Sylvia's bed. Callie was holding her mother's hand as she explained what they were going to do.

'So you'll get a sneak peek of this little grandchild of yours. Sienna is going to show us all now.'

Sylvia turned wondering eyes at the four smiling faces and another tiny tear slid down her sunken cheek. 'I can't wait. And I love that you're all here to share the moment with us.'

Callie lay down and Eve helped her pull her blouse up so her taut, rounded belly was exposed. Sienna squirted the gel and Callie sucked in her breath at the coolness of it.

Sienna squirted some more. 'I keep it in the fridge, you know,' she said as she smoothed it over the white skin. 'To be mean.'

Her voice was more gentle than Eve had ever heard it as she explained to Sylvia, 'Callie's baby is thirty-five weeks, so big enough for us to see the movements in real time on the inside, and for Bennet to feel them easily on the outside.'

Sienna floated the hand-shaped transducer across the gel and the screen came to life with grey and black images. She zoomed in confidently. 'A little hand.'

The fingers were clenched, but Sylvia gasped as they opened like a miniature starfish and seemed to wave. The picture of the fingers dissolved and a small flexing foot came into focus.

'Now foot and ankle and toes.'

Eve glanced around at her new family and felt the sting of tears. She watched Callie's terrified joy and Bennet's wonder, and took a quick snap on her phone of the sweet anticipation on Sylvia's face. It was pure pleasure, unshaded by disappointment that this was all she would see of her grandchild, just delight as each new facet of the child she would never hold was revealed to her.

'Look at the little nose.' Sylvia smiled mistily down at Callie. 'It's your nose. Your father's nose.' She glanced around at the three girls facing her. 'All your noses.'

And that was when Eve realised she was going to be an aunty – something she'd never thought she'd be. She saw the moment of non-professional wonder in Sienna as their eyes met but then her sister focused and was an obstetrician again.

Eve suspected that Sienna, despite kicking and screaming all the way, was being sucked into the Red Sand vortex, and they were becoming a family. A trio of sisters. And they owed a lot to this absolute darling of a woman who was fading away in front of them.

'So here is the mouth and the cheeks.' Sienna zoomed the magnification out and the whole face crystallised into focus and they saw a tiny baby suspended in the dark pool of its mother's womb. She used the machine like a musical instrument, dancing with the fluid so the baby took on a three-dimensional clarity. It was nothing like Callie and Eve's fumbled attempts to gain focus and zones.

Sienna glanced at Callie. 'Do you want to know the sex?'

Callie looked at her mum. 'Do you?'

Sylvia shook her head. 'It doesn't matter. I've seen your baby. Keep the surprise.'

Callie shook her head. 'Then no, thanks.'

'No problem.'

Sienna ran down a shoulder and showed them the little beating heart, but Sylvia was tiring now and she lay back from where she'd been leaning to see. Sienna flicked a glance at Callie, who unobtrusively lowered her fingers to stop the examination.

Sienna shut the machine down. 'Everything I saw looked perfect. Congratulations on your gorgeously growing grandchild, Sylvia.'

'Thank you. Thanks to all of you. You have given me such a precious gift.'

Eve helped Callie wipe down and then sit up. The bustle of rearranging furniture began again. Bennet carried the machine to the kitchen table, ready to return it to the medical centre when he went, and Sienna washed her hands at the sink.

In the background Sylvia lay back with her eyes closed and a pure, sweet smile on her face. Callie pulled the easy chair back next to her mother now the lounge had been restored and sat there quietly, holding her mother's hand as the other two returned the room to normal.

Sylvia drifted into sleep but her smile stayed. Her breathing slowed and for a brief moment she opened her eyes and rested her gaze on her daughter, then looked past her to a shadow beyond.

'Soon,' she whispered to the shadow.

TWENTY-EIGHT

Eve woke as the sun peeped over the horizon, and, with her skin prickling, tiptoed out to see how Sylvia and Callie were doing. Callie sat holding her mother's cooling fingers with tears trickling down her face.

Callie turned her head as Eve came closer. 'She's gone,' she whispered. 'I was dozing in the chair when her breathing changed to a sigh. Her eyes opened and she smiled, that beautiful smile, and then she slipped away.'

The huge lump in Eve's throat made it hard to talk. 'I'm so sorry, Callie.'

'She'll never say, "Hello, darling," again.'

Eve didn't know what to say, so fell back on the answer she gave all the women she cared for. 'I know.' She came across and rested her fingers on Callie's shoulder. 'She went peacefully and with dignity, as she did everything else. And you were here so she was happy.'

Callie just nodded wordlessly.

'Do you want me to phone Bennet?'

'No. Not yet.'

'I'll make a cup of tea.' Incredibly sad herself, Eve had to do something with her hands or she'd pull Callie out of her chair and squeeze her. She'd grown to love Sylvia. Who didn't love her? Even Sienna had been surprised how little she could blame Sylvia for drawing Duncan back. Life was too damn tragic. And her half-sister was too damn nice for these things to happen to her.

The last eight months had been incredibly challenging, but certainly uplifting – and a lot of that serenity had come from Sylvia.

Then there was the birth to think about.

Bennet would go back with Callie to Brisbane for the four weeks until the baby was born. They'd arranged to stay in Eve's flat. Eve would follow as soon as she had relief for the centre. Two of her midwife friends from Brisbane were keen. In fact, she would probably come back to Red Sand for the first six weeks after the birth and watch for postnatal depression. With the loss of both parents in a year and a previous loss of a baby, Callie would definitely be at risk. But Eve would be there for her.

But for now, Callie had a funeral to arrange, and Eve would stay in a supportive role until she was needed.

The funeral, three days later, was everything Sylvia and Callie had planned. It was a celebration of a loving woman, and the photos she'd chosen included almost all of the congregation, from a smiling tableau of Country Women's Association afternoon teas with everyone dressed in multicultural traditional costumes, to bake-offs, to the grinning faces outside the pub at the annual camel races.

Eve had to smother a laugh in the church when a photo of Sylvia and Blanche, dressed in magnificent hats for the fashion stakes, had a background focus on Old Mick from the pub leering at their legs.

There was one of Callie and Eve and Sylvia, taken by Sienna, and in every second photo their dad peered out, smiling, embraced in the warmth of the woman who had never stopped loving him, and his joy in the person who was Sylvia shone clear.

There was even one with Callie and her parents at a Christmas lunch, and next to Callie sat a very young and debonair Bennet in brown moleskins and checked shirt.

Then there was the photo taken by Eve on the day of the ultrasound, with Sylvia's hand on the screen and her family around her, delight captured on every face. Even Sienna was there.

The last photograph stayed up: a single, softly focused portrait of Sylvia, and her smile at the congregation was so tender and wistful Eve thought she was going to sob out loud.

After the wake the house felt empty, apart from the mounds of food people had brought, and Eve covered laden paper plates with plastic and froze the cooked meals that had been pushed their way. She had no doubt the food would last Callie for the next year. Eve wondered how Callie could bear the sadness, and she wasn't the only one – the townspeople continued to pop in with yet more food.

For the first few days after Sylvia's funeral Eve looked after the house quietly in the background of the passing visitors, heating the meals of macaroni cheese and spaghetti bolognaise and shepherd's pie she'd frozen, because her cooking skills managed reheating nicely.

Callie packed her bags for her time away and they all realised the baby would be here soon. Or maybe Callie had had enough reheating because on the seventh day, as Eve took another meal from the freezer, Callie put up her hand.

'About tonight.'

'No frozen meal?'

'No meal. Bennet's just rung to ask if I'd like to go to the farm for the night. It's the last night I can go before I leave for Brisbane. He and Adam are coming to pick me up soon, if you think it's okay for me to stay there until tomorrow?'

Eve looked around, pretending to see if anyone could hear this scandalous conversation. 'You mean you're going to sleep over? With a man?'

Callie had to smile. 'I know. I'm silly.'

'Not like you could get pregnant.'

'I hate leaving you alone.'

'I could ask Sienna if she wants to come over.'

'Maybe Sergeant McCabe would like to come too?'

Eve's relaxed evening began to look a little less likely. 'They spend their time bickering.'

'But it's usually pretty funny.' Callie tilted her head. 'You could probably do with a laugh. It's been pretty miserable here for you this last week.'

'As if I haven't wanted to be here.'

'I know. Thank you. Don't think I haven't noticed.'

'Don't think I need a thank you. Go. Have a lovely evening with Bennet and Adam. I'll see you tomorrow.'

Callie's face lightened as she remembered. 'We're celebrating thirty-six weeks of pregnancy tonight and he's promised roast.'

'Fresh roast? Whatever you do, don't let him freeze the left-overs. Just bring them home for me.'

Later that afternoon Bennet and Adam arrived, and Bennet made a beeline for Callie and took her in his arms. The way she closed her eyes and leaned into him made Eve's throat close.

Eve took the little boy for a walk around the garden and let him hose Sylvia's plants while the couple had a quiet chat before their drive back.

When she waved them off she wandered around the empty house and it came to her that this was the first time she'd been in her father's house on her own. But all she could think of was Sylvia and her sweet smile.

The void Callie's mother had left seemed impossible to fill. Sienna and even Douglas were looking good as company and she hurried over to the phone, but before she got there she heard a voice at the door.

'Lex?' She opened the screen door. 'Where did you come from?' She could not have wished for anyone better. He must have seen it in her face because the smile he gave Eve wrapped around her like he was already inside the house and holding her.

Then he stepped in and did it for real. 'You okay?' His chest was as solid as the big oak dresser in Sylvia's kitchen, and just as wide. She rested her forehead on the V of his shirt for a few brief, healing seconds until she remembered they weren't really at the 'hug on view' stage.

'Sorry.' She stepped back. 'I was feeling very fragile and you arrived at a bad moment.'

'And here I was thinking I'd arrived at a most auspicious time.'

'Auspicious? Where did you go to school?'

'Geelong. And I was homesick the whole time.' He smiled again. 'But I'm learning to be more of a here-and-now kind of guy. Gotta be happy when a woman throws herself at your chest.'

She smiled at that, but didn't quite know how to go from the hug to normal conversation. 'Callie's gone to Bennet's for her last night in town. She leaves for Brisbane tomorrow. How are you here?'

'Spent the night in Roma. Cattle sales. I was flying back and thought I'd drop in to see how you were all going.' He glanced around. 'I've got an hour if I want to get home before dark. Do you want to stay in or get out?'

The man was a mind reader. 'Out? Just a walk would be good.'

So they strolled the length of the town. Lex bought her an ice-cream, they discussed the ambulance and the few minor call-outs she'd had, talked about how Lily was settling in at Diamond Lake, and Blanche's latest plans for the centre. They laughed a bit over Henry's latest girlfriend, the unlikely pairing of Sienna and Douglas, and a little about the sweetness of Sylvia. Nothing groundbreaking, but by the time Lex left Eve felt as though she'd had a holiday. She kept telling herself not to read too much into it, that Lex hadn't known Callie was gone, and he was making the best of the company he'd found. But inside, she couldn't help whispering that he'd come to see her.

TWENTY-NINE

When Eve got the call to the car accident the next morning her fingers shook as she raced to unlock the door of the ambulance. It was still cool, even though the sun had been up for a few minutes. Her first big disaster: a day she'd hoped would never come.

'Car versus road train,' she muttered as she swung herself into the driver's seat almost overshooting the seat in her haste. She knew who would have won. Shakily she pulled on the blue gloves they'd told her she had to don every time she turned the engine on.

Apart from Gracie's run off the road and her baby's subsequent birth, Eve hadn't had to deal with any MVAs. A chest pain, a snake bite and an adventurous ten-year-old's duel with a chainsaw had all been treated methodically via the set protocols she had, and her patients were flown out by the flying doctor as soon as they'd been able to come.

She reversed the cumbersome vehicle out of its carport and swung it backwards, out onto the strip of tar, narrowly missing the telegraph pole. In her gut she knew this promised to be nightmare-bad. She wished Callie had been home to help her but her belly probably would have just got in the way. Her mobile rang beside her and she shut it off, then saw Sienna, out for a run. She flagged her down.

'Tried to ring you. You going out?'

'Car versus road train.' Eve hated the way her voice shook.

She heard Sienna sigh and ridiculously her hopes rose. 'I'll come.'

And Sienna jumped up onto the seat beside her, and the laces on her running shoes caught in the door as Eve stomped her foot on the accelerator.

'Seatbelt, please.'

'You sure you can drive this thing?'

Eve didn't answer, just concentrated on getting out of town without running over any dogs or – heaven forbid – people, as she wound the speed up on the outskirts. The long ribbon of tar cut through the red dirt, and the khaki scrubby landscape became more defined as the sun rose.

She glanced at her sister. 'Thanks.'

Sienna drummed her fingers on her leg. 'I think I've been looking too deep for the answer. I think it must be something really simple.'

Eve had no idea what she was talking about. Her mind was running through possible scenarios. 'It's three people in a car. One's a child.'

Sienna must have picked up the vibe because suddenly she got it and focused. 'Okay. Sorry. What do you want me to do when we get there?'

Right, because Eve was so experienced at this. She swallowed. 'We probably won't have enough hands. I'll check the road train driver. He's the one who called in the accident and likely to be the least hurt. Once I can confirm that, maybe he can help. Don't want him exsanguinating from something simple while we're busy.'

'So you want me to assess the car?'

'They told me to just triage, go for the most critical injuries and stop bleeding. I'll be quick. Hopefully we can stabilise everyone until help arrives. Can't worry about what we can't do. The flying doctor is on the way as well. Whatever we do has to be better than nothing.'

She wasn't sure if she was talking to Sienna or herself. Goodness knows how ambos did this full time. It terrified her every time she went out, not knowing what she'd find.

'The flying doctor will probably land on the road.'

Their vehicle crested the final rise and they saw the wreckage.

'Shit.' Sienna got the word out before Eve.

'Yep. I seriously hate this part of the job.'

'You do it well.'

Eve dragged in a huge breath, and then another. 'We will both do the best we can with what we have.' Like a mantra. 'Okay.' She looked at her sister. Pale in the morning light.

Eve licked her lips as they sped towards the rear of the road train, which lay across the road on its side. 'It's huge.'

The trucks looked big enough when they drove past, but stationary, with only one trailer over on its side, this one seemed to go on forever. Eve shuddered as they drove along it towards the front. She couldn't help but wonder how anyone in a car could survive hitting that thing.

She reached forwards and threw Sienna some gloves. 'Put them on.'

There wasn't much to see on this side of the wreckage so they drove off the road and over the thick red dust until they could park near the remains of a white twin-cab four-wheel drive utility, the type you saw about fifty times a day out here.

Except that they recognised the tiny emblem on the door. Eve gasped. 'Bennet's truck.'

Sienna jumped out as soon as their vehicle stopped. 'Stay on plan. Check the other driver, then meet me here.'

Eve sprinted to the cab of the truck. She didn't want to check the other driver but it was protocol when two medics were present. She sure as hell didn't want to look in the car either.

The driver was sitting on the side of the road, dazed and clutching his upper arm. Blood oozed around his fingers and a stripe of it ran from his forehead down over his cheeks and onto his neck. There was a small puddle in the dirt, at least a couple of hundred millilitres' worth but he wouldn't die if that was all he'd lost. Eve knelt down and opened her pack. She pulled out a thick trauma dressing and eased his fingers away. Blood instantly welled thickly but it didn't spurt. She put his fingers back over the dressing.

'I feel a bit faint.'

'Not surprising. Lost blood and shock.' She wrapped his dressing in place firmly. Checked the forehead gash and gave him another wad to push onto it. 'You hurt anywhere else?'

Another car pulled up and Eve waved the elderly couple inside over to her.

The driver of the road train was staring in the direction of the white dual-cab with a quivering lip. 'They will be.'

'Yep. Going there now.' She pushed him gently to lie back against the little bank. 'Keep your head low and you won't feel so faint.'

'Eve!' Sienna's voice.

She lifted her head towards the car. 'Gotta go.' As she ran she prayed. She slowed as the elderly couple stepped gingerly over what Eve assumed were pieces of Bennet's truck that had spread across the area. 'Can you get him further away from the truck? He should be fine.'

'Now!' Sienna's voice was hoarse.

'I'll watch him,' the lady assured her. 'My husband can go with you. He used to be a paramedic. I'll call if I need help.'

Eve nodded and kept running. The elderly gentleman hurried as fast as he could behind her and she hoped he wouldn't have a heart attack.

'Here.' Sienna's voice was strained as she held a wad of tissues against Callie's neck and Eve gulped as she came around to crouch beside her sister on the passenger side. Callie was awake and Eve took that as a good sign as she glanced across to Bennet, who was unconscious with a purpling bruise on his forehead. His legs looked trapped beneath the steering wheel where the front of the car had been crushed into the cabin. But he didn't look seriously injured at first glance. 'Can you take him?'

The older man nodded. 'Got him.'

In the back, his white face shocked and eyes wide and fixed on his father, Adam whimpered and shook like a little rabbit, miraculously safe in a pocket of the car that didn't seem to have been damaged at all.

'It's all right, Adam.' Incredibly, Callie's voice was calm, if a little spacey.

Eve let out her breath in relief. She leaned in to ask Callie how she was when she saw the blood. Litres of it. Her stomach rolled and she hoped she wasn't going to be sick.

'She told me to look at the kid first.' Sienna's voice shook.

Eve clamped down on the panic. 'Uterine?'

'She's losing the baby. I can't do anything to stop the blood.'

Another car had pulled up and a young man and his girlfriend hurried to them. Eve stood up and spoke to them. 'Can you help me get the boy out? Take him to that lady over there,' she said, pointing to the older woman beside the truck driver. 'I want to lay this front seat back.'

The guy swallowed when he saw the blood. He wrenched open Adam's door and reached in to unbuckle his lifesaving seatbelt and lifted him out easily. Adam began to struggle but the guy shushed him.

'It's okay, mate. We can help by getting out of the way.'

'Daddy?'

'The lady has to help your mummy.'

'She's not my mummy.'

Eve winced at the words as Adam was carried away. 'And back the ambulance over here, will you?' she called after them.

It didn't look like Callie would ever be anyone's mummy. But she couldn't think like that. She wouldn't. *Disassociate.* This was not her sister. This was an unnamed woman. Then it was as if a new clarity sharpened every sense. She would not let it happen.

The next few minutes seemed to pass in slow motion. Without the necessity of keeping Adam calm Callie suddenly let go of her tenacious grip on consciousness. Her eyes rolled back and she shuddered as Eve helped Sienna lean the seat back to get a little more blood to Callie's brain before she blacked out.

Callie's eyelids fluttered and her skin shone white as a cockatoo's wing as her lifeblood seeped away underneath her. Too little too late.

'She's going into heart failure.' Sienna's voice was harsh with an underlying panic.

They heard the ambulance backing closer, and sensibly the young man had jumped out and opened both rear doors before he ran back to Eve and Sienna. Eve glanced across to where the older lady and the young girl had Adam between them. She heard a siren.

Douglas. *Good.* More hands, but they were running out of time. *Do the best you can.*

There were pounding footsteps as Douglas ran up to them.

'We need to get her flat so we can work on her.' Eve glanced at the two men. 'Lift her out as fast as you can. Don't worry about anything. We just need her flat on the stretcher in the back of the ambulance.'

'We can't move her.' Sienna shook her head.

'We have to. She's going to arrest and we can't save her in the car.'

'We can't save her.'

Eve pulled Sienna away. 'Take her, guys. Now.'

They looked at each other and between them managed to get a limp and blood-soaked Callie maneuvered from her awkward position into their arms. The young man's eyes widened in horror as he realised she was heavily pregnant.

Eve sprinted ahead and climbed into the back. Grabbed an oxygen mask as the men heaved Callie onto the stretcher. Sienna seemed to shake herself as she saw what Eve was doing. Her emergency maternal resuscitation procedures must have flooded back into her shocked brain because now she spoke smoothly.

'Wedge one hip. Roll her a bit to get the weight of her uterus off the big arteries. Get the blood from her legs into circulation.'

Eve handed her a cannula and a tourniquet, and gave the bag of fluids to Douglas to sort once the line was in.

Sienna nodded and bent to the task while Eve ripped open Callie's shirt and stuck the monitor leads on her chest. Frantic, high-pitched irregular heartbeats raced across the screen.

'Hold this bag upside down and squeeze while I stab it with this line connection,' Eve said to the young man and he grabbed the floppy bag of fluid as Eve thrust the line connection into her bag. The man squeezed the air pocket in the bag into the filling chamber and the line of life-giving saline raced down the tubing as Eve hung it downwards. 'Kink the line to stop it when the fluid gets to the end, and give it to me when I ask for it.'

Eve bent and inserted the intravenous cannula in the crook of Callie's arm and held out her hand for the connection. She taped down the line and handed the tape to Sienna, who did the same on her side. At least they had started to replace some fluids.

The frantic heartbeat accelerated and then Callie stiffened as her heart stopped.

'*Noooo*,' Eve said fiercely. 'Douglas. Cardiac massage.'

Sienna squeezed past Douglas and grabbed the oxyviva bag and mask to ventilate two breaths after thirty compressions, but the only change in the cardiac rhythm was the spikes of compression from Douglas.

Four minutes, four cycles and no change. Eve grabbed an emergency pack from the shelf and stared steadily at Sienna. 'Crash caesarean.' Then she leaned across and yanked Callie's skirt down to expose the shiny white mound of her veined stomach.

Sienna seemed to shake herself and then she nodded.

The young man crossed himself. 'Holy Mary, Mother of God.'

Eve glanced at him. Too focused for sympathy. 'Jump out and lean over from the front so you can do the bagging while Sienna and I do this.' She caught his eye. 'She's lost too much blood. There is *no* chance without this.'

The young man jumped out, and Sienna pushed past Douglas again so she could come around to the other side.

Eve opened the pack. Not much in it. Fresh gloves. A scalpel, some heavy sponges for holding back the abdominal layers, a pre-threaded needle and forceps for suturing that she'd made up herself. In memory of a young mother many months ago. Two forceps for clamping the cord and some scissors for cutting it.

Eve splashed antiseptic liquid straight onto Callie's belly and swirled it over the bulging skin with a large dressing. Her eyes met Sienna's and she saw her sister's gaze sharpen and focus on the task at hand. Relief swelled in her chest. If anyone could do a slash and grab in record time it was Sienna.

Two minutes later Sienna passed the limp body of her half-sister's baby girl to Eve, scooped out the placenta from the pool of blood behind it, squeezed the uterus empty, and shut and sutured it with huge figure-of-eight stitches, packed the rest so they could get back to keeping Callie alive.

THIRTY

Eve lay the lifeless little girl on her back on the folded sheet on the side box, the only space left to work. She briskly rubbed the tiny baby with the towel and watched the blue limbs wobble with the movement, but nothing else.

She settled the miniature bag and mask over a snub nose and sagging mouth and began to inflate the tiny lungs. One a second. *One, two, three, four, five* . . . She didn't worry about cardiac massage because it was more important to get air into the lungs during this first thirty seconds. Meanwhile Sienna taped a wad of dressing over Callie's wound for repair later. Or not – Callie wouldn't bleed if her heart wasn't beating.

Douglas kept pumping and the young man kept squeezing air into her flaccid lungs. They nearly missed the extra beat of Callie's heart because the baby tensed and opened her hand and Eve gasped, almost dropping the green bag she was squeezing. She steadied herself and kept bagging but the skip of her own heart reminded her to breathe herself.

The baby wriggled again, and another beat on Callie's monitor, closely followed by another, had all eyes turn incredulously towards the green blips on the screen. The sudden surge of blood that had been rerouted from the uterus returned to the mother's circulation like a bolus blood transfusion.

The fluids began to run again, the baby gasped and cried, and whether or not the sound penetrated the mother's unconscious brain, the rhythm of her heart steadied and fell back into pattern – it was too fast, but Callie was alive.

Douglas slumped back from the heart that didn't need compression any longer.

Sienna eased the bag and mask from the young man's death grip and slid the mask back up Callie's porcelain face. She connected the oxygen as their patient began to breathe for herself.

The drone of a plane in the distance penetrated the tense airlessness and the sweating ambulance occupants began to look at each other and return to the real world.

For Eve, the thirty minutes after the RFDS arrived and took over – when she saw Callie, still breathing but unconscious, being transferred into the aircraft, her face the colour of the white sheet beneath her – seemed to last forever. And yet it was over in a flash.

Another small helicopter landed and Lex, appearing beside her, took her hand, turned her to him and pulled her into his arms so that she stopped the sway she hadn't realised she was doing.

'Callie nearly died.' Her mouth seemed stuck together as reality set in. Her vision blurred.

'I know,' she heard him say. He kept patting her. 'I know.'

Eventually. Distantly. When she was ready to listen, he asked, 'Would you like me to fly you to Charleville?'

She blinked. Focused on the fact the RFDS aircraft had taxied away. Callie would have another operation to get through. She could still die, though her chances of survival were good. 'Yes, please. Now.'

Then she looked back at the scene, slumped, and realised she couldn't leave yet. She still had a job to do.

The huge trailer was still on its side. She was glad it hadn't been a cattle carrier – dead or dying animals would have made things even more gruesome – or still more ghastly, one of the three-trailered fuel tankers. The general freight that hadn't been damaged would be unloaded and the crane from Charleville would be here in a few hours to right it.

But she had an ambulance parked beside it. Already she could see Douglas talking to volunteers for directing traffic off the road and around the blockage.

'I can't. I have to take the ambulance back.'

'Sienna can do that. You can come with me. You've all been incredible, from what I've heard.'

'Sienna might not want to.'

But when Eve asked her, Sienna took one look at her face and nodded. 'Sure. You go with Lex. Ring me later when Callie is out of theatre. I'll stay with Bennet now that he's conscious, until they can cut him out. Go.'

So she went, her mind filled with images and a mix of disbelief and horror until suddenly she thought of that morning all those months ago, when she'd come out of work and wondered what good could possibly come of a mother losing her life in such circumstances.

This time Eve had had Sienna, skilled and able to respond, the stalwart Douglas and the brave young man; she'd been driven to take a leadership role by heartbreak at the prospect of not succeeding. But without the trigger of Eve's memories from that long-ago day, the experience of that sequence of events, they would have lost Callie.

A new father would have been left to weep forever.

One day she would find that other father, Jason, and thank him, just so he knew what a gift his wife had given.

THIRTY-ONE

Lex landed at Charleville and ushered Eve into the shed that held his car at the airport. Before they left, he took her to the little toilet block and helped her wash the blood from her skin and hands, and stripped off her blood-stained shirt. She saw his eyes widen as he noticed the blood soaked into her bra, saw him wince at what she must have seen.

He gave her one of his own R. M. shirts and helped her shaking fingers button the front and roll the sleeves. The shirt swam on her and she probably looked like a lost waif, but she was at least externally free of gore.

During the drive to the hospital she still trembled in shock, but incredibly, as if a switch had been thrown, when they arrived she straightened and slowly morphed into the determined Eve she wanted to be.

But the unexpected obstacle of an officious nurse who denied them entry had her shaking again. That was when Lex came into his own. He demanded to see the nursing supervisor. Told her who he was. Who Eve was. What she'd done. And Eve listened like it was a tale about somebody else. But the result was impressive.

She just needed to see Callie. Had tunnel vision.

On the way the apologetic woman reassured them that the baby had settled into the neonatal intensive care unit and would be able to come out when Callie was able to feed. Eve looked at Lex and thanked him with a touch on his arm, and he squeezed her fingers back at their tremendous good fortune as they followed the supervisor to high-dependency.

There Callie lay, her face pale, her eyes closed, amid the beeping and alarms of machines, in a private room.

Eve stared at her sister. At the machines. At the proof her Callie really was still alive. She tried not to think about brain injury from extended loss of oxygen. Would she even wake up?

The supervisor explained quietly that they had taken Callie back to theatre to properly repair her caesarean wound, give transfusions of blood and blood products, and massive antibiotics. Callie's observations and bodily responses looked very promising but she was heavily sedated. Even Lex understood the gist of that.

Distractedly, Eve noticed that Lex hung back from the myriad of drips and drains and monitors and tubes, and she could see he was trying not to think of the horror smash he'd only seen parts of.

Distantly she'd heard him arrange her accommodation. Some food. Ensure she was given the respect she deserved. She couldn't imagine the logistics of being with Callie without his help.

But she didn't care about any of that just now. She needed to question the intensivist nurse with the chart, peer over her shoulder at the patient records. See improvements in the vital signs.

Eve glanced from her sister to Lex, saw the reflection in his eyes of all the women she'd briefly mentioned to him, the ones she'd fought for over the past few years on her high-dependency roster. She could see he knew her fear for Callie, who miraculously breathed for herself while she slept off her anaesthetic.

Eve just wanted to know that when Callie woke up she'd be fine – and, as if in answer to an unspoken plea, Lex stepped up to Eve and rested his hand on her shoulder, gripped it, and she could feel his conviction that she had saved her sister and niece. Lex's faith that all would be well, a cross she usually bore for others, was now being given to her. She closed her eyes and allowed herself to be reassured.

A nurse came in and updated them on Bennet's progress. He'd been freed from the vehicle, was stable and conscious, and had arrived in Charleville for orthopaedic surgery. Lex left her then, promising to return, but Eve forgot Lex as soon as he was out of sight. She didn't take her eyes off her sister.

Callie knew she had to wake up. There was a reason she had to fight the grey mist and reach for the pain that hovered at the edge of her awareness – something that filled her with a cold dread that she needed to know.

She wasn't alone because she could hear small sounds – a chair shifting, the rustle of paper – and she forced her heavy eyelids to lift just a little.

Light. So it was daytime. The heaviness descended again and her world dimmed. Until she remembered the roaring horror of the accident, the shock of the impact, the non-response of Bennet, Adam's cries.

And then she remembered the blood. And that she was going to die.

Her fingers clenched on the sheet and as the power to move slowly returned to do her bidding, her hand inched from her chest where it lay, down to the source of her pain. Her abdomen. A hollow abdomen, like seven years ago when she had woken, and she knew her baby was gone.

*

At four o'clock Eve turned from the window and saw Callie's fingers clench and stretch and her eyelids flutter. Eve's own heart fluttered in response.

She took a precious few seconds to slip out to the desk and ask them to phone the nursery for baby. When she hurried back Callie's eyes flickered and then slowly opened.

Eve reached down and gently took Callie's hand in both of hers as her sister's eyes focused. 'It's okay, Callie. There was an accident. Bennet and Adam are fine.'

Callie blinked and shifted her head on the pillow. Her mouth moved in a small circle of distress as she shifted her position. 'Eve?'

It was a croak but to Eve's ears it was the most beautiful sound in the world. Callie recognised her. Eve's throat felt thick and clogged and she wanted to answer but the words wouldn't come. All she could do was nod enthusiastically and squeeze her sister's hand.

Then Callie's eyes welled with tears and her distress filled the little room like a swarm of black moths. 'My baby's gone? Again?'

Tears burned and stung as Eve shook her head vehemently. She'd so hoped to spare dear Callie this. 'No, no. Not gone. Coming. She's beautiful.'

And just then the sound of a hospital bassinet's wheels rattled in and, even better, the sound of an unhappy baby filled the little white room at the end of the intensive care unit. Callie gasped and tried to see and Eve hurried to raise the head of the bed and scoop the baby up in full view.

'Here she is. Look.'

The world slowed down again. Callie's dry lips parted in wonder as her small pink bundle of a baby was placed in her arms. And the baby stopped crying.

Callie held her awkwardly in the crook of her arm, drips and monitors at risk of dislodging as Eve unwrapped her so her mother could see perfect hands and feet.

Callie dripped tears on her owlish baby, as big round baby eyes – so much like Bennet's – stared solemnly back. The baby's tiny rosebud mouth opened and closed and every now and then a soft crimson tongue poked out like a little pink lizard.

'Oh my.' Callie stroked one tiny finger. 'She's a miracle. I'm so blessed.'

'We all are.' Though, Eve thought a little tartly, she'd seen much easier births. She snapped a photo on her phone of mother and baby and sent it through to Bennet, Sienna and Lex, and then remembered to make sure all the lines and monitors were not endangered.

Callie drooped as the adrenalin of seeing her baby wore off and the fatigue took over. 'When is Bennet coming? And Adam?'

'He's here. Downstairs, just out of surgery and stable. You'll see him tomorrow probably. And Adam will come tomorrow too.' It wasn't the time to go into Bennet's injuries. 'I'll help you feed this little munchkin – you don't have to do anything – and then you can have another sleep. Just know everyone will be fine as soon as you get well.'

She could see a hundred questions half formed in her sister's eyes but she could also see the absolute exhaustion.

Callie closed her eyes for a few seconds and then forced them open. 'Let's.'

A few pillows, a lot of help from Eve, and a voracious appetite from the youngest Wilson girl, even if she was a couple of weeks early, and soon there was a very contented baby and mother as they both drifted off to sleep.

Eve looked down at them and her shoulders slumped. *God, they were so lucky.* And she was so tired herself.

She felt a hand on her shoulder and turned, knowing in her heart it was Lex. The man had perfect timing and she relaxed back into him, feeling the absolute bliss of allowing herself to let go of responsibility. She turned, leaned into his solid chest and closed her eyes as his arms came around her.

'They look very peaceful,' he said softly into her hair.

Eve just held him. Buried her nose in his chest and let the tears fall. Eventually, calm came after the storm that had needed to break.

'A peace hard come by,' she said, rubbing her eyes and stepping back. 'You are an amazing man with perfect timing.'

'Happy to be of service.'

Eve smiled mistily. 'She remembered me. She's going to be fine.'

Lex's shoulders dropped with relief and he steered her towards the chair. 'Nobody survives that without scars but Callie is one of the strongest women I know.' He smiled at her. 'It's a family trait.'

'Sylvia, you mean?' Eve thought about that, immediately feeling the sadness of loss for a woman she had grown to love. 'That's true.'

Lex laughed softly. 'Yes, Sylvia.' He squeezed her arm. 'But I meant you. Even the atrocious Sienna is one tough woman. I expect all you Wilson women would have survived out here with the pioneering Duracks 140 years ago. Though I have my doubts about your oldest sister enjoying the experience.'

'Sienna's the toughest.' Eve shook her head, remembering. 'You should have seen her perform that caesarean. I've never seen one so skilled and fast. We would have lost Callie and her baby if it wasn't for Sienna.'

He pointed to the chair and handed her a sandwich wrapped in paper and a bottle of iced tea. Maybe he didn't want to think about it, so she let the subject drop.

He said, 'Eat. Drink. You must be exhausted too.' Then he muttered, more to himself, 'I heard we would have lost Callie if it wasn't for you.'

She brushed that aside. 'Have you heard how Bennet is going?'

'He's out of theatre. Surprisingly simple fracture to one leg but plated and stable now. They hope he'll be well enough to visit tomorrow.'

'And you said Adam was fine and with Delta?' She thought back. 'He looked shocked but healthy.'

'Didn't get a scratch. The big fright he might lose his dad after losing his mum hit him hard. It might take a while for him to get over the shock.'

'Poor little man. At least now he's seen how tough they are.'

'He's spoken to his dad on the phone.'

'When Callie wakes next time we'll ring Bennet and she can talk to him. He'll be beside himself.'

Lex watched her eat absently, not tasting, just doing what she needed to do to stay alert. 'How long are you staying?' he asked.

'Until Bennet is well enough to take my place. I can help with the baby, which means Callie won't miss out on the little stuff. She doesn't deserve to miss out on anything.'

He nodded. 'Of course.' There was dryness in his tone she didn't understand. 'I have to head home now.'

Oh. She hadn't thought of that. It had been so easy having Lex streamline everything. She needed to get out of that mindset.

'Thank you for bringing me.' It didn't touch the sides of the huge assistance Lex had given her. She wished he wouldn't go but hesitated to ask him to stay. 'I would have been beside myself if I had to wait to get here.' She glanced at the room they'd been ushered straight into, thanks to Lex's authority.

'You're welcome. Do you want me to fly back tomorrow and pick you up?'

She had to smile at that. Her own personal helicopter pilot. A girl could get spoiled.

'You've got too much to do. Sienna can come to get me after clinic tomorrow.'

'As you wish,' he said formally, and Eve wondered if she'd offended him, then brushed that silly thought away. Lex didn't need her dramas. Probably couldn't wait to get away.

He seemed to be waiting for something and Eve waved to her lunch. 'Thanks for the food. Great thought. I was feeling a bit weak.'

He smiled wryly at her. 'I know you like to eat. And they have a bed in the nurses' home for the next few nights if you want it. The supervisor will drop off the key later.'

He shook his head at her, glanced once more at the picture of mother and baby and then lifted one hand in farewell. 'Phone me if you or Callie need anything.'

'Thanks again, Lex.'

'Yep,' he said simply and left Eve staring at the empty doorway. Had she missed something?'

THIRTY-TWO

At the crash site Sienna was left with the ambulance.

After Bennet had been prised from the wreckage and stabilised before being flown out, she'd spoken briefly to him about Callie and the baby. Now that he'd gone, Sienna knew she had to drive the bloody ambulance home.

Thankfully Douglas had turned the cumbersome vehicle around for her after she'd stalled it twice, because this ghastly beast was nothing at all like her little red baby car, and she shuddered at the thought of having to clean it when she got back. She guessed she'd have to because she couldn't leave it to Eve. And she couldn't pay some kid fifty bucks to do it, like she did with her car, though she wanted to. She grumbled and moaned all the way home and told herself she wished she was back in Melbourne, but all she really wanted was to not think about the last four hours.

Back at Red Sand she drove the vehicle awkwardly into the parking bay and the whole horror of the situation crashed in on her. Her head sank into her hands on the wheel and she shuddered for a few long seconds.

If Eve hadn't been there, so single-minded and determined that Callie would live, they would have lost her in Bennet's car. She would have bled to death and cardiac-arrested right there as her blood supply seeped rapidly away from the sheared placenta.

She opened the door and climbed wearily out. Reluctantly she opened the rear doors, sighing at the gore.

Clean. It wasn't going to happen unless she got started. She reefed the linen off the stretcher and bundled the sheet and towels into the skip at the side of the carport. Grabbed another towel and swirled it over the stretcher and floor, grabbed another to do it again. Poured the cleaning agent straight from the bottle and splashed it around rather than use the piddly little spray.

God, she thought as she scrubbed and cleared the traces of Callie's fight for life from the vehicle. It should have been her to see that the emergency caesarean was still a chance. It should have been the hotshot, wannabe director of obstetrics, not Poor Eve the midwife, who couldn't even sort her own world. Sienna may have done the surgery but Eve had saved Callie's life, without a doubt.

She dragged herself into the shower at the medical centre; no way was she walking down the street covered in blood. As the cleansing water poured over Sienna's face and turned dried blood to red trickles that ran down her legs and between her toes, she scrubbed the blood from beneath her nails and wished she could scrub the memories.

All she could see was Eve grinding out instructions. Directing her, Sienna, who should have known without being told, that it was the only chance they had. Eve had made them get Callie out of the car to somewhere they could work. Forced them all to consider that they still had a chance when Sienna had, in truth, given up in weak horror.

Why hadn't she seen it?

Being too close to the victim didn't cut it as an excuse because Eve had been on the ball. How had her little sister remained so focused that she could see immediately after Callie's heart stopped that they wouldn't be able to get her back without removing the baby?

It was such a big risk but Eve had called it within a doable time frame and despite the slim chance the stats were enormously better than if they did nothing.

'Nothing' was irretrievable. That was what she couldn't forgive herself for.

Maybe she needed to rethink the little sister who she'd always assumed had her priorities wrong. God forbid if Sienna was the one with the screwed ideas.

Suddenly it didn't seem so important that she became the youngest director of obstetrics in Australia. What was she going to do with it? Whose life would she change? What happened when she retired from the job in twenty-five years' time?

More interestingly, who would be there to care if she faded away like Callie's mother?

She knew she shouldn't have come out here.

Bloody unsettling place.

But if Sienna hadn't been there, Eve couldn't have done the caesarean – she might have known what was needed, but didn't have the knowledge to do it herself.

She was fiercely glad Callie hadn't died at the side of the road.

Her half-sister. She'd better get used to it because it looked like Callie was going to be a part of their lives forever, even if she was thousands of kilometres away. And Sienna realised that she for one was very happy to be a part of Callie's family.

Sienna turned the water off and grabbed the blue towels that, as Eve had pointed out, matched the walls. She stared at the painting of a sunrise over a red sandhill.

Who would have thought she'd be doing a perimortem caesarean when she came out here? She was supposed to have been doing research, except every day seemed to have a time-consuming crisis or dilemma that drew her away from her work.

She'd never had so many in-depth conversations with pregnant women before. Sienna had begun to gain an insight into the isolation, the improvisation required when things weren't available, and grudgingly realised women out here had 'let's manage anyway' down to a fine art. Eve seemed to have picked it up instantly while Sienna still battled with the shortfalls.

But it did bring home the disadvantage the outback women worked under, and not just the medical staff.

She thought back to the mail run Douglas had taken her on. His recounting of the history of Irish settlers with horse and cart and bullock drays, who struggled through drought and flood and the tyranny of distance. Pioneers she had a whole lot more respect for now.

He'd told her of women birthing on the road to untamed land, of losing babies, children and limbs in accidents, no refrigeration, wounds that turned septic with heat and pestilence, while there was no place to swab a wound, no way to treat it with antibiotics. That brought her back to why she was here. Saving babies. But really, from all the medical records she'd read and data she'd collected, it was clear the RFDS and the flying obstetrician and the outreach clinics did an amazing job.

The only minor improvement the clinic could possibly make would be keeping an extra tab on sexually transmitted infections. Chlamydia was prevalent, with staggering numbers of eighteen-to-twenty-five-year-olds carrying the infection, and the asymptomatic infection could cause the premature rupture of membranes, as well as damaging the fertility of women who remained untreated. Maybe some were being missed on the swabs? They could do a second test for it mid or late trimester as a safe guard. There had been another centre where this had happened. Sienna remembered the root-cause analysis she'd sat in on.

Otherwise the service these women received was covering all bases. Blanche could spend her money on something else. Sienna had checked every single thing; this new clinic would more than make up for any shortfalls the location caused, and she was ready to go home.

Sienna retreated to her office down the end of the hallway. There was no way she could talk to people today. She planned to bury her nose in writing her report and hide even from herself. In the past she had managed that very successfully.

She stood up. Walked to the window. Saw Douglas outside, peering into the window of the ambulance, and her breath stilled. She began again as she took a step towards him, then stopped. The door rattled as he tried it, and then came a heavy knock.

He'd been amazing today. As solid as one of those big boulder opals they were so proud of around here, but not as colourful on the inside – there was a darkness in Douglas that called to her but she doubted she had the capacity to bring that light out in him. She'd tried. Sort of.

Sienna had been knocked back for her pains – except for those kisses on the mail run, if she remembered rightly. This place had certainly been good for bringing her down a peg or two. Or six.

Now he was one of the few people who she would share today's more graphic moments with. She peered out the window again but he was gone and her chance to talk about it gone with him.

It would have been good to debrief. She shook her head. Since when had she started wanting to do that? This place really got to you and she couldn't wait to leave.

She glanced at her watch. Unbelievable; it was four already.

Callie would have been to theatre, where they would have repaired her classic caesarean wound. Sienna had never done a classical incision before – straight down the middle instead of bikini line – but it had saved minutes on the way in and that was what they'd needed. Callie should be waking up now. She'd ring Eve later to see how it'd all gone.

Just then the message came through, and there they were: her half-sister and her new niece. She stared at the picture. Swallowed the huge lump in her throat and let the thoughts she'd been fiercely withholding fly out the window. They were both fine! *A miracle.*

Sienna's mouth curved upwards and she let out a sigh. The day had been worth it.

She texted back her thanks and congrats to Eve and then put her phone on silent. Next thing Eve would be texting and ringing, and Sienna couldn't talk to Eve just now.

She'd better go feed those animals. She thought about the smelly little hens and having to touch the still-warm eggs, of her long-lost father's dog that would need the water changed in its bowl.

Maybe she could use the washing-up gloves from here and replace them tomorrow. The shop did have washing-up gloves.

Then she smiled. Okay, so she seriously was not an animal person and she doubted she ever would be, but she could just wash her hands afterwards. And the dog would be worried with everyone gone. She actually had some sympathy for it because she was a bit worried and lonely herself.

Sienna decided if she could do lifesaving surgery on loved ones, which was not good practice because it stuffed with your head, then she could wash a dog bowl. But the smile fell off her face as she remembered the morning again, so she shut down the computer and hurried to the animals.

Douglas found her as she came back along the street from Callie's house.

She didn't see him coming, was on autopilot, thinking only of making it back to the B&B, hopefully avoiding Fran's questions and slipping into her room and under her covers. The idea of spending a few hours with the sheets pulled over her head was extremely attractive.

'Sienna?'

'Douglas?' God, he probably thought she looked like an escaped mental patient dressed in this hospital gown – she hadn't found anything else in the medical centre to change into. She looked up. Had to look up because up was where he was, and she never got sick of the novelty. Today the solid frame of Douglas looked even better; she couldn't help but think that his masculine chest looked a good place to hide.

'Are you okay?'

Her eyes filled with tears but she tried to speak normally. 'Of course.'

He just looked at her. Stepped forward and took her hand and pulled her in next to him so he could tuck her fingers in over his arm as he turned towards the police station.

'Come with me, madam. I have a few questions.'

'Bloody constabulary,' she murmured weakly, but he was squeezing her fingers in sympathy so that the bones were crushed together, as though in a vice. But the pain was good compared to the mush in her brain.

He must have realised he was holding her hand too tightly because suddenly his grip loosened. But he didn't let go.

'Sorry.' And he quickened his step.

He bypassed the police station entrance and instead went up the dusty path to the police residence, pausing briefly as he unlocked the front door, and then ushered her into the house she'd been trying to get into for weeks. She heard the door lock behind them.

'Kitchen or bedroom?'

God love Douglas. 'Bedroom, for pity's sake. Even if you just hold me and I can close my eyes.'

'I was hoping you'd say that.'

'Bedroom' or 'just holding'? she wondered vaguely, but it felt so damn good to be steered. To let go of directing the play, always working towards an outcome. All she wanted to do was close her eyes, forget today, and if she could do that in the circle of this honey of a man's arms she would be forever grateful – or at least grateful today.

Douglas drew her by the hand down the hallway into an immaculately made up bedroom. *The army strikes again*, she thought with a semi-hysterical giggle, though she barely had time to acknowledge the scarcity of the furnishings before he sat her down on the bed.

To her surprise he knelt down in front of her and took off her sandals. They were Eve's sandals, which she'd found at the house and were a little tight. His strong, cool fingers gently massaged the marks where the straps had indented her feet. She sat there like a statue, too drained to even sigh at the bliss, but she did look at the thick swirls of black hair just out of reach and promised herself she would run her hands through it later.

He stood her up again, slid the patient gown over her head, tossed it on a chair so she stood before him in her bra and pants that were still damp from rinsing.

He let his breath out slowly as he slid one finger down the hollow between her breasts. 'I always imagined lace under there.'

'Did you now?' Her mouth was dry and the smart answers were

a little harder to come by as his gaze swept over her. The fire in his eyes briefly made her, of all things, blush.

Then his hand lifted as he bent, threw back the covers and, again to her surprise, reached forwards to put his arms around her shoulders and knees. He lifted her into the middle of the bed like she was a child. In the sweet novelty of the moment she didn't care that he hadn't taken off her underwear.

Nobody had ever lifted her into bed, or if they had she'd been too young to remember; maybe her father had but either way the sting was back in her eyes and she blinked rapidly to clear it.

'You'll do your back in.'

'Can't think of a better way of doing it.' His tone was matter of fact as he swiftly removed his boots and socks and unbuttoned his shirt. Now she was the one to watch and admire. She sucked in her breath as he undid his belt, slid off his trousers to expose long, strong thighs and a pair of well-packed black trunks before he shifted in beside her. More underwear. But still lots of hot, solid skin blissfully pressed against hers as he pulled her closer.

'Come here.' Then his arms were around her, crushing her in the most delightful way and she buried her nose in his gorgeous chest and for the first time since she was a tiny child, she felt safe and protected in a man's arms.

And then she wasted it all as she began to cry.

THIRTY-THREE

Eve didn't bother with the nurses' home bed; she spent the first night in the chair in Callie's room and it felt like a night shift.

Eve finger-brushed the little dark mop of hair that spiked out of her niece's bony skull and felt a rush of love for this scrap of humanity. So precious, so fragile, yet with a fierce will to live that confounded half the staff in this hospital. The other half were born outback and expected it.

The time she'd spent here had changed her perception of the world, but more importantly it had changed her perception of herself.

She wasn't different here, she fitted. She didn't feel adrift, she felt anchored. A big part of that was Callie and the bittersweet memories of Callie's mother, and another part was the feeling that she'd come home. But it wasn't her home. She couldn't be a part of Callie's family because Callie already had Bennet and Adam and now a baby too.

So she savoured every moment because soon it would be time for her to decide if she was going to go back to where she came from.

By lunchtime Callie seemed to have recovered her resilience and had already spoken to Bennet on the phone, reassured herself he would be fine, and vice versa, and excitedly confirmed his agreement to name their baby Amari, a name suggested by one of the midwives that meant 'a miracle from God'. Her second name was Sylvia.

Late that afternoon Bennet would be able to come in a wheel-chair to Callie's room. Callie had done some transferring of her own and was resettled into a lovely single room in the maternity ward after her first assisted shower.

Callie complained that Eve had needed to help her, and Eve just laughed. 'You know you sound like your mother when you showered her?'

'I do not.' Callie looked mutinously at her sister.

'So if I were the post-operative one, would you help shower me?' Eve snapped her fingers. 'Ha. If I hadn't lived with you I might have lost that battle.'

'Hmm,' said Callie, smiling. Then her face saddened. 'Do you think Mum can see our little Amari Sylvia?'

Eve had no doubt. 'I'm absolutely sure of it. And I can even feel her smiling.'

Callie stared at her sister. Eve seemed so confident in her conviction. It was a comforting thought. 'You're amazing. I can't believe how it feels to have you in my life.'

Eve shook her head. 'I'm lucky too, you know. Hence the determination not to leave you in peace until the cavalry arrives this afternoon.' She helped her sister back to bed, where Callie sighed into the fresh sheets.

'I can't wait to see Bennet.'

'I know.' Eve handed her the pain-relief tablets the nurse had just passed across. 'If you're managing okay I'll probably go home tonight. Give Sienna a break. She says she's finished her review.'

Callie looked up. Despite the dark rings around her bruised eyes there was still a sudden glow of interest. 'About the prem labours?'

'Yep. She's coming in late this afternoon to see you. And then we'll drive home.'

'You called it home.' Callie reached out her hand and caught Eve's fingers. 'Red Sand could be your home, Eve. Have you thought about settling here and not returning to Brisbane? Your niece would be growing up without you.'

'I know. We don't need to talk about this now. But if I did go back I'd visit heaps.'

Right at this moment she didn't ever want to leave Callie but that wasn't the real world. She had no idea how she would settle back once she returned to Brisbane. Or even if she would. But she couldn't live alone here, either.

When Sienna arrived several hours later, she was present for the tearful reunion with Bennet.

After spending time with Bennet yesterday, sharing insights she hadn't been able to avoid, she'd glimpsed the depth of love he had for her half-sister. Not surprisingly there was something about a man trapped in a vehicle that opened the floodgates and for Sienna the hardest part had been preventing Bennet from injuring himself more as he tried to free himself to get to Callie.

'Amari looks good in your arms, Bennet.' *And you look better than yesterday*, she thought, and her gaze was drawn to Callie. It was a miracle to see her talking and smiling, albeit carefully, and still leaning her head back on the pillow to conserve her energy. Sienna knew how close it had been.

This was the problem with families. Emotion.

*

Eve watched Sienna's face, unusually visible emotions flickering on it as she absorbed the stories in the room. For Eve the family felt complete again, except for the missing presence of Sylvia. But Eve genuinely believed Callie's mother was hovering somewhere anyway.

Sienna looked like she couldn't wait to leave, but that was okay. Eve was ready to leave herself now, because Callie would recover. Callie had her family and her happiness with Bennet.

Eve thought of Lex and his unobtrusive help, which she was just coming to realise had made it all happen so seamlessly. How she'd got from the crash site to Callie's bedside, the parcel of clothes and bathroom items that had arrived for her and for Callie. A man who didn't say much, even after he'd kissed her. How depressing was that? She needed to see him, and at the very least thank him, but also hopefully hug him – because she needed a Lex hug something terrible.

There were tearful kisses all round as they prepared to depart, and one last cuddle with Amari, which even Sienna demanded a turn of. Eve's last look back saw Adam sitting on the bed, snuggled up to Callie, and Bennet, crutches cast aside, holding his new daughter in one arm and Callie's fingers in the other hand.

'Thank God we got out of there.'

Eve spluttered back a sob that turned into a laugh. She patted Sienna's shoulder. 'Poor Sienna. You did very well. All that disgusting emotion.'

Sienna stopped. Looked at Eve's shaking head and smiled herself. 'Okay. It does make me uncomfortable but I am pleased for them. Very pleased.' They reached the outside door and crossed the hot car park. 'But it's been a pretty tough couple of days for all of us.' She stopped at her tiny dust-covered sports car and the lights flicked on as she opened her door. 'It's been a tough couple of months.'

'Too true.' Eve opened her door and climbed awkwardly into the low vehicle. Glanced across at her sister, who slid behind the wheel with the elegance of a film star.

'How do you do it, Eve?'

Eve had been thinking the same question about her sister. But they probably weren't referring to the same thing, and she grinned at the idea of Sienna wondering how Eve could be so elegant.

'Earth to Eve?' The old Sienna, exasperated. 'How do you do it?'

'Do what?'

'Stay warm and fuzzy, and give so much, and still be sane?'

'Who says I'm sane?'

'Good point.' She reached for the key and then let her hand fall. 'No. Too easy.' She looked levelly at Eve. 'You were very sane getting Callie out of the car. Very sane calling for the emergency caesarean. I'm sorry I was so slow.'

Eve blinked. 'God, Sienna. You were awesome. There was a lot going on.'

'I know. So it blew me away that you recognised the right course of action and I didn't.'

The memory of that morning so many months ago had been the reason for that. The gift she'd been given in the guise of death. 'Have you ever been involved in a caesarean like that?'

'Never.'

Eve nodded. 'I have.'

She saw the relief on Sienna's face as she got it. 'Oh.' Her sister leaned forward and started the car. 'Not something you'd forget.'

'Nope.'

For the rest of the drive they discussed Sienna's findings.

'There's really nothing to tell. The antenatal care in the past was excellent. I believe the previous losses were incredibly bad luck, and

I think the care you give now will make outcomes even better. The clinic is a good thing and these women certainly deserve it.'

'So nothing at all?'

'The only slight variation I would suggest is rescreening women in their second to third trimester for chlamydia. It's a simple test and that's turned up twice in the notes: both women had premature rupture of membranes.'

'We screen at first visit, but we can do that again. Easy. And Callie wants a sexual health and women's health clinic as well.'

Sienna nodded. 'At least we've ruled out factors like fertilisers and familial genetics.'

Eve looked thoughtful. 'As far as the STIs go, we may have a serial offender who doesn't know they have something they could pass on.'

'Yep. Always the way.' Sienna pulled over onto the gravel to let a caravan and trailer going the other way stay on the road. 'Some foetuses just don't seem to be worried, regardless of the environment they grow in, while others perish. But because your birth numbers are so low in a small community, every baby who died flagged that something wasn't right.'

Eve shuddered and ran over it in her mind. 'The good news is the women who birth here did get fabulous care and the clinic is making access easier.' She thought about the two million dollars. 'Blanche accidently got it right in a very expensive way. Poor Lex.'

Sienna laughed. 'But I'll write a paper on it. Get word out there in case STIs are a risk somewhere else. Blanche might save more babies than she expected.'

'Whether this will help the grieving parents I'm not sure. Hopefully Blanche is satisfied enough to feel she made sure there wasn't a causative factor. Still, I categorically believe your Red Sand mums will have the same positive birth outcomes as in any other town.'

That was wonderful news but it also sounded like closure. 'So you're going soon?'

'ASAP. I've done my job. It's up to you and Callie now.' She lowered her voice but Eve still heard her. 'I just need to get the hell away from here.'

Eve glanced across. 'What about Douglas?'

'Nice guy.' There was silence for a long moment. 'Very nice guy. But he lives in the wrong part of the world.'

'And here I was thinking you were going to sponsor a nail bar and settle down.'

'Ha! Not a hope in hell.' She glanced at Eve. 'But I might be a better sister to you now that I appreciate you.'

'So you appreciate me now?' Eve grinned. 'You're not too bad yourself. I'll miss you.'

THIRTY-FOUR

Sienna packed her room and was out of there by lunchtime the next day.

Eve and Fran waved her off, and Douglas was conspicuous in his absence. Sienna had promised to drop in to see Callie when she reached Charleville.

The winds of change were sweeping across Red Sand like the rainless clouds that were sweeping across the blue sky.

That night Eve had a phone call from two midwives she'd worked with in Brisbane, asking if she needed a replacement. They'd be willing to come out in the next two weeks if she did. She could be home for Christmas.

Two weeks. Would that be long enough for Callie? Or would that mean too much of Eve now that her sister had her new family?

The next morning Eve woke before the sun and knew she needed to think about the future. She climbed out of bed in the empty house, glanced at the trappings of her other family's life, and pulled on her favourite purple tights and green top. Slung a yellow scarf around her neck.

The day before, Sienna had told Blanche about her results; Eve had passed the findings on to the hospitals and Fran had booked appointments for the at-risk women to have extra tests on Monday.

Sienna had left the rest for Eve to sort. But Eve needed to sort herself first. Blanche wanted to come in but she could wait another few hours. This morning Eve just wanted to drive. Get lost. Be left alone so she could get it straight in her head if Brisbane was where she was supposed to be. Or whether she should she stay here and fight for the very slim chance she could edge under the outback reserve of Lex McKay and convince him to give a city girl like her a shot.

An image of that red sandhill drifted into her mind – all that serenity of sand, the peace of the sunrise from there. She could have faith in a decision she made out there.

So she drove, uncaring of the darkness of pre-dawn and the coolness of the air, avoiding the grazing wildlife as she soaked in the solitude and the open road. Finally she drove up the track and around the fence line, then parked under the spotted gum that she and Lex had eaten their lunch beneath so long ago.

Eve needed to think about Lex because he, like Douglas, was a guy who lived in the wrong part of the world, and she really didn't know if she had a chance. Or was it that he lived in the right place and she didn't?

When she turned off the engine there was just the sound of the occasional galah screeching for his mate and the lowing of a rangy white Brahman calf that was silhouetted against the hill line.

The dawn broke as she opened her door. Like a promise of resolution. A red sand sunrise greeted her as she walked up the sandhill with the day's first warmth on her face, red crystals flicking into the air behind her with each footfall. Those tiny trails marked in the sand made by bird claws, snakes and dancing crickets patterned the flawless canvas like a child's scrawl and reminded her again of the day with Lex. Everything reminded her of Lex.

Enough with the reminding.

Her breath puffed out as she tramped up the slope, footprints breaking the purity in the middle of the slope, while the edges that fell away to the paddock below rippled from the wind in beautifully spaced precision.

There was something about the harmony with nature when she stood up here that made her feel as if she were joined to it all. Just one more grain of sand in a world of sandy particles.

The sleeping giant of the glittering ochre hill embraced her as the new sun warmed the chill off the air. The breeze cooled the shaded side of her body and even the two temperatures seemed right. She sank to sit with her knees drawn up and lowered her chin as she shut her eyes. Breathed deeply and felt the tension ease. Breathed again and felt her teeth unclench. Had she been that stressed?

She let the questions all disappear into the air around her and was at peace.

An hour later the sound of the helicopter rotors vaguely penetrated her fog but it wasn't until she heard the swish of someone approaching up the sandhill that she realised Lex had found her.

A long, akubra-topped shadow stopped next to her. 'I saw your car as I flew over. Was looking for it. But you look very settled up here all by yourself.'

'Surprisingly I am.'

'You look beautiful.'

She blinked. 'Really? I thought I looked like a budgerigar.'

'It's funny.' He crouched down beside her and smiled, staring slap-bang into her eyes. 'I had no idea that budgerigars were my favourite bird.'

He looked so good. 'I don't know what to do, Lex.'

He sat down next to her and handed her a spare hat. Then he rested his elbows on his knees. 'What about?'

'Leaving.'

That snapped his head up. 'When?'

'Two weeks. Two new midwives have offered to relieve me. They're good. I know them and Callie doesn't need me now.'

He lifted his hat and ran his hands through his hair. Put the hat back on as if happy now he'd ordered his thoughts. 'We'd miss you. It's nearly Christmas. I thought you'd rather spend it with Callie?'

'Bennet wants to take her and Adam and the baby to see his mum. I might fly down to Melbourne to see Sienna or she might come to Brisbane. We seem to have found a sisterly love we were missing out on before.'

Her throat was getting tight. 'It seems the magic of Red Sand has touched us too.' She finally met his eyes. Those black brows of his were drawn together. 'You look shocked?'

'Well, we have a big breakfast on the station for all the hands. Always have had. Then the family has Christmas lunch. Blanche and I, and Lily and Henry, we'd love to have you join us.'

'I'm not part of your family, Lex. And I'm not part of Bennet's family.'

He put his finger under her chin and raised her face so she couldn't hide. 'Eve Wilson. You are a part of every family for a thousand kilometres. And you always will be. Most definitely you are a part of our family.'

She tried to look away to the distant hills but he wouldn't let her. *That's right*, she thought, *just for Christmas lunch. Nope. Too painful.*

'Eve.' He lifted her chin higher so that she was facing him. 'Look at me.'

She looked. How could a man with such strong features be this beautiful? His powerful jaw was set, as if determined to have his way, yet a pulse beat under the dark regrowth he'd missed in this morning's shave, and undermined the certainty in his voice.

Was Lex uncertain?

Was he unsure of her response? Lex – who was sure of everything! A man undaunted by drought and flood, weathered by the wild distances he'd ridden and flown, happy to take on a Brahman steer or a hospital supervisor, and now he couldn't complete a sentence.

'I'm not very good at this. I mean, don't go at all. Stay. As my wife.' The last three words were barely audible.

She spluttered in her own shock. 'Wow, you really, really aren't very good at this.' Eve realised she'd said that out loud. Maybe she wasn't very good at it either. But there was a great big bubble of happiness that wanted to explode out of her.

'Sorry? Wife? You're asking me to be your wife? So I won't miss Christmas dinner?'

He took her fingers in his big hand. Shook his head in amusement.

'Not for Christmas dinner.' Now the words were stronger, feeding on the emotion he'd finally let loose. 'Marry me. Stay here. With me.' He bent his head as he lifted her hand to his lips and kissed her palm. 'Be my wife. My life. My love.'

'You can't love me.'

'How could I not?' He rolled his eyes. Squeezed her fingers. Shook them a little. 'For Pete's sake, woman. Look at you. You amaze me. Inspire me. You make me feel ten feet tall.' He stroked her fingers in his. 'You're so wise, and silly, and surprising. I want you by my side when I wake. I need to know you're safe in my bed when I'm out at camp during muster. I need you with me forever.'

He drew her fingers down with his until both their hands lay over her belly. Stroked it. 'I want to see you holding our child. Our children. Marry me. Can you do that, Eve? Can you stay with me until we're old and we've handed on all our cattle to the next generation?' He smiled gently as he reminded her of their last conversation here in this spot.

She had to believe him. Lex didn't lie. 'It's sudden, Lex.'

'No. You've been blind. I've loved you since the day we flew to Charleville. But I admit I fought it for a long time.'

'You wouldn't even look at me.'

'I looked at you all right.' His searing look at her right then said he liked what he saw very much, and she could feel the warmth of it in her belly and on her skin. 'And I wouldn't let Henry take you on your first flight.'

'You arranged that?' He nodded. 'Did Blanche make the picnic basket?'

He shrugged. 'I asked her to. And she knew why.' He picked up her hand. 'So will you?'

'Will I what?' She was feeling very breathless here.

'Live through droughts and floods and impassable roads and good seasons and bad. Until we are so old, all we can do is sit on the verandah and rock and watch the sun set over Diamond Lake. It's a lot to ask, but can you love me back, Eve?'

Eve blinked and the red particles of sand she'd dug her other hand into fell in a shower as she lifted it to touch his face, to make sure this was real and she wasn't just in her bed dreaming, soon to be woken by the cockatoos.

A flock of iridescent green budgerigars took off from the spotted gum below the sandhills and she could feel her own emotions take flight, like that first time he'd kissed her. A huge *whoosh* of feelings.

'Um. Yes. Please. To all of it.' She could barely speak. 'Lex, give a girl some warning if you're going to take her breath away.'

He smiled down at her. 'Warning. I'm going to kiss you and I hope like hell I take your breath away.'

THIRTY-FIVE

Sienna flew back to Red Sand for Australia Day. She had to because her sister was getting married, though Sienna didn't know what the rush was.

The flight wasn't too bad. Douglas met her in Longreach, and people glanced at her as she walked across the tarmac. Police escort. It was hot – typical – but then again, so was the man meeting her. H.O.T.

'Never thought I'd be back here.'

'You look good.'

She raised her brows. 'You look good yourself.'

He took her overnight bag from her, changed hands, and then took her fingers in his. Very firmly. 'Come with me, madam. I have some questions.'

They didn't leave Longreach until well after lunch.

At Diamond Lake Station Blanche was ecstatic with her new daughter-in-law to be, and bestowed a promise that while she wasn't moving out of the homestead, she would travel at least six months of the year and leave the young ones in peace.

Lily was also very pleased with her father's choice, and Eve had told her not to even think about calling her step-mother 'Mum'.

Henry was happy because Eve had talked to Lex about the racing stables and they were all flying to Brisbane after the honeymoon to scope out the options.

But the happiest person there was Lex. His usually grave features were carved into a permanent, if subtle, smile. Especially when his eyes rested on his Eve.

Eve, who had managed to slide into the hearts of everyone on the station in just two weeks. Who had already mastered the basics of riding the quiet mare he'd picked out for her. There was talk of her first helicopter pilot's lesson – which Blanche disagreed with, but she was learning not to disagree quite so much.

For the wedding the only thing Eve had insisted on was that it be held beside the lake, so when Blanche wanted to fly in a hairstylist, a beautician, Eve's dress and trousseau, flowers and the men's suits, Eve really didn't care. She just wanted Lex.

On the night before the wedding Lex was banished to Bennet's farm, where the men were being looked after by Bennet's sister.

Callie, still looking fragile but luminously happy, arrived the afternoon before the wedding, not long after Sienna. Lily fell instantly in love with Amari and carried her everywhere, desperate to be babysitter.

To avoid the military campaign Blanche was running in the house, the three sisters escaped to the small rustic pavilion beside the lake after Amari had gone to sleep with her solicitous new cousin in attendance.

A sunset over Diamond Lake with a bottle of very expensive Champagne from Sienna was too good an opportunity to miss. As they clinked their glasses, Blanche called to a stockman in the distance and her voice drifted across the paddock.

Callie glanced over her shoulder. 'I'm sorry, Eve, but I'd pass out if she was my mother-in-law.'

Eve grinned. 'Blanche is a classic. I love her.'

'Good that someone does,' Sienna added in a droll aside. She glanced around. 'So this is the Diamond Lake it's all named after?' She didn't look impressed. 'Does it have emus?'

'Hordes of them,' Eve assured her and she caught Callie's smile.

'By the way,' Callie said, changing the subject, 'congratulations on your appointment, Sienna. Australia's youngest director of obstetrics.'

Sienna shrugged. 'Apparently there's a bloke down in South Australia who's younger. But thanks.'

Eve rolled her eyes. 'Sergeant McCabe looked pretty pleased with himself when he drove off.'

Sienna wasn't going there. 'Aren't all men pleased with themselves?'

Eve looked at her, her sister, the sometimes bitingly brilliant woman she so admired. Then she turned to Callie, gorgeous and steel-cored beneath that gentle exterior. And she knew she was so lucky to have these two incredible women in her life.

'Well, the men in our lives have good taste.' She raised her glass. 'And so have we. To Red Sand. To Diamond Lake. And to family.'

ACKNOWLEDGEMENTS

With sincere thanks to the people who helped make this happen with their incredible support.

To my husband, always my hero, who suffers when I'm on deadline, and just like the song, is the 'wind beneath my wings'. To my five sons, who have the world before them and can make me laugh just like their father does. To my mum, Catherine, who had her own heroic breast cancer journey and a beautiful smile just like Sylvia. To my dad, Ted, my first hero, who would have loved to read this book. And to all the medical men and women who do an incredible job caring for Australia's unsung heroes of the outback.

To my writing friends, especially Anne Gracie, Barbara Hannay, Kelly Hunter, Marion Lennox, Carol Marinelli, Trish Morey, Alison Roberts, Meredith Webber, Lillian Darcy and my mate Bronwyn Jameson, who have been such a part of my writing journey. My agent, Clare Forster from Curtis Brown, who quietly creates magic. My Penguin angels, Belinda Byrne, Sarah Fairhall and Jo Rosenberg.

To the local writers, Annie Seaton, Karly Lane, Elle Finlay, Jenn McCloud, Suzanne Brandon, Dianne Curran, and to Romance Writers Of Australia conferences – the go-to place if you want to write anything.

To the birthing women, young, older and mothers earth, and their families, who always inspire me with their strength and joy. My fellow midwives and doctors at my small country hospital, with special mention to Dr David Lunnay, my ALSO colleagues, and those flying doctors and flight nurses I cornered who, with such patience, answered my hypothetical questions.

And to all the amazing people we spoke to on our research trips, like Monique Johnson at the Cosmos Centre in Charleville, the publicans, and the people who live and love the land.

Thank you all.

The Homestead Girls

After her teenage daughter Mia falls in with the wrong crowd, Dr Billy Green decides it's time to leave the city and return home to far western NSW. When an opportunity to pursue her childhood dream of joining the Flying Doctor Service comes along, she jumps at the chance. Flight nurse Daphne Prince – who is thrilled to have another woman join the otherwise male crew – and their handsome new boss, Morgan Blake, instantly make her feel welcome.

Just out of town, drought-stricken grazier Soretta Byrnes has been struggling to make ends meet and has opened her station house to boarders. Tempted by its faded splendour and beautiful outback setting, Billy, Mia and Daphne decide to move in and the four of them are soon joined by eccentric eighty-year-old Lorna Lamington.

The unlikely housemates are cautious at first, but soon they are offering each other frank advice and staunch support as they tackle medical emergencies, romantic adventures and the challenges of growing up and getting older. But when one of their lives is threatened, the strong friendship they have forged will face the ultimate test . . .